SWIFT RIVER

ESSIE CHAMBERS

SIMON & SCHUSTER

NEW YORK LONDON TORONTO SYDNEY NEW DELHI

100 YEARS

SIMON &
SCHUSTER

1230 Avenue of the Americas
New York, NY 10020

First Simon & Schuster hardcover edition June 2024

SIMON & SCHUSTER and colophon are registered trademarks of Simon & Schuster, LLC

Simon & Schuster: Celebrating 100 Years of Publishing in 2024

An earlier version of Chapter 8 appeared in *CRAFT*.

Lucille Clifton, excerpt from "far memory 2" from *The Book of Light*. Copyright © 1993 by Lucille Clifton. Reprinted with the permission of The Permissions Company, LLC, on behalf of Copper Canyon Press, coppercanyonpress.org.

For information about special discounts for bulk purchases, please contact Simon & Schuster Special Sales at 1-866-506-1949 or business@simonandschuster.com.

The Simon & Schuster Speakers Bureau can bring authors to your live event. For more information or to book an event, contact the Simon & Schuster Speakers Bureau at 1-866-248-3049 or visit our website at www.simonspeakers.com.

Interior design by Carly Loman

Manufactured in the United States of America

10 9 8 7 6 5 4 3 2 1

Library of Congress Cataloging-in-Publication Data has been applied for.

ISBN 978-1-6680-2791-2
ISBN 978-1-6680-2794-3 (ebook)

For Christine

someone inside me remembers

—From "far memory" by Lucille Clifton

PROLOGUE

Picture my Pop's sneakers: worn-out and mud-caked from gardening, neatly positioned on the riverbank where the grass meets the sand. This is the place where the Swift River is at its widest and deepest, where a jungly mix of trees makes you feel like you're all alone in the wilds somewhere, even though the road is so close you can hear cars humming on the other side. We'd come here as a family on hot summer nights—the one spot where we could splash around freely without people staring at our black, white, and brown parts. Ma even swam naked sometimes, her pale body like a light trail moving through the dark water. Pop couldn't swim. He'd stand hip-deep, hold me high in the air, and launch me out from his arms like a cannonball. Over and over again I'd paddle back, his proud, fluorescent smile my beacon.

July 1st. The current is extra strong and the water is churning—restless, as my Grandma Sylvia would say, from summer rains. Pop leaves early that morning, long before Ma and me are out of bed. He forgets to make me breakfast before he goes. He leaves the car in the driveway. When Ma comes downstairs she frowns at the door, wrestling with something on the other side of it. She moves to the window and beams her worried look out into the distance. I decide not to put sugar on my cereal even though no one's paying attention. Answers come to questions I don't ask: There isn't enough gas in the car for both her and Pop—she has to get to her job and he has to go find one. He must be off on foot somewhere.

Two days later, his shoes turn up. Tucked inside them: his wallet and house keys. Pop is gone.

All through the next week, men in boats drag long hooks and nets across the river. They look like the fisherman we saw in Cape Cod two summers ago, except these nets are out to snag a person, my person. The men pull out a tricycle, a mattress, and a dead deer whose antlers were stuck in mud. But no Pop.

The search moves outward from the water, farther and farther away from those sneakers—to the deepest parts of the surrounding woods, to the abandoned factories up and down the river, to hunters' cabins and tool sheds, under porches, and inside our house, all through the dank, dirty basement Pop wanted to turn into a TV room one day. Then back to the water again, where it fizzles. Soon summer is gone, too.

Fall comes and I start the fourth grade—life snapping back to its normal ways as if I don't have a missing dad and a mom who's afraid to let me leave the house but also forgets to feed me. At school, we read *The Adventures of Huckleberry Finn.* I am the tallest and the smartest one in my class. I am also the only Black person at school, and now that Pop is gone, the only Black person in the whole town. The kids call my dad "Nigger Jim" because: he's Black, he's somewhere in a river, and he has no shoes. Mrs. Durkin hands out detentions, hugs me, and pulls her long fingernails through my knotted curls, saying, *Kids can be so cruel but if you just ignore them they'll leave you alone.* I cry into her chest because she's so nice and so wrong, and I wish I didn't know this with such certainty. Pop stays gone.

Gone hangs in the air without landing and, after time (a summer, a fall, a summer), gives permission to fill in gaps with meanness and nonsense.

Like: Pop was murdered by a racist serial killer who scalped him and used his Afro as a dust mop; or, he went for a swim and was pulled out to sea by a water Sasquatch; or, he faked his own death and is off somewhere with stolen money, a new life, and a new white wife.

Years pass and the story turns one last time. Now Ma and me are the beasts. We hitchhike through town seducing men, robbing them and jumping out of moving cars. We wander along the banks of the river at night, looking for some secret thing my father buried before he took off. When the fireflies are so thick they look like mini lanterns, and a stray pulse catches a passing car, they say that's us—Diamond and Ma—up to their old tricks, out with their flashlights digging for treasure.

I don't hear this dumb shit until I am long gone from that place.

Back to us three. Before I am a riverbeast, before the kids hold their breath as they pass my house, before I lose my name altogether. Before all of this. I am a small brown girl in the back seat of a VW Bug, watching the pavement flash through the rust holes in the car floor like it's TV. Ma and Pop are in the front. "Cut that out," Ma says without turning around, as I toss things through the holes experimentally: a smooth stone from the river, a penny, a broken Happy Meal toy; they clack against the bottom of the car. We are on one of our Sunday two-days-after-payday-full-tank-of-gas drives, a family luxury. I lift my head to catch the side of the road action flying by: farm stands and yard sales, wood piles and jerry-rigged rabbit coops, dumb dogs tied to trees, choking themselves trying to nip at our tires.

"What if we just keep going and never come back?" Pop asks us.

3

"What about my toys?" I say after some thinking.

"Come on now. We can always get more toys," he says, winking at me in the rearview mirror.

"We can't leave my mother alone in this town," Ma says. She's not in on the joke.

"We can always get another mother," Pop says.

I can't see Ma's face, but when Pop reaches out to touch her cheek she swats his hand away.

"Diamond and her toys need space in the back seat, so we'll have to strap Sylvia to the roof," he says. I picture one of Grandma's beige stockinged legs, thick ankles puffed out around her sparkly dancing shoes, dangling next to my window. Ma tries not to crack, but when she chuckles, her whole body shakes.

Time is bent. Everything I could ever want is in this car, except for Grandma Sylvia. I calculate that loss and decide to embrace what's here—Ma's feet out the window, her donkey laugh. Pop's off-pitch humming of no recognizable song, his big hand rubbing the back of Ma's neck with careful fingers, like he's afraid he might snap it.

Time is shaken. We've never even lived in this town; we're just passing through. Where we're from, all the people are kind and brown like me.

Simon and Garfunkel on the radio: "The Only Living Boy in New York." I am the only living girl in Swift River Valley.

A mosquito trapped in the car chomps out a constellation on my legs. I dig into the pink bumps with my nails, carving out tiny blood crosses. I'm excited for the scabs to come so I can pick them.

"Should we keep on going, sweet pea?" Pop says again, looking in the back seat at me. Ma the nag is locked out of the conversation now.

Yes! Yes! Yes! I say, stomping my feet against the front seat partition. *Keep going!*

Time is folded in half. There is no "us three." Black people live here, they call this town home. They are millworkers and cobblers, carpenters and servants. A "Negro" church sits next to a "Negro" schoolhouse; the mill bell carves up their days. They fill the streets of The Quarters, voices calling out to each other *Mornin'* and *Evenin'*; clotheslines stretch across yards like flags marking a Black land.

In one night, they're gone. Those were my people.

This isn't a mystery or a legend. It's a story about leaving.

It starts with my body. My body is a map of the world.

1

1987

The summer after I turn sixteen, I am so fat I can't ride my bike anymore. So I let it get stolen on purpose.

"You got a new boyfriend?" Ma the smartass yells out the living room window, laughing through her smoker's cough when she sees me lying on the ground in front of our house, wrapped around the bike with a bucket and a cleaning rag.

"Are you humping that thing?" she asks. I ignore her and she leaves me be, puffing away on her Newports—a faceless blob in the dirty window screen. The whole house looks like it's having a cigarette.

It's hot out, and the bike is fiery from lying in the yard all morning. I'm curled around the frame so I can get to all of its parts; it's the only position my body will allow. I scrub at the street grime until a bright red frame pokes through for the first time in years. It mocks the rest of the junk around it: skeleton lawn chairs, broken push mower, Pop's dead car in the driveway.

"You trapped under there?" Ma shouts as she watches me struggling to stand. She is testing my forgiveness with her stupid jokes. An hour ago she told me she got herself fired again, this time for telling off her boss at the fertilizer store after he refused to pay for another sick day. Now we will have to live off my check from the Tee Pee Motel, the same job she had when I was little. I keep reminding her we'll have to choose between electricity and heat once the winter comes, but she tells me not to worry myself, that adults plan things and their kids don't always know about it. "I have my ways," she sings from her crater in the couch.

Ma is a break in the long line of a family who worked the same *one* job their whole lives. I am a break in their pure Irish stock; the first Black person, the end of the whites.

"Something blocking your ears?" She tries again. I decide I will not speak to her for two days.

As I push myself onto all fours, a laser-like sunray jumps across my hand, spilling onto the grass in front of me. I turn to see my neighbor and her friends—dumb freshman girls—out on the front lawn in fluorescent bathing suits laughing and trying to beam me with the tinfoil tanning reflectors they hold under their chins. They are close, only two houses away, but their faces are a blur of baby oil and braces. I like to think that if I wanted to, I could stroll over there and dump my dirty bike water on their ratty towels and pale, greasy bodies. Slap a face or two. But I'm not like Pop; I can't fight everything, everyone.

"Thank you for all our times together." I touch the wheel of my bike. "I made you pretty again. You're free."

Later that afternoon, I lay the bike gently against a light pole outside the CVS like an offering. Ma has sent me there to get her monthly prescriptions, which takes about five minutes, but I sit in the back of the magazine aisle for an hour reading *National Gardening Magazine* and *Seventeen* until the cashier tells me to buy something or go find a library somewhere. When I come outside and see the empty space around the pole, my panic is not for the bike, it's for the basket. I've forgotten to take out the ribbons my Grandma Sylvia had woven in—rows of bright red, white, and blue stripes that purred in the wind the faster I went. They're the same ribbons she braided into my hair when I was little, when my kinky curls just wanted to feather like the rest of the girls. I'm still sick over Ma throwing away Grandma's sewing supplies after she died. Ma does not like the clutter of feelings. She saves empty Coke bottles ("they make pretty vases"), old *TV Guides*, and a garbage bag full of travel-sized lotion she stole from the Tee Pee when she worked in housekeeping. But her own mother's things get tossed.

In this moment, I'm so mournful for Grandma Sylvia's yarn and zippers and buttons and scraps of cloth that smelled of Jergens lotion that I feel dizzy and heavy, like the full weight of me—two hundred and ninety-eight pounds last time I checked—might fall out on the sidewalk. For a second I consider yelling *Police!* into the empty street, but I remember the feeling of my legs pressed into my stomach with each spin of the pedal, my body no longer making room for my lungs so that I can breathe. My three stomach rolls have filled out into one solid ball. I am unbendable. My legs are heavy ghosts that move me from place to place. The bruises and stinging raspberries all over my body from weekly falls are constant reminders that the bike doesn't want me on it anymore; we don't want each other.

Goodbye, Grandma ribbons.

It's a two-mile walk home from the CVS—a new, ugly brick building on the south side of Main Street. It stands apart from the long row of old-timey storefronts that follow, with their thick, hazy glass windows and cutesy signs hand-painted by someone's cousin who can do calligraphy. The paper mill, where Pop used to work, is close by. Ma and me live all the way north, in one of the identical houses that once belonged to the French Canadian mill families. White people call it "The Quarters," but there used to be Black people who lived there before them—they ran the textile mill. They called it "Little Delta," because the area was shaped like a triangle and reminded someone of their old Southern home by a river. They all left except my great-aunt, Clara. She died before I was born, so I never even got to meet her. Pop says she was a midwife. Every now and then someone says, *Your grandma delivered my dad!* And I wonder why that doesn't make them treat us any different, any better.

I don't call Ma to come get me from the CVS. She can't drive, and taxis are expensive—just to be used in an emergency or on payday. We're the only people in town who actually walk to get somewhere. There are no buses except for school buses, and the only real sidewalks wind themselves around the mile of stumpy blocks that make up the downtown. Sometimes you see Homeless Richard hugging the edge of the road near the entrance to the highway, skip-kicking imaginary rocks at the entry-ramp sign like he's testing the limits of a force field. Ever since the start of the deer overpopulation we call "Deerpocalypse," you also might see a few deer on a street corner, shuffling around like bored teenagers. Otherwise, it's just us out there, single file on the left side against traffic when we don't mind the walk, and doubled up in the right-side flow of it when we're hitching.

On my bike, the stretch of town between Main Street and home had been a haze of places to pass without stopping, all the shitty memories of each fuzzed over by the air on my face and the pounding in my chest. Now, on foot—all kinds of terrible in sharp focus: here comes the barbershop where they refused to cut Pop's Afro; there's the moldy-smelling department store selling stale saltwater taffy and Garfield the cat figurines; or the diner where Ma and me used to come for splurge Sunday dinners until I was accused of stealing tips off of tables.

If I'm on foot, people stare so hard it's like I'm on fire. Heads in cars flip all the way around. Workers in shop windows stop what they're doing to look at me blank-faced—as if I'm not their daughter's classmate, their friend's co-worker, like they haven't known me my whole life. When I forget the spectacle of myself, I look behind me to see who is the me. Sometimes Pop used to stop in his tracks and stare back, saying nothing, until they turned away. Mostly he ignored them until the final bad months. Nowadays, Ma might yell something like, *What, are you jealous?* and then swish her skinny ass in their direction.

Halfway home, I take a break at the only pay phone on Main Street. It has a seat and the doors close and I'm grateful; everything hurts. Feet, knees, swollen sausage fingers—the pain throbbing out a code: *Rest until you're ready.* This has been happening a lot lately, where an ache plucks at some body part and then a message shoots right to my brain. Not like my inner genius or God speaking; just a clear, steady voice that's me but not mine. That's how it came to me—I may be too fat for my bike, but I'm going to learn how to drive. I haven't told Ma. The thought is like a puddle with a river inside it.

I flip through the phone book, wishing I had someone to call to come get me. We don't have friends as much as people who do us favors. I have one friend-like person: Fat Betty. I don't know her phone number because we've never spoken except about books and library business. Betty is an adult woman—our town librarian—who used to weigh four hundred pounds until she started going to the Diet Center a year ago. She's half of her old self now, but people still call her Fat Betty. I don't think her new body will ever earn her a new name in this town, where everything that's ever happened to you is a stain that fades but won't come out.

Betty is very encouraging of me—tucking cheery, handwritten library slogans inside the books I take out. As she got smaller and I got bigger, she started leaving her old clothes—nice ones from Lane Bryant that we could never afford—at my door; first anonymously, and then with her friendly-style notes attached. *Self-confidence is the best outfit!* Then came healthy snacks and books she thought I'd enjoy, like *Sophie's Choice* and *The Color Purple*. She's like a wise person from the future, come to tell me things I'll need to know, give me things I'll need to fight my way out of here. "Here" being this town and my body.

For kicks I look up our phone number instead. It's still listed under *NEWBERRY, Robert*. Right next to it someone has scribbled, *NIGER*. I pull a pen out of my purse and finish the sentence—*The third longest river in Africa!*

Even after sitting for a few minutes I can't catch my breath; no more thoughts are coming to help me. Only doubt bouncing around my head. *Was I supposed to hang on to my bike?*

"Aw, that sucks, sweet pea," Ma says when I tell her it's gone.

She's standing at the stove cooking dinner in a bra and cutoff sweatpants tied at the waist with a shoelace, her permanent morning hair going every which way. Whatever it is that she's stirring gives off a confusing smell—sweet and fishy, like she took what little food was left in the house and threw it all in a pot. She's not the worst cook in the world, but if she strays from the basics—sloppy joes, fish sticks, tuna casserole—it's anyone's guess what will end up on a plate. Straying means she feels guilty about something.

"Get in here and try this." She motions to the kitchen table with a gunked-up spoon. "Your mother is a food magician."

"That's it?" I say, still standing in the open doorway, pulse jumping out of my neck. I forget I swore off speaking to her. She doesn't notice I'm wheezing so hard each breath is a whistle. She doesn't ask how long it took me to walk home (two hours).

"Your overweight friend must have sent you something again." Ma points to a package addressed to me sitting next to the front door.

"Pop would have gone out there, found the bike, and kicked some ass," I say.

I don't use Pop that often, but right now I want to make contact, and I do. From the back I see Ma's body droop, like she's been unplugged. She sways a little, as if dizzy. This is what gets to me: the curve of her back, on its way to the scoliosis hump Grandma Sylvia had in her final years, spine nearly a right angle.

"Stand up straight, Ma," I say more gently.

"Kicking ass never helped," she says, arching her back but still not looking up from the stove. "Only made it worse."

I shake the CVS bag full of her pills like a maraca, and her head whips around for the first time.

"I got your Tic Tacs," I say.

We call Ma's pain meds Tic Tacs. She planted the joke, working it so often I was forced to partake against my will. We don't talk about her pain, which is from the accident we don't talk about either.

"I'm sorry about your bike," she says.

"My basket," I say. She nods.

I line the prescription bottles up on the windowsill behind the sink where Grandma Sylvia used to keep her chia pets. The chia hedgehog was my favorite. Ma once had a fit when Grandma brought home a chia man with a wide nose, giant lips, and a green sprouted Afro; she threw it out the window because she said it was racist, Grandma was racist, and how could she even live with herself knowing she had a Black granddaughter. I felt bad for Grandma; she looked so confused, like she just couldn't put the two together. "Did I do something wrong?" she whispered to me later in my room as she kissed me goodnight. "Yes and no," I told her, because that seemed like the right answer.

We sit down to eat what turns out to be Spam and gravy with boiled potatoes. Normally I have snacks I take from the vending machine at work hidden throughout the house for when there are dinners like this, but my stash is gone. To help it go down, I drink powdered milk and Pepsi like Laverne from *Laverne & Shirley*. I always wanted a best friend like that.

"I'm gonna get you one of those grocery carts," Ma says. "I'll make it look pretty, like your basket."

I know Ma doesn't have the money to buy a new cart, or a new anything. There's always cash coming someday, except this is the summer it's supposed to be real. It's been almost seven years since my dad disappeared, and Ma says we can finally declare him legally dead, then get his life insurance money. She calls it my inheritance. This has crept around every hope-for-the-future conversation we've ever had—it's the thing that pulls us up but leads us nowhere. "By next year the house will be ours again!" "We'll get your knee fixed and buy waterbeds and recliner chairs!" "Soon we can buy ten of those!" she says about any one thing we want to buy. Each time Ma passes by the six-month-old *Bank Owned House for Sale* sign jutting out from our yard weeds, she gives it a good kick. She dreams of the day we can throw a pile of money on the banker's desk and tell him to suck it. She seems to think it will be for sale forever, instead of this fact—we could be out on our asses any day now.

Lately I let myself think about the money, too, careful to pull back my hopes as soon as they wander out too far. By the time I turn seventeen I want: a birthday party with German chocolate cake and friends, new clothes with the store smell still in them, shoes that fit. I imagine buying an Atari at Caldor even though I don't like video games—just to have it around for visitors to play. Tossing extra change in a jug like I won't need it that day, that week. Leaving this place, leaving Ma. That thought hurts too much and I pinch it down to nothing.

We move to the living room so the TV can take over our brains. Ma wants to watch *Perfect Strangers*, but I win with a tape of *Good Times* reruns because it's a Black show and that will always shut her up. We slurp up melted Cool Whip and laugh at this world we don't really know. I think about how Ma has met more Black people than me, which is very unfair. I get up and grab a box of glazed donuts to dip in the Cool Whip.

Our rusted metal tray tables are unsteady on the blue shag wall-to-wall carpet, so our knees do the balancing. Grandma Sylvia let Ma choose the carpet when she was a little girl. Ma thought it looked like blue grass. I've always loved how it felt to roll around in it, even now. Ma also picked out wallpaper to match, with enormous blue flowers on twisty green vines against a yellow background, now faded to gray on gray. Grandma gave us this house when I was little because she moved into an apartment building for seniors. Over the years, Ma has tried to get rid of all the sentimental snow globes and ancient china figurines, but there's still the same fifty-year-old furniture coughing up dust, the same sagging tin ceiling, squeaky twin beds, and checkered linoleum kitchen floor. Even the wooden plaque painted by Grandpa Joe still hangs above the front door, a happy-looking four-leaf clover welcoming all to the home of a long-gone family: *The O'Briens, Luck of the Irish!* Like we're babysitting for ghosts. Or living somewhere we don't deserve, yet.

Only my room feels like mine.

I escape TV time with a stack of Ritz-Cracker-and-Cheez-Whiz sandwiches carefully balanced in one hand, kicking the box from

15

Betty into my room and shutting the door. As I plop down on the bed, my head bumps the wall's hollow wood paneling and I hear Ma shout, "What happened?" from the living room. She does this every time. The paneling gives the room the feel of a ship's cabin from the movies. Or a giant bulletin board. I've made it into both.

There is only enough space for a single bed, a dresser, a tiny desk, and a few footsteps in between each. On either side of my bed, I have pictures of portholes I tore from a book, *Cabin Class Rivals: A Picture History*. They almost look real if you turn away quickly. The rest of the wall is covered with pictures of places I want to visit: the pyramids in Egypt, Stonehenge in England, the redwood forest, the New York Botanical Garden. "Why go all that way to see plants and trees? We have those!" Ma says.

She keeps giving me things she hopes will make it onto the wall— torn-out pages from a stack of equestrian magazines Mrs. Konkol threw out, with *We'll be riding these someday!* written across the prancing horses. Old photos of us standing stiffly in front of the house when it was still pretty, ads for diamond rings from a Zales insert, with Ma's note: *They got nothin' on you!*

On my nightstand is my tape recorder. Ever since I quit chorus last year, I do this weird thing where I record myself singing a song, play it back, and harmonize along with it. Ma says I have a perfect voice, but she's supposed to say that—she's my ma. The chorus teacher said it, too, but the chorus kids would sometimes *moo* when I sang.

As I lie back with a tower of cracker sandwiches on my chest, I notice that the black specks on the ceiling are spreading down the wall toward an old Yoda poster. I used to imagine the specks were distant planets, the water stains clouds in a night sky. Now I see mold and a rotted-out ceiling from a leaky roof. When this was Ma's room, the ceiling was painted blue and the walls were covered in posters of "heartthrobs" from corny shows where there were always enough brothers and sisters to form a band or a baseball team.

My stomach feels dangerously full.

I touch the skin on my belly—tight and hot, a volcano of food gurgling beneath. White jagged stretch marks look like lightning bolts striking across my middle. It hurts in there and I wonder what it would be like to go too far. I wait for it to settle.

I pull out a driver's ed manual from its hiding place under the mattress and start reading the "Safety First" chapter. I've been studying "License Classes" and "Restrictions," and plan on having memorized all the laws before I start class next week. I already aced my permit test and forged Ma's name on the application like all things needing parent approval. I'm trying to focus on brake lights and turn signals when I see a person-sized shadow pass by my window. People nosing around the house isn't unusual, especially since the *For Sale* sign went up. But normally they just stand in plain sight, looking into windows and poking at the rotted wood shingles as if no one lives here. Ma sometimes screams at them, *If you buy this house we're comin' with it!* Right now, the thought of somebody out there makes me so mad I'm up and out the door before I can even think about my bursting tummy. I can hear Ma snort-wheezing inside, so I know she's fast asleep on the couch. That sound—usually annoying—is a comfort now, like a rope that ties me to the house so I can't be pulled out too far into the night.

I stand a few feet from the door on the walkway that splits the yard in two, listening for the sounds of a sneak about to be caught—twigs snapping underfoot, an uncontrolled sneeze, the giggle trail of a kid running away after a stupid prank I'd hear about later from some neighbor who felt sorry for us.

I look over at my dad's once red, now brownish VW Bug, parked in the back of the driveway close to the edge of the woods behind our house. We called it Ladybug. I half expect a car door to be open, or some other sign of a person passing through. I'm prepared for nothing, but I'm hoping, as I always do, for something else.

"Who's there?" I say.

I want to call out to my dad. Weirdo thoughts like this are always with me, but never more than when heat and summer smells make me feel like something is missing or about to happen. I don't even know who I expect to answer—dead man or live disappeared person. I've said this to Ma a few times when I was feeling mean and wanted her to be confused, too. *They never found his body, Ma. Doesn't that ever make you wonder?* She's not a person who wonders.

I'm sweating so much the drops are like tiny fingers moving up and down my back. My shirt is soaked. Sometimes if I'm looking extra gross, I imagine what he'd think if he saw me now. He probably wouldn't even recognize me.

"Hello, someone?"

The answer comes in the form of an especially long snort from Ma inside, like she's laughing at me for standing out here in the dark, trying to catch some idiot who's probably long gone.

"Whoever you are, leave us alone," I say to no one.

When I get back to my room, I nearly step on the torn-out magazine page Ma must have slid under the door earlier. It's an ad for Nature Valley granola bars. In it, two friends riding bikes through the countryside stop on the side of a tree-lined road for some tasty treats. They're looking at each other in a knowing, happy way, like the bars are the secret to all that country goodness. I've had those dry, wannabe cookies, and they are not the secret to anything. If this were my friend, we would both spit them out, spraying each other with crumbs, and then laugh at our foolishness for thinking fake dessert could satisfy us after a long journey. The bikes are real beauties, though. One is metallic blue and the other is silver—not a trace of dirt or any sign they've been ridden anywhere. Just the girls' thin legs casually hooked around them. Carefully written in pen across the bottom of the page, almost as if it's part of the ad:

Us. Real soon. At least 10 of these. Love, Ma. I tack the bike girls above my desk and vow to stop speaking to her tomorrow.

I pull the Betty box onto the bed. I notice that, unlike her other packages, this one was sent through the mail, not dropped off, and there is no return address on the front. Inside, a bunch of random stuff—records, a quilt, a miniature sweater. And an envelope. On the front of it:

To: Diamond, From: Auntie Lena.

2

June 15, 1987

Dear Diamond,

First, I'd like to apologize for the intrusion. I know your mother doesn't think too much of my family, and I'm not sure what ideas you might already have in your head about me. Certainly, you could live a fine life without us ever crossing paths, but your daddy always said he wanted me to check on you more, make sure you were OK. So here I am, your Auntie Lena.

How odd it must be to see the name of a stranger here, calling herself your aunt, your kin? I'm actually your second cousin, as you probably know—your father's first cousin. My mama—"Sweetie" is what they called her—and his daddy were brother and sister. Our people call older relatives and friends of the family "Auntie" and "Uncle" as a show of respect. I have a hundred of 'em, at least, in Woodville alone. Can't go to the mailbox without tripping over one. For you, I'm what you might call an auntie cousin.

To tell you a little about myself, I'm a trained nurse, and I usually live in Atlanta, but I'm temporarily back in Woodville

managing Newberry Fine Fabrics, our family business started
by my great-uncle, Henry Newberry (your great-great) and his
brothers, when they all came back from Swift River in 1915. We
started out with a textile mill, but it went under for all kinds of
complicated reasons and they had to sell it to some white folks. I
know it might seem like a step down, going from running a mill to
a fabric store in Woodville, GA, but at our best, we had three stores
across the state. Our women were the best seamstresses in Georgia.
They made clothes for mayors and debutantes and all of James
Brown's backup singers if you can believe it. Now we just have the
one store, here in Woodville. I hope someday you can come see it.
We can make you an outfit or some of those legwarmers y'all wear.

There are some gifts in here for you—my mama's Lena Horne
album collection, a quilt she made for your daddy, and his baby
sweater. If I'm being honest, this is a big part of why I'm reaching
out to you now. Mama passed about a year ago, but I'm just
getting around to going through her personals. I couldn't bear it
before. Her smells all mixed in with everything, her handwriting
everywhere. She put aside a few things she wanted your father to
have, hoping she'd see him again someday. I'm sure you already
know that she raised him like he was her own child for the first
seven years of his life. That was before his daddy took him to Swift
River so they could live with our Aunt Clara. It broke Mama's
heart when he left. She never forgave his father for taking Robbie
away from her, especially to go to Swift River, of all places. Hating
that town is like inheriting your granddaddy's eyes—it's in the
Newberry DNA, crouched down inside every cell. I'm sorry to
speak in such a way about your home, but that's the truth. Do you
know the story of what happened to our people there? That place
crushed your daddy, took every bit of his light. I was mad at Aunt
Clara for taking Robbie in. Until I found out that she was left

22

behind, too. I'll send you some of her letters if you're interested—
they're hidden all over this daggone house! Aunt Clara wrote the
letters to my mama, Sweetie, who was her baby sister. The first date
on them is over a year after The Leaving. That's what they call the
night all the Black people left Swift River.

Aunt Clara had been raising her siblings since they lost their
own parents. I can't imagine what it must have felt like to see them
go. I've grown fond of her as I'm reading them. I think you'll like
her, too.

I don't want to overwhelm you with all of these things, so do tell
me if this is OK. I started with the quilt because I hear those New
England winters are very cold. I hope you'll write me back. Tell me
about yourself. Like what puts a smile on your face, or what it's like
to live in Swift River, now. And even about your mama. I'd like
to know about her, too. Send me a picture of yourself if you can. I
hope you've had a good life so far, Diamond. And I hope to meet
you someday.

From,
Auntie Lena

3

1987

Early morning light cuts through the bent-up kitchen blinds, slicing the wall in front of me into jagged strips; I count them as I wait for Ma to get out of the shower.

I have Lena's letter in front of me, and I'm looking at the only photo that exists of Ma and Pop's wedding day. Ma had told me a thousand times how she'd dreamt of getting married at the Swift River Country Club, with a party afterward in a grand reception hall draped in streamers; white-table-clothed tables polka-dotted across the room. Rows of foil-covered trays would line the walls, steam poofing out from the Swedish meatballs, pigs in blankets, and baked ziti. There'd be shrimp cocktail and lobster on ice and a band playing the Rolling Stones and the Beatles—only music you could dance or jump to.

But Pop wanted to get married under a tree. They didn't have any money, so Pop won. He pleaded for a weeping willow, his favorite; there was one on the north side of town behind the Top Dollar, surrounded by the greenest moss you've ever seen. Apparently, Pop's Aunt Clara told them about the spot, said it was special. Ma said OK, even though the leaves and branches looked like wet hair. They went and got their marriage license first. They were both eighteen years old.

It rained, hard. Ma said the rain was good luck. To me, this sounds like what you say when you have the crap luck of rain on your wedding day.

The photo also looks rained on. Some careless dipshit must have spilled Coke or something on it, because now it's stiff and curled up at the edges, like a potato chip. Much of the background has melted into a splotchy, electric blue. The center of the photo, where they stand in front of the tree with Grandma Sylvia and Aunt Clara, is still crisp and clear; an island of people surrounded by a cartoon sea. They are all soaked. Pop's father had died a year before, so this was it, the whole family. This is the only photo I've ever seen with Aunt Clara in it.

Ma has on a long white dress with lace sleeves; Grandma Sylvia made it for her, even though she didn't approve of the wedding. The dress is rain-soaked—see-through and too sexy, like she's outside with just a nightgown on. Her bouncy curler curls are spoiled, stuck to her face in limp waves. Pop has on a baggy suit, also plastered to his body. There is a flower tucked into his Afro. He's trying to be goofy. They are holding on to each other at the waist, heads tilted and touching. Their faces make me think of a sigh—relief, disappointment, happiness. Aunt Clara and Grandma Sylvia stand on either side of them, both squinting, confused, hands covering their own heads like useless umbrellas. They all look like they are trying to make the best of things.

It has never occurred to me to ask Ma, *Where are all the people? The friends? The bridesmaids in ugly dresses?* Something about the photo makes me feel queasy and embarrassed, and I have to look away. They seem *so alone* together. At the beginning of so much alone together.

This morning as I stare down the photo, I remember that someone else related to Pop was supposed to come to the wedding, too.

Supposed to drive all the way from Georgia. The day had started out so bright and shiny, Ma says the sunbeams coming through the trees looked like *Star Wars* light sabers. They waited and waited for Pop's person. Waited until the clouds joined together and the sky turned a solid gray. Then they all fought about waiting and then it started to pour. Aunt Clara complained about her ruined church shoes. Pop yelled at Grandma Sylvia for saying, *This is what happens when you get married too young. God always has the last word.* Ma cried.

And then just as the thunder kicked in, Pop swooped Ma up in his arms and carried her off into the woods, telling the minister to go home and the old ladies to wait in the car. When Ma and Pop came back thirty minutes later, the rain had let up; Pop was still carrying Ma. They were smiling and clingy. They said they were hitched. Ma won't give me the part of the story where they somehow married themselves, says it's too special, too private. I know she was nuts about the swooping up into Pop's arms part. She loved how he always treated her like a delicate lady (we all know she is neither one of those things). She told me what came next—Pop getting the grumpy ladies from the car, carrying each one over puddles and mud, one at a time, back to the tree. A passing jogger took the pictures for them. The down-South relative never came. It rained on and off all night.

Lena.

It comes to me like someone kicked in the door to my brain. It was *Auntie Lena* who never showed up. Lena who wrecked Ma's curls and made Pop yell on his wedding day. Lena who made it rain.

What if she had come? Would a sunny wedding photo with curls and smiles and one more person at their side have made a difference? *The* difference?

What would my life have been like with her in it?

I try and picture her face and Thelma from *Good Times* pops

27

into my head. This is something I'd get pissed at Ma for saying out loud, but I let myself skim through random Black TV people for a visual; I settle into Weezy Jefferson because she's more of a comfort. Just as quickly, my thoughts turn against Weezy, circling around her face like a bunch of angry villagers. *Why didn't you show up for the wedding? Do you know what really happened to my dad? What's your problem with my mom? Where have you been all this time? Why didn't you help us?*

I put her away in the place where people who let me down all huddle together in my mind, fighting for another chance. The wedding photo goes right inside the box along with everything else.

"If there's no hot water left, I'm not going with you," I yell in the direction of the bathroom. I don't really mean it; there's no way Ma can get through today without me. We're going to meet with an old classmate of hers, Jerry, who is a lawyer now. Ma says he'll help us get a death certificate for Pop, and later Pop's insurance money. We're going to make Pop officially dead.

It's a Thursday, my new day off from work at the Tee Pee; I got it in a trade with Dana Lambert, plus her shitty early morning shifts, so I can make room for driver's ed in the afternoons. I start class tomorrow. I still haven't told Ma.

"Your turn, sunshine," Ma says, popping her head around the corner. "Go get your butt clean!" She snaps her towel against the kitchen table, where I sit, and it releases a moldy smell. She King-Tuts it into the center of the room wearing only underwear and a towel turban, then walks back and forth "like an Egyptian"—neck bobbing, hands poking air, wet feet slapping the dirty floor. Now that song is stuck my head.

"You're not even doing it right," I say. It's hard to believe she used to be a dance teacher.

"You don't like my boogie?" She gives me jazz hands and a sad high kick. Her saggy boobs, on constant display, point down to loose underwear puddled around her waist, the worn elastic limply hugging her body. Faded period stains creep up from the front and back of her crotch like old wounds, and I have to look again for reasons I can't explain.

"Too much. No more," I say, putting my head on the table.

"Can't your ma be happy on a day like today?"

It's true that today could set a new life in motion. But it feels weird to be doing high kicks; it's the seven-year anniversary of Pop disappearing. Usually we ignore the day, fumbling around spaced out, not looking at each other. Ma might stare into an open closet for twenty minutes. I'll walk into walls, stub my toe on some furniture and start crying. Sometimes Ma disappears and comes back the next morning with a dozen Dunkin' Donuts or a fun pack of Butterfingers. Then it's over. Rinse, repeat.

This year, Ma goes full-on in the opposite direction. She slides an index card under my door—an old French vocabulary flash card she swiped from my desk. She'd crossed out *Ou est la bibliotheque?* and written above it, *You're invited to a celebration of life!* Today we're going to the Goodwill to get new dresses. This evening she wants to go down to the spot at the river where Pop's sneakers were found. Light a candle. Say some nice things. "I'm not making a speech," I tell her. Afterward she wants to go for a swim.

I think about those sneakers, not the actual ones still sitting in the back of Ma's closet, but the ones from the picture in the newspaper. The newspaper sneakers haunt me. They're just regular old Pro Keds from The Shoe Barn, but they look like lone, stunned witnesses to a crime. They should belong only to Pop, to us; something private turned inside out.

Pop's wallet was tucked under a sneaker tongue. It held two dol-

29

lars, his license, a packet of snapdragon seeds for the garden, a grocery list from Ma, and my school picture. When the cops finally gave
us back his things, I ate those seeds—swallowed the whole envelope
full of black speckles, nine-year-old Diamond hoping a real dragon
would sprout up inside me, fire blossoming from my belly.

The current had been strong that summer, too strong for swimming in places. A few people claimed they saw a floating body whiz
by in the foamy water. Ma says it probably got hooked onto a steamer
headed out to the ocean. *He couldn't swim. He never learned to swim.*
That was the last thing she said before she laid face down in the front
yard and cried into the grass for a whole day and night.

As awkward neighborhood people brought us Rice Krispie
Treats and casseroles, they whispered, "*Nobody* deserves to die like
that. It's all just so *strange*."

But he was not dead enough for the courts, even years later. They
declared him "missing." This was one of those confusing situations
that fall somewhere in between people trying to mess with us and
something too complicated for Ma to manage. *Trying to fix this is like
swimming in mud*, she always says.

We were pissed but didn't know where to put it, so we mastered
the wait for revenge. We made lists of the people who would regret
messing with us. We made lists of the things we would do to the
people who had messed with us. We crumpled the lists and replaced
them with faith in karma, God's own boomerang for the assholes
who had messed with us. We lit our Karma Kandle and prayed with
eyes shut tight for it to do its work.

Except that I don't pray for those people to let my dad be dead.
Instead, I picture him waiting for us in an actual place—maybe
deep in the woods near the caves, in a barn hiding behind haystacks,
or sitting in some diner a few towns over. He plots his return. He
watches over us at night. The things that keep him from us by day

are as murky in my mind as what keeps him "missing." I want it that way. Ma is trying to swim in mud; I just let it hold me.

Ma's mood is what decides whether or not we hitch or walk to get somewhere. Hitching is for days when we run out of ride-favors from our neighbors. Ma rallies me with a *Let's hit the road!* like we're Bo and Luke Duke but without the General Lee. We don't go with just anyone: no pickup trucks or broken car doors, no more than two men or one college bumper sticker, no beards, no booze, and nothing that tows a four-wheeler behind it.

When we first make a pick from a distance, Ma flashes a friendly wave at the driver, and we shuffle backward in slow motion; putting your thumb out is old-fashioned and only happens in movies when someone needs to be killed off. The town's small enough that if we don't know the person, we probably know someone who knows them. Ma's lived here her whole life. So did her parents, and their parents. A-holes joke that she's the town's version of a Native American.

Ma always stays on the outside closest to the cars to protect me in case some drunk guy clips us on his night swerve home. Sometimes a wiseass slows down just enough to fake us out, and Ma pounds on the side of the car door and screams like she's in pain as he speeds off. I bet there's a whole fleet of right-side-door-banged-up cars driving through town courtesy of us, the serial denters. I'm always scared that one of these times the brakes will screech and some nutbag will jump out and pound on us or have us arrested. Ma says they wouldn't have the guts to stop, because what if they'd really hit us?

She pretends that hitching is a treat.

"Let's catch a ride to the Goodwill, save our energy for later," she says, turning around to face the cars. Seeing the panic in my face, she tries to distract me with our game.

31

"I call it on the white Toyota Corolla," she says, nodding at the one coming toward us. My stomach drops as I scan the car for signs of safety. It's not foolproof. You can't *really* tell until you get in it, and by then, it's buckle up.

Being inside someone's car is like going in their purse or bedroom with permission but no advance notice. Ma made up Cargame, where right as a car is slowing down deciding whether to pick us up, we guess what kind of music will be playing, how it will smell, if it'll be clean or grimy, have a kid's car seat, a loose-change cup. It's easy when they have bumper stickers on the front, like *I Heart Cats* or *I wish my wife was as dirty as this car.*

"Stuffed animals, nut snacks, wet wipes, and Fleetwood Mac," Ma guesses confidently.

One for four. The lady is super nice, offering us salted peanuts, and asking if we want the air turned on. Ma thanks her, saying, "I never was one for driving," like we decided not to use our chauffeur today.

"How far are my girls going?" the lady says cheerfully, making sure to look us both in the eye each time she speaks. She's wearing a bright green dress with matching sandals, and her short red hair is forced back into a stubby ponytail with gel and a plastic green headband. I think she might be my classmate Brian Doherty's aunt, but I decide she's the cousin of an elf—she even smells like the color green. I can tell Ma likes her. There's something about breathing in normal people who are also nice that makes you feel better than you actually are. The way Ma has one arm hanging out the window and the other wrapped around her headrest, we could be a bunch of pals on our way to Friendly's for an ice cream sundae after a makeup party.

"We're just headed to the Goodwill." Ma says it with a fancy lady accent. Elf lady doesn't know what to say. "Diamond and me like to dig for treasures."

32

"Diamond is a lovely name." Elf lady looks back at me with an apology on her face.

"Tomorrow night is movie night for us. Diamond and me had a taste for steak and pasta. There's plenty if you'd like to join," Ma says.

Elf lady gets suddenly busy looking for something in the glove box.

"I could make some of my famous garlic bread?" Ma says after more silence, and I realize this dinner invite is real. "You'll join us?" she says with a shaky voice.

I see Elf lady's eyes get darty in the rearview mirror, and I grab on to the door handle as if that will protect us from what might happen. This is the start of a tricky thing that happens to us. Ma is tough and weirdly optimistic until she's not. She can run top speed into a wall ten times and laugh, unhurt, but on the eleventh, she just explodes into dust.

"How generous. If I didn't have to cook dinner for my husband, I'd take you up on that. It would be my cheat night!" She says it so sincerely Ma smiles, and I let myself think of all the things I'd eat on a cheat night.

"Diamond, haven't I seen you in town riding a bike?" Elf lady says.

"Yes, ma'am, that was my preferred mode of transportation."

"Some ass-hat jacked that bike, right out in front of the CVS!" Ma says it like gossip. "She was too old for it, anyway, don't you think?"

"God is making room for new things in your life, Diamond," Elf lady says.

"That would be cool." I lean forward into the back of her seat, gripping the edge of the headrest close to her shoulders, as if I have something important to say. I picture her as my ma—both of us wearing different shades of green to complement each other, everybody at school making jokes about elfin magic, but we wouldn't care. My current ma is the kooky aunt we look after, and me and Elf Ma just shrug when she says something stupid, like, *What are we gonna do with this one?* She would let me practice my driving in this very car.

Ma pipes in, "You know, a diamond doesn't just come into the world blinding folks with its beauty. It takes years for it to get like that." She looks back at me wide-eyed, as if this weren't the hundredth time she's said this.

I want to tell Elf lady that new things are happening; room is being made. But I can't say it in front of Ma. We both have our secrets.

"That's a good one, Ma." I smile at her.

I hang my head out the window and my hair makes a purring sound in the wind.

We get to the Goodwill early enough that it's still possible to find decent things. Morning is when they put out fresh donations. If you get there after noon, it's like picking through actual mounds of garbage. In the mornings, the clothes are still hung neatly in color coordinated rows with just a light mothball-dusty smell in the air. When the pizza shop next door opens in the afternoon everything smells like sadness and cheese.

I go right to the blues and grab the only dress that could fit me. It's a shimmery fabric with a small pocket on the chest. "Fancy-casual!" Ma says like we hit the jackpot.

Next, she makes me walk with her to the bank for free coffee before we head back home, calling it our "powerwalking workout" for the day, as if we have a choice between that and Jazzercising at the gym. The only other powerwalkers I've seen live across town— an after-dinner flock of ladies who drive to the park with their mini dumbbells and their swishy sweatpants, flapping their arms in unison as they loop around the dried-out duck pond.

Ma isn't playing around about today; she's arranged a ride in advance with our neighbor, Lottie DeStefano. We head around the block to Mrs. D's place, Ma with a bop in her step, proud that we managed to get out of the house clean and dressed on time. She looks like a stranger in her own clothes; they're tight and loose in all the wrong places. If I were as skinny as she is, I'd just wear my bathing suit, a short jean skirt, and crisp white Tretorns, like the girls I see sunbathing by the river or hanging out in the Cumberland Farms parking lot, spread across car hoods and bumpers like birds in uniform.

She has on the same dress she wore to Grandma Sylvia's funeral—black-and-white striped, short-sleeved, and shoulder-padded. I have a Swiss-cheese memory of the funeral day, the holes all filled in with pictures taken by one of Grandma's friends. I know that's the dress Ma wore because of the photo she keeps on her nightstand, the two of us in our new funeral gear—nude pantyhose and hard shiny shoes, mouths half-open because some dummy told us to smile and say, *Two all-beef patties special sauce lettuce cheese pickles onions on a sesame-seed bun*. Proof that you can't choose what you remember. Her pantyhose have a thick run down to her toes, probably from that same funeral day.

"No one will know when it got snagged," she says when I point to it. "It could have happened in the waiting room for all they know."

She's carrying a worn brown briefcase that belonged to her father, who died before I was born. He was a foreman at the textile mill. Ma loved her father the most. He was the last person to have real hope for her future. That's what Grandma Sylvia always said when she fought with Ma. *Your father had such hope for your future.*

I'm wearing the Goodwill dress. I look lumpy, and the tiny

pocket on my left boob only emphasizes the giant mound it sits on. I'm wearing flip-flops, but I can't see my feet anymore—a scary new line has been crossed.

"Don't we look like businesswomen," Ma says, as we stand at the edge of Mrs. DeStefano's empty driveway, ready to leap into her car as soon as it pulls in.

"Not really," I say.

Fifteen minutes go by, and Ma is swelling up with panic. She slashes at a pricker bush using a stick she found on the road; tiny red berries rain down on the ground. Our appointment with the lawyer is in five minutes. It takes about that long to get there by car.

"She's doing this on purpose," Ma says of Mrs. DeStefano, the closest thing to a friend she has, which isn't saying much. If you listen to Ma tell it, they both want only the very worst things in life for each other. They're usually in a fight or recovering from one.

"Maybe she got the time wrong?" I say, without much conviction.

"She knew exactly what time. She knew this was important. Crucial."

"Think she's waiting at our house?"

"This is where we always meet. *We* come to her majesty." She throws down her stick. "Goddamn it to hell! She's just getting her revenge because I owe her money."

I'm tired. I feel like ten years have passed since this morning.

"Eff it. Let's hit the road," she says.

"We'll never make it in time." It's a thirty-minute walk.

"You want to drive us over in your dad's car?" She looks at me so hard, for a second I think I'm found out.

"Why don't *you* drive us?" I say.

"Let's go. Now," she says, walking ahead of me.

"It's embarrassing going so late. And my knee hurts."

My knee does not hurt. It could easily start hurting any minute now, but sometimes I lie about the pain until I feel it. Ma does not turn around to look. "I might not make it all the way," I say.

"I'll carry you on my back then," she says, cracking herself up.

We walk ten minutes or so and cross over to River Street. Our heads turn at every sound as we scan the road, hoping to hitch a ride. Every few blocks we leap over piles of pebbly black deer shit, pristine, like tiny eggs in a nest. "Poop dancing!" Ma cackles, well into making-the-best-of-things mode.

This is the ugliest area along the riverbank—mostly abandoned factories and warehouses, with their crumbling brick and checkerboard windows caked in grime. The lawyer's office, about a mile away, is part of a new complex in a building that used to be a tool-and-die factory. With views of the river in the back, and old warehouses on either side, people look up to it with cautious hope and burning jealousy—as if the building itself is some rich family moving in to clean up the run-down neighborhood while holding its nose. I can't even count how many car-ride small-talk sessions turn into *I've been saying they should build up River Street for years*, and *No one wanted to listen when I said those factories are worth a fortune*; the knowingest people who ever knew nothing about something until it stood up and proved itself.

"I always knew Jerry would be a success," Ma says to me over her shoulder—I am a few feet behind her. My knee is catching up to my lie, slowly filling with fluid, stiffening up and forcing a little limp. I feel the heat from the sidewalk through the flimsy rubber bottoms of my shoes.

"He always thought the world of me, too," she says.

"What did he think you would do?" I ask.

"That's not what I meant," Ma snaps. "I was an excellent dancer. And I was nice to everyone. Treated 'em all like I would want to be treated, even the bad ones. Just how I teach you to be."

"Was Jerry the same as you?" I ask.

"Of course. We're all the same on the inside," Ma says.

"No we're not. I'm not." I stop to catch my breath. I spit on the ground. She hates that.

"Maybe we can get you one of those motorized chairs," she says.

"A wheelchair? That's so mean, Ma."

"No, silly. Like a go-cart. The teens ride them around. Safer than a car."

"Why would I want a go-cart?"

"Because people with money buy nice things for fun." She pauses, waiting for a reaction. "Diamond, do you understand that your whole life is about to change?"

"I don't know," I say. She wants my hope and I won't give it to her.

"This was what your dad wanted," she says. "This is for you."

I take her hand and squeeze it. This is the moment to pounce on her optimism, wrestle it into working for me.

"I was thinking maybe I should learn to drive," I say. "A car." I'm scared to look at her face.

She sighs deeply, like she's channeling centuries-old wisdom. "That's not a good idea," she says, holding my hand tighter, pulling me along as she starts walking again.

"Why not?"

"Having a car is too expensive."

"I can save up, fix Pop's car."

She snort-laughs. "That car is not fixable."

"I just want to learn. Take driver's ed. See what happens."

"Listen." She stops and grabs me by my wrists. "It's not the right thing for you, not right now." She speaks in a clear, knowing way that momentarily wipes my brain clean of the want. I lean into the Ma who knows what's best for me.

"Remember what happened last time I drove?" she says, whipping up her dress to show me the deep scar that wraps around her leg like a snake. Then she points to the top of her head where I know there's a white, shiny knot, a hairless island that can knock her silent for days. *Migraine, shhhhh* is sometimes all she can manage.

"I'm not gonna lose you," Ma says.

Too, she might as well add.

"Your father wouldn't want you to do it, either." She looks at me wild-eyed, like she's in a fight for her life and all she can find is a shoe to throw.

What she wants to say: *You're not gonna leave me.*

"OK, Ma. I won't do it," I lie.

"We'll talk about it next year, OK?" she says. "I'll be able to buy you a new car by then."

We stop at a parking lot in front of a deserted warehouse where a handful of druggies are rumored to live. I can't catch my breath, and my knee has a heartbeat. I lower myself to the curb, knowing full well what it will take for me to get up again. Ma does, too. She looks desperate.

"Sweet pea, you know you'll get your dress dirty like that. Come on," she says softly. She stands and holds out her hand as if coaxing an animal from under a car.

"I can't," I say. I stretch out, rubbing my puffed-up knee. My legs are lifeless, swollen and sprayed with a delicate red heat rash. It'll take at least a week for them to get back to normal. I'm hit with a feeling of so much tenderness and pity for them, it's like they're my sick children. I'm happy to cry for them, and I don't care if Ma sees it.

Except I look up and she's gone. Before I can turn my head all the way around, I hear metal wheels on gravel and then the shuffle of Ma's heels.

She's standing in front of me with a busted old Queens Shopping

Center shopping cart. The front has been cut out, so it almost looks like a wheelbarrow.

"Get in."

"Ma."

"We're almost there."

"That belongs to Homeless Richard," I say.

"He won't mind. He's saving us. We'll thank him later."

Ma's wheeze and the metal clanking is all I can hear as we fly down River Road. My legs dangle stiffly from the front of the cart, my poor fat kids out for a joyride.

"Take it easy on the bumps," I yell back through the wind as she nearly dumps me on the sidewalk.

"There, there now," she says, making mothery sounds I've never heard before.

I close my eyes and listen to the noises leaking out of her as if they're what's propelling us forward. I consider kicking off a flip-flop so I'd be forced to wait outside the office, a one-shoed embarrassment.

"I don't want a death certificate, Ma," I say quietly enough that I leave it up to the wind to carry it to her, or not.

"This is your very first meeting, sweet pea," she says in my ear, excited. Someone drives by and shouts something about groceries, but Ma acts like she doesn't hear.

We ditch the cart once the office is in sight. All of the building's shiny glass reflects back the decay from the old factories that surround it. Patches of green—weeds, ivy, moss—sprout from rusted crevices and shimmer in the new windows like a water garden.

"Pretty," Ma says, pulling out a cigarette when she sees people in front of the building on their smoke breaks. I'm holding on to her for balance.

40

"Do I have to say anything at the meeting?" I ask.

"You don't have to talk about your father," Ma says. "You were too young to remember anything. Just tell Jerry how when he was alive we always had a good life, never wanted for anything at all."

"But how would I know that if I can't remember anything?"

"Don't ruin this, please, Diamond," she says in a small voice, so I shut up.

"Aren't you a sight?" Jerry Polaski says as he grabs Ma in a bear hug, looking genuinely happy to see her. We're standing in his very full waiting room. Ma looks around to make sure everyone is taking note. Jerry is basketball-player tall, with arms that seem like they could wrap around her body twice. He looks years younger than Ma, like he's her friend's baby brother. This is the first time I've ever seen a man in a suit with a ponytail.

"You're so tiny." He holds on to her stick-thin arm, his fingers easily encircling the whole thing. Then he looks over at me like I've eaten half of her, sucked some bit of life out of the girl he knew. It hits me that as I've gotten bigger and bigger these past few years, she's gotten smaller and smaller.

"Is this—"

"This is my daughter, Diamond. She's a really smart girl. Way ahead of everyone else in her class." Ma says it proudly, even as I stand there panting in my sweat-striped dress, plucking fabric out of my folds. He offers me a cool air-conditioned hand and I give him a damp shake. He ushers us through the waiting room and I catch a nod at his secretary like some secret-code agreement, obviously having to do with Ma and me. I wish I hadn't seen it.

"Can I help you sit down?" he asks when he sees me limping.

"She had a bike accident, but she's almost all healed," Ma says. "So how's Candy?"

We're sitting on a leather sofa in a corner of his office, facing the river. I can only think about sitting perfectly still so I don't make the wet static sounds every time my bare skin lifts off the surface. He sits on the arm of his thick leather chair across from us, peeling an orange. The smell fills the room.

"We split up a few years ago." He's smiling and nodding.

"Oh, that's right. I knew that. I'm so sorry."

He offers us an orange slice, but it's an afterthought; he only has three pieces left.

"We have a lot of catching up to do then, don't we?" Ma says. Sometimes I remember that Ma used to be pretty. It peeks through her smile, like now.

"Anna, I'm sorry I don't have much time left. We were supposed to meet at one o'clock. I'm already running late for my next meeting."

"Could we come back tomorrow?"

"No, Anna." He laughs a little. There's a flatness to his voice, and I find myself wishing for that liquidy softness we hear from men in cars.

"Oh," she says, looking crushed. "We had a little mix-up with our transportation."

"Of course. I understand."

"Well, I think we can both make some money here," Ma says.

"Anna, let me stop you there. You insisted on this meeting, so I thought we were clear that it was just an introduction. You still have a lot of paperwork to get me, and that's only the start of the process. I want to manage expectations—"

"But I was thinking we could sue the original judge, the cops, the town—"

"Seven years is the law for death in absentia. Sometimes they make exceptions, but there are enough red flags in this case—"

Ma pulls a crumply piece of paper out of her briefcase, and I can see that her hands are shaking. I recognize the original police report. My eyes always grab on to the same things: *July 1, 1980* and *Negro with local wife and child* and *colored man with no known employment* and *last seen by the Swift River*. And *Assault and battery with bodily harm, June 22, 1980.*

"I thought this was what you needed." Ma tries to hand it to him, but he waves it away.

My heat rash prickles with Ma's shame. Our shame.

"Come back in a few weeks after you fill out the forms and get your witness statements. Maybe check in with his old friends and family," he says. "Put the death notice in the paper. There's a lot you have to do, Anna."

Ma stares straight ahead with her dead-eye look, so I nod yes.

"I'll help you file the petition with the court. But you need to come with two hundred and fifty dollars for the processing fees. And the bank still needs to do their due diligence, checking for bank account activity and possible sightings—"

"Account activity? Account activity!" Ma laughs so hard the secretary pops her head inside and then back out again.

"Anna, I have to ask. Have you ever tried to find him?" Jerry looks embarrassed. "You know, the investigation and all . . . and there has been talk . . ."

"No." She cuts him off.

"You said he had an aunt in Canada and a sister in Georgia."

"His aunt is dead, and it's his cousin, not his sister," I say, my voice quivering. A new feeling twists in my chest—I both need Lena and hate her for being gone.

"He was an only child," Ma adds, like that was the key missing piece of information.

"Anna, you have to know that people still say they see him from time to time."

Ma is muttering something about the two hundred and fifty dollars. I pinch her leg to try and snap her out of it.

"These racist pricks think *any* Black man they see is Rob."

"Excuse me, Mr. Collins says he can't wait much longer." The secretary is back, holding a takeout bag. The sweet orange smell is replaced by the armpit scent of fast food; it still manages to make my mouth water.

Jerry gets up and walks toward us with the same big smile. As he stands over us, looking down, his smile cracks and the sigh that leaks out of him catches me like a contagious yawn; I sigh too. Ma doesn't move from the couch. She stares at the police report, her hands still shaking.

"Surely you have five more minutes for us—"

"Ma, come on. Let's go."

"Anna, I wish I did." He holds out his hand to pull her up from the couch. She doesn't budge. He looks at me.

"Ma, please." I stand up.

"Oh boy." She suddenly grabs hold of his arm and jumps up with weird enthusiasm. Looking up at him, she reaches around and tugs on his ponytail. Hard. His neck snaps back.

"Look at that thing," she chuckles, running a few fingers through it like she's petting an animal. He jerks his head away and steps back from us, shocked.

"Time to go, ladies," he says. Strands of his hair have fallen out of the ponytail and I can't help feeling like we just tore his shirt off. He doesn't move to fix it.

"I'll go tell Dad to pull the car around," I say, and give a laugh that sounds like I'm crying with a smile. I want to rip the ponytail off his head because he won't fix it.

"Diamond, my jewel. Let's hit the road."

* * *

We are headed home, down River Street toward the cart, holding hands. I let mine be limp.

"Suing the town?" I scream at her.

She shrinks. We always bicker, but I never shout.

"A book I found at the library had a case—" All I can think is, *Ma was at the library?* And then a car is honking next to us.

"Anna, what are you doing?" Mrs. DeStefano yells through the open window. She's waving like crazy. "Hellooooo?"

Ma won't look at her.

"I said I'd pick you up at the lawyer's office at two o'clock. Why are you walking?"

"You said you'd *take* us there. You promised." Ma still won't look at her.

"I said no such thing. I told you I had to take Frank to the dentist today. Big fucking baby that he is."

Through her scowl, Ma's face shows a flicker of remembering.

"Anna? Get in the car. Diamond, tell your mother to get in."

We both say nothing.

"What's the matter with you?" She lets her mouth hang open.

"We don't need your goddamn help!" Ma screams it straight ahead at something in front of her.

"Aw, Anna." She punches at the horn a final time. "Diamond, your mother is a piece of work."

"We both are," I say. "Pieces of work." I give her a little wave: a *thank-you* wave, a *don't-drive-away* wave, a *leave-us-alone* wave, a *don't-give-up-on-us* wave. It will be months before they speak again.

We are waiting for night to come.

It's hot inside the house—a heavy, bossy heat pushing us from room to room as the afternoon sun moves through. When night comes we'll blow up our giant kiddie pool, fill it with water from the hose, and cool ourselves outside. No daytime eyes on us. No nosy DeStefanos. The rest of the town turns on their air-conditioning or goes to Crescent Lake on hot nights like this, loading up their trunks with sandy beach towels, boom boxes, and six packs of beer. We travel through the dark of the house to the patchy grass in our own front yard. We wait for it.

I lie in the cool water by myself while Ma gets ready, looking out at the mountains. Swift River is a valley town. Once the sun starts to set behind the two ranges that surround us, they look like outstretched, muscly arms, tricking us all into feeling protected. Keeping us from ever leaving.

"Make room for your ma!"

She comes out of the house in a long T-shirt, with probably just underwear underneath. She'll say it's a bikini bottom if I ask. She's carrying our Karma Kandle, a flashlight, her cigarettes, and a Sears catalog. We like to circle things we're going to buy someday.

I'm wearing a bathing suit with a T-shirt that goes down to my knees. Our legs are a brown and white tangle. My belly rises above the water like an island. Ma's too-big underwear puffs out around her like a cloud.

"How's your knee feeling?" Ma asks.

"Much better."

I hold up my feet and wiggle them.

"Such pretty feet you have, Diamond."

Ma's pale, flat stomach peeks through the surface of the water like a smooth stone.

"You came from here," Ma says, patting it. "You came from me."

I click on our flashlight and make shadow puppets on her boob. A bird. A one-eared rabbit. An elephant with a stubby tusk. She laughs and splashes me.

In the distance someone is calling for a lost dog. A flashlight scans the yard and catches us briefly, like criminals. We hold our breath and wait for it to pass.

Back in my room, I flop down on my bed, waterlogged and bone-tired. My excitement for tomorrow feels both bright and heavy, like a first chuckle after a long cry. By the light of the Karma Kandle, so Ma can't tell I'm still up, I write Lena back.

4

July 11, 1987

Dear Diamond,

I was so grateful to hear from you, and of course I understand
your feelings about me taking so long to show up, breezing in with
a letter like I wasn't gone your whole life. I'd be sore about that,
too. I guess I didn't know what to say that was good enough, that
was sorry enough. I've been thinking about the fact that families
split apart over one thing, but the thing that keeps them apart
is something else entirely. Toss in guilt and shame and then the
years stack up like bricks in a wall you can't climb over. I don't
want to be a woman who loses her people, Diamond. I wish I had
been there for you as a child, given you a bigger circle of family
so it wasn't just you and your mama and daddy on an island by
yourselves. It sounds like you have a very full, happy life with your
mama now, and maybe there's not much room for another person,
but I'd like to try to make up for it if you'll let me?

To answer your question, I only heard from your father four
times during his whole life up there. After they left Woodville, my

mama and his daddy stopped speaking. At first, they put up an effort so we could all keep up with Robbie, but eventually adult problems just trickle down. Once, your daddy asked me to take you in for the summer. Mama was already sick by then. I know he was having a hard time with money. And he said he was struggling to show you who you were, scared to death that you'd get lost without knowing your Black family. At first I said yes, and we got to making plans. But then I started to think, *What would I do with a little girl?* I was in nursing school, living in a one-room apartment in Atlanta with just a pullout bed; you would've been sleeping with me. I had nightmares about rolling over and suffocating you in your sleep, scary as anything real. Your father had sent me a picture of you—prettiest little thing I'd ever seen, and I don't mean in the way they describe all light-skinned, curly-haired girls. You were lit with a shine like armor. Like you didn't need a mirror to make you happy, and it couldn't ever bring you pain. You looked nothing like me. What if someone saw us together and thought I'd kidnapped you? What if no one believed you belonged to me? Some say I'm a peculiar woman, Diamond. What if you didn't behave? Or like me? I called your daddy back and told him no, the timing wasn't right. I'm not proud of this. I imagine you must have been very disappointed.

Diamond, I didn't know your daddy as a man, but I missed him every day of my life. As kids, we tore through Woodville together, ate it up. The woods were ours—trails, forts, shortcuts— our bare feet knowing every mossy, rocky, leaf-filled inch. The streets belonged to us, too, even the ones we weren't supposed to walk down—the ones troubled with white people dangers. The house, with its one hundred and one places to hide, singing ghosts, and a slew of kids. The dipping creek that rose and fell with the rains. After he was gone, I could never make it all just mine again.

As time passed, I got angry being stuck to something not there anymore.

I wonder what missing him has been like for you?

I'm sorry, Diamond, about your daddy. That's how I should have started with you. But this is how we got to here.

I'm happy you want to learn more about our family. I think our story is gonna fill you up, make you stand straighter. It's a good one.

Lena

5

1980

When I am eight years old, Ma and me start to keep secrets from Pop. He is leaving us in slow drips. In six months, he will disappear.

It's deep winter, and the snow has painted our house normal again. Gone is the missing row of roof shingles, the overgrown grass, the junk-filled yard; we are buried under the smooth white lines that cut through the neighborhood. Drifts as tall as me hide broken toys and buffer the cars that dare to skid down our curvy street. All that whiteness is loud and sharp. Pop has gone quiet and still.

Ma puts a curtain around the two of us girls, shielding him from our noise and fumbles. Inside the curtain we are messy and break stuff by accident; we do things we're not supposed to do and we don't get punished. "It's OK. This is just between us," Ma says with a soft voice and a pinched face when she gets called into school after I wet myself in class because teacher wouldn't give me a pass to the bathroom. Ma's eyes dart toward the living room to make sure my badness has not broken the spell between Pop and the TV.

This goes against my nature as a teller of everything, a tattler on myself and others. Pop has always been my best audience. Nestled under his armpit on the sofa, I would describe what I heard and saw from my hiding place under the porch: a woman going through the neighbor's trash, a man dragging his wife by the ponytail, two cats fighting a raccoon.

Sometimes I didn't have to snoop; I could be invisible in plain sight. "You're like a goddamn ninja," Ma said, jumping when she realized I had been watching her stare at nothing for fifteen minutes. I would melt into walls, as quiet as breath, as breath being held. Or I made playing sounds—dolls talking, cars *vroom*ing. Adults thought my ears had been shut off.

"I got hemorrhoids the size of meatballs," I said to Pop. I pushed out my belly to imitate the pregnant Mrs. Duffy, who hung out her kitchen window to smoke cigarettes while talking on the phone. Pop never made me feel bad for having a chubby tummy; he patted it like there was a baby inside.

"You're a born comedian." His belly laugh vibrated through my whole body like we were the same person. "Or a spy."

This same reporting to Ma was met with sleepiness, a kind of tired that seemed directly inspired by my talking. If she had just come home from work cleaning rooms at the Tee Pee Motel or teaching a dance class at The Creative Talent Dance Studio, sometimes she responded by putting a finger to her mouth, *Shhhh*. With my dad, I was the most interesting person who had ever spoken words.

Once, while reading him my book about the brown Indians, I asked him if we were supposed to have our own private language, too. Pop is the only other brown I know. No one else in town has dark skin like ours, not even Ma, which is what makes our family different. In the book, the Indians talk to animals, the wind talks to the trees, and the wolves talk to fire so it will never leave them.

"No, silly," he laughed. "We speak English."

Instead, Pop taught me a language called Nostralis.

Two flares of the nostril means "Hello." Three means "Your breath stinks," and so on.

He invented this language with his cousin when they were my same age so that they could plan secret adventures right in front of parents or aunties and uncles. In the town where he spent the first seven years of his life, he told me, they didn't have hobbies, daycare, or time-outs. Children looked after themselves, fetched cigarettes and bottles of pop at the store for the adults, did chores around the neighborhood for anyone who needed help, and listened to grown-ups tell stories on screened-in porches at night. They lived in a cluster of families on a dead piece of farmland, their houses squeezed in close to each other, making one long row of boxes like teeth across the mouth of the street. Some of the families moved around "like gypsies," he said, a new box and a new landlord each time the money ran out.

"We are not gypsies," Ma said when I asked, since we run out of money, too. "This will always be your house, Diamond." It was where Ma had grown up, where her own Ma had been raised, and her mother before that. "These are your roots."

I pictured all of those women holding my ankles so I wouldn't float away.

Pop does not want this house, these roots.

"I need *my* family," he says as I listen outside their bedroom door one Saturday morning. "And Diamond needs to be around people who look like her."

"When's the last time you spoke to them? They don't give two shits about us. *We* are your family. Me and Diamond."

"We could send her to Georgia this summer. Lena would take her, just for a few weeks."

"You haven't seen her since you were a kid," Ma says. "We're not just gonna *send* her our daughter."

"You don't . . ." Pop is out of words and his voice falls into a hole. Everything else is whispers.

The next morning I ask Ma if Pop wants to give me away to another family.

"No, baby. You're not going anywhere," she says. "Your dad doesn't want you getting hurt, is all." She pinches my arm. "Now mind your business and stop listening to grown-up conversations."

Ma never comes right out and says, *Don't tell your father things*, but she doesn't have to. She is careful with him; he is limp and polite—a tired visitor come in from the cold. Whereas his deep voice used to push itself into every corner of the house, everywhere at once, now Pop takes up almost no space. He comes home from work at the mill and crumbles into his chair. He shoos me away if I'm playing too close to him.

Ma explains that someone at the mill is saying mean things to him, accusing him of things he didn't do.

"Imagine that meanness making cuts all over his body that his clothes cover up," she says. "Sometimes you can accidentally bump into a sore spot and not even know it."

I am gentle with him, too. I make my indoor games quiet games. I fold myself in half.

I am angry at the mill for taking our old Pop, leaving us with this new one.

One day, a blond-haired boy calls me a nigger during recess. I don't know what this is, and I feel the sharp-edged newness of the word; I've never heard it spoken before. I can tell he's new to it, too. The way he says it, *nig-ger*, enunciating each syllable; something off of his vocabulary list he's trying out. It sounds ugly, and his mouth looks all wrong with the word in it.

I react to the reactions around us—jaw drops, squeals, titters. I have just been shot with an invisible bullet.

I go home and tell Ma. She cries and says she wishes she were Black, would give anything to be Black like me. "Look at my ugly white skin," she says, pinching at her arm violently. But it's just her pinkness and freckles, the Ma skin I love, nothing ugly.

I want to tell Pop. Ma says don't, but that night after dinner I work up the nerve to put my face in front of his, one long flare of my nostrils for *Help*.

"Not now," he says, barely looking at me.

Ma pulls me away.

"Let's find the ugliest white thing we can think of to call this boy," she says after my bedtime story.

"Call him an asshole, sweetheart," Grandma Sylvia says, resting her chin on my bed as she sits on the floor. She's on a surprise visit from her apartment across town.

"We don't use that language in this house." Ma angles herself to give Grandma her full back.

"My house, you mean?"

"Happy to give it back to you, Mom. We'll go somewhere else. Say the word."

"She should be kicking him in his little nuts," Grandma starts to wind up but stops herself. I wonder if Ma and me will one day get stuck in the same fight forever.

"How 'bout a fish belly? They're white and gross," Ma says. "I saw a Jamaican guy in a movie say that to a white man. Call that boy Fishbelly."

I think of the slimy translucence, the perfect evenness of the belly bulge, the whisper of skin barely covering the inner parts. The way you can see the breath—actually see the breath—like the skin is a part of the air moving through its body.

"It's not ugly enough," I say.

"We'll find something else, then."

But we don't. And when I march up to the boy the next day on the playground and spit my newly created insult in his face, he pokes me in my gut and calls *me* Fishbelly.

"Then you're the nigger!" I shout.

To the other kids, this is the funniest thing I've ever said. More jaw drops and squealing and laugher. The boy punches me in the arm, hard.

For the next week he's called Nigger Boy and I'm called Fishbelly, until his parents threaten to sue the school if they don't do something about it. Emergency meetings are had. He is made to say, "I'm sorry," and I have to say, "I accept your sorry and I'm sorry, too." This is the end of it, for him. I am still called Fishbelly.

We don't tell Pop any of it.

A few weeks later, me and this same boy play "making love" after school at the Boys & Girls Club. All has been forgiven over graham crackers and disco lessons, and Ma has just filled my head with the book *Where Do Babies Come From?* In it, an enormous, naked white man and woman rub their fleshy parts together. Out come cartoon, dancing sperm with top hats and pretty lady eggs swimming around in a colorful, swirly womb. There's an explosion of some kind and they make a glorious sperm-and-egg sandwich.

The no-clothes part doesn't translate. Me and the boy have on our boots and snowsuits. We've just finished our disco lessons, and I'm still wearing a sparkly disco crown. We know enough not to make love out in the open, heading instead to the shrubbery in front of the parking lot. It has just started to snow.

He lies on top of me and I hug him.

And then, my first kiss, stiff lipped and spit drenched, held for at least thirty seconds. Our eyes are wide open the whole time, and I marvel at the delicate whiteness of his eyelashes; they are the only things in focus. I feel the air move up through his stomach and into my mouth; we puff each other's cheeks out for fun. I breathe in his day through my nose: ivory soap, orange juice, and melting-snow-on-sweater.

"That's it?" he says finally, rolling off of me.

"I think there's more," I say. I don't want him to leave.

It's getting dark, and the light from cars passing through the parking lot washes over us in speckles through the bushes. We are hidden from view. A horn blast jolts us off the ground and we stand up, dizzy and scared.

My dad is leaning up against our car with his arms folded. He's far enough away that I can't make out the look on his face, but I know he is staring right at us. He is tall and lumpy, and I can tell he's wearing his layers of clothes to keep warm—T-shirt, long john shirt, two sweaters, sweatshirt, scarf, and his rain jacket. He likes to peel himself like an onion. Sometimes Ma peels him, too. I feel a rush of love for him. And panic.

"Get over here," I see his mouth say.

The boy looks back and forth between Pop and me.

"It's OK," he says, and then kisses my hand.

"What's OK?" I ask. He's already off and running.

"That your dad is a nigger," he calls over his shoulder.

The night is thick and holding its breath.

Snow comes down in mini fistfuls, looking like cotton balls piling up in Pop's Afro.

"What were you doing in the bushes?" His eyes are furious, but his voice belongs to the flat and lifeless Pop who lives with us now. As the club's door opens and closes in the distance, a Bee Gees chorus yelps into the cold. I feel suddenly protective of the fun times we have in there.

"I can't tell you."

"Who was that boy with you?"

I am quiet until we're all the way inside the car.

"I can't say."

"What was that he said to you?"

"I can't . . ."

"I'm gonna ask you one more time."

He doesn't ask and I don't answer.

The car fills up with our silence. I stare at his face, waiting for what's next. A winter cold rattles in his chest, and he coughs uncontrollably as the heater kicks on. The whole car smells like his cherry cough drops and the pine air freshener dangling from the mirror.

"OK then," he says.

His hair sags as the snow melts into his eyes and drips off his mustache. He blinks back the water and leans into the windshield, clicking on the wipers. They paint half-moon roads in front of us. It's only snowing inside the headlights.

By the time we get home, it has turned into light rain, forming a crispy crust on the top of the snow. My boots make popping sounds through the ice skin, leaving giant holes behind me.

"Go straight to your room and don't come out until you're ready to talk," Pop says without looking at me.

"What happened?" Ma calls after me as I run to my room without taking off my snowsuit or snow boots. I flop face down on my bed.

I listen to their voices in the kitchen. Pop is fuming now, his voice thawing like the snow. Ma is whisper-yelling. A few minutes later she sits on my bed and takes off my wet things, not getting mad even though my covers are soaked.

"Come tell your father what happened."

"I can't," I say. I'll just take my punishment. I know if I tell he will send me away to the other family.

"Please, Diamond," she says with the voice of a little girl.

I am not allowed to leave my room. Not for school. Not for Boys & Girls Club. Not for disco lessons. Not for anything except going to the bathroom. I drag out each trip across the hallway, taking the tiniest of baby steps, my eyes grabbing at all the things I took for granted. *Hello, my old friend dirty clothes hamper. I miss you, Ma's broken exercise bike.* I stop to touch Grandma Sylvia's watercolor painting of mallard ducks in a pond.

"You're gonna be pissing in a bucket if you don't keep it moving," Pop threatens from the living room, his voice wobbly.

Three times a day Ma brings me food like I'm a prisoner from TV, begging me, "Please tell your dad what happened so this can end. Please." She looks at her lap when she speaks and says nothing of the fact that until now she has been my partner in keeping secrets. In the mornings I wake with the loose memory of her cool hands touching my forehead, checking for signs of damage while I sleep.

In my room I dig out my old Fisher-Price village from when I was four. The people are small and hollow with no arms. Their skin is a pale peach color, except the dog, who is white with black spots. Two at a time, they make love to each other. Even the dog gets to play. On top of the farmhouse. At the general store. In the fire station. Sometimes my finger is the penis, poking inside their hollows.

Day and night trade places. While it's light out, the house is silent. Darkness hits with a storm of sound. First: the flutter of Ma's footsteps, pierced by the loud clanging of a pot or the closing of cupboard doors; then static fuzz finds music on the portable radio she carries from room to room, shaking away silence from dusty corners. Doors slam, and Pop's voice climbs a ladder, rising like it's coming from somewhere deep underground. He is back to life, yelling at Ma. She is selfish. She is bad. She is going to ruin me. She talks back to him calmly, as if part of a different conversation. I am too far away to hear her side, and too scared to sneak out of my room for a better listen. Things are smashed and walls are pounded; an avalanche of plaster-crumble follows each thud. It sounds like a giant bird—a *Microraptor*—flapping its wings. I imagine the patch job to come—a new raised sheetrock square joining the others spread throughout the house, painted over like poorly hidden doors that make me think, *What's inside there?* even though I already know. I picture other ruined things: books I tore to shreds, dolls with their eyes poked back into their heads, the baby hole I punched in my own bedroom wall, covered up by a Yoda poster. I wonder what I will be like as a ruined girl.

After a week, Pop comes to see me in my room. He looks nice and new in what he calls his "church pants" and a stain-free white shirt with a big collar, like he dressed up just for me. Also new: a look on his face I can't read—wild and groggy, like someone shaken from sleep. He joins me on the floor with my Fisher-Price lovemaking village.

"Nice tiara," he says, touching the sparkly wreath around my head.

"It's a disco crown," I say. He nods as if he's learned something important.

"You want to talk about anything?" he says.

"Not really."

His new face crumbles.

"For chrissake, I'm your father! You don't keep things from me!" he says. "Tell me what happened!" He snatches off my disco crown, like maybe this will allow good sense back into my head.

"I want to stay," I say.

"Stay where?"

"Stay here in our house. I don't want to give it back to Grandma. I don't want to be sent to the brown family."

"What kind of nonsense has your mother been telling you?"

"You ruined my skin!" I yell.

It comes so fast and loud, I scare even myself.

Pop looks at his hands, like he's silently asking them what to do. He puts the disco crown back on my head.

I didn't mean it, I want to say, but can't.

A tear slides down his face; I stretch up toward him to wipe it away with a Fisher-Price cowboy. He takes it from me before I reach him.

"They can't even give them goddamn arms?" He picks up the fireman, who's making love to the farmer's wife in the stable.

His voice is limp, again.

I want to kiss his hand, a peck for each knuckle, even the ones blackened with scabs. Instead, I pick up the dog and make him punch the fireman in the face; I add a sound effect, *Pow!* Pop smiles. And then we cross over to the other side of something. Not bad to good. Just bad racing toward something else.

Later that night, I look out my window and see him standing in the yard, smoking his pipe as the snow comes down. A curlicue of smoke floats past me and escapes into the night sky. Soon, he's covered.

6

1987

It's not lost on me that Ma needs two hundred and fifty dollars to file our court petition, and I'm about to have two hundred and fifty in my hand that I won't give her. About a year ago, when I was still getting paid under the table, I asked my boss, Tim, to put aside a few dollars every payday and to return it to me only after I'd saved up enough for driver's ed. That way I would *technically* be giving Ma my whole check each week. Today, I collect my money. It's my first day of driver's ed. It'll be the most I've ever spent on anything. I get five weeks of classes, three weeks of driving lessons in a car, a license, freedom.

Classes for Get in Gear! Professional Driving School are held in the basement of the Elks Lodge. On my way to the stairs in the back of the building, I peek through a window into the smoky main hall, with its dark wood-paneled walls, card tables, and butt cracks framed inside the backs of metal folding chairs. I stop to watch two pot-bellied men fold a tattered American flag into a triangle. Another tapes a party streamer to the wall. The rest drink beer, eat sandwiches, and argue with their mouths full.

When I was little, this was one of those places we would speed-walk by with our eyes on the ground. Ma and Pop never gave that order out loud, it was just something I knew to do—keep moving until Pop loosened his death grip on my hand, until Ma resumed her patter of gossip and complaints, our three bodies on pause until we could pass. I didn't know what we were afraid of, just that we couldn't be ourselves again until we could.

Today, I feel the same nerves, but not just because of the Elks.

I haven't seen my classmates in over a month. I'm having the terror that usually comes with cooling weather and back-to-school Goodwill clothes. Summer always pulls me far enough away that I forget this thing: me in the sea of them. The shock of my dark summer skin against theirs. My body squeezing itself through the narrow rows of chair-desks, ass-plowing into people even when I shimmy down sideways. No fun summer vacation stories to tell. No boyfriend to brag about. Every year, I fantasize about a newer, better version of myself who will show up on the first day of school—skinny, Jordache jeans, and tame hair, fresh off of a summer adventure—but she never comes. I'm fatter than the last time they saw me. Much fatter. Like, I'm off the actual scale—it doesn't go higher than three hundred pounds. I comfort myself with the fact that July is the in-between time, when anything can still happen.

This is the only driver's ed in all of Swift River Valley, so it's full of kids from area high schools. I see a handful of people I know and try not to catch anyone's eye.

"Earthquake!" a kid with a patchy mustache yells when I scooch by him. He looks around wildly, waiting for his meanness to catch fire. He gets a couple of laughs, but mostly eye rolls and head shakes. "Fishbelly!" he tries next. Gets nothing.

Ma comes to me in these moments; for a second I wish I could tell her about the stupid driving posters covering the walls—a cartoon squirrel behind the wheel of a people-sized car, squeaking out safety tips. She would have some corny thing to say, like, *Squirrels can't drive, pea-brains!* and then elbow me. I would elbow her back and then she would try to tickle me and I would grab her hand and then someone would get hurt for real. We are a good team when it comes to pretending something bad isn't happening.

A girl throws a Cheeto at me and another mouths, "Oh my god," but otherwise I make it to the very back of the room uninjured. I sit against the wall, right in front of a giant *Penguin Crossing* street sign. A girl who goes to my school, Shelly Ostrowski, sits down next to me in front of *Danger*. We haven't spoken since fifth grade, but here she calls me "Di" and looks at me every time our teacher, Mr. Jimmy, says something dumb, rolling her eyes and dramatically mouthing things I can't understand. I just laugh. Mr. Jimmy calls us by our street sign names. Shelly whispers that he does this gag in every class; I quickly understand that she wants to be "Danger" more than she wants to sit in the back next to me.

"I failed the stupid test two times, which is why I have to take this stupid class again," she says, in between bites of cuticle skin.

Shelly has long blond hair that thins out as it travels down her back in split-ended wisps, the front of it teased out and hair-sprayed frozen, like a wreath around her face. She is skinny, with hard, muscly legs, big boobs, and full lips that I'm sure make most boys think of sucking things. She is a knockout from almost every angle, except for one droopy eyelid, which makes her seem pretty in pieces, kind of like me.

At school, there are popular sluts and then there are slutty sluts. Shelly is a slutty slut. I don't know if she slept with the whole football team or just the wrong girl's boyfriend, but her locker is always decorated with *whoreface*, *dishrag*, and *one-eyed monster*.

In the same way that sometimes I like being invisible, Shelly seems to like being a slutty slut. Or at least she isn't bothered by everyone being so bothered by her.

Like now, Shelly is asking for it. It's gross how she's flirting with Mr. Jimmy.

"Hey, Danger, when you see a flashing yellow light at an intersection, what are you supposed to do?"

"Come on, Mr. Jimmy, you know I don't do slow. Ask another question."

Everyone groans in the same note. "Skank," someone coughs into their hand. The room gets loud with hoots and snorts and barks.

Mr. Jimmy smiles and puts a hand up, like, *Pump your brakes, people*, but he doesn't tell anyone to stop. He's happy to be here with us, among us. In fact, he doesn't look much older than us, until you get up close and see the moist-looking bags under his eyes, the yellow teeth. He has shaggy, bouncy hair and a mustache that curls around his top lip. He says things like, "Dude was bitchin' on the corners" and "Yo, take a chill pill." Mr. Jimmy explains that he was supposed to make everyone call him "mister" plus his last name, but the only mister-plus-his-last-name he knew was his father, a mean old bastard, so he was going to half follow the rules and go by mister plus his first name. But there'd be no rule breaking for us. *When you're driving, lives are on the line!*

"So what's my name?" he says, hyped up like this is a pep rally. Everyone looks around, confused.

"Mr. Jimmy!" he says. Then waits. "I said, what's my name?"

"Mr. Jimmy," everyone says back quietly, not in unison. I just mouth the words.

"Who's ready to drive?" he says.

Yes, me, let's go! Everyone roars. I have to admit I get the chills a little.

* * *

At eight o'clock, the class pours out the back of the lodge and into the parking lot. The Elks are leaning against the window, watching us and laughing. Muffled sounds leak out of the waiting cars, and I hear a father yelling at his son for throwing a half-eaten McDonald's burger out the window. Suddenly I realize I'm hungry, that I haven't eaten in hours. The limp, gray piece of meat, ketchup-soaked bun, and shredded lettuce clumps are scattered next to the car. Something sad and urgent pulls at me; I want to eat that thing right off the ground. It's like curling up in my bed, covers over my head—hiding and comfort at the same time.

"Were you going to hitchhike home?" Shelly is next to me. Speaking but not looking directly at me. I wonder if she might be talking to herself.

"I was just deciding," I say, though I honestly don't have a plan. While I'd hoped a neighbor or someone I knew might offer me a ride, I also don't feel like making adult chitchat.

"I have enough gas. I can take you home," she says.

"But you don't have a license yet," I say, confused.

"I have a car, though." Shelly smiles and shrugs. "Nobody cares."

As she leads me through the parking lot, I have this stupid feeling that I don't really know how to walk next to someone, especially since we aren't looking at each other; I worry I'm too close and might whap an arm into her by mistake. When I hang back a little she turns around and says, "Get moving, Di!" And then I'm the fat girl who can't walk fast enough. I catch up and she smiles right at me.

Her car is an older Buick, mud-colored and no power anything, maybe something she inherited from a grandparent. Oh, but the inside! It smells like flowers and cherries. Everything has been magically repurposed to be of service to makeup: mascara and eyeliner are tucked into the pink, fur-framed visor; a bouquet of lip gloss fills the cup holder; a tiny perfume sample kit is Velcroed to the dashboard.

I notice a pillow with a faded Strawberry Shortcake pillowcase and a red fuzzy blanket folded up on the back seat. On the floor: an A&P paper bag with a pair of sneakers, some pink Daisy razors, and a few cans of Beanee Weenee franks and beans. I remember that Shelly lives in a house so filled to the brim with junk, you can see it piled up to the tops of the windows. The porch is covered in broken furniture topped with bursting black trash bags. The whole thing looks like it's sinking into garbage quicksand.

"I don't bring boys in here," Shelly says quickly when she sees me looking at the blanket and pillow.

"Oh, I didn't think that," I say. My stomach gurgles.

"That blanket looks soft," I offer.

"It's OK," she says with a shrug. "I like to sleep outside, by the river sometimes. Like camping," she says. "Except now I'm afraid I'll get raped by a fucking deer."

"Camping is cool," I say. "But without the deer rape." I don't know if this is the right moment to tell a camping story, if it's my turn to say more than three words, but I want to. "My family went camping once," I say. Shelly doesn't respond.

I'm suddenly scared that I stink. I consider asking her if I can try some of the perfume. In the summer, heat bumps erupt in places I can't reach, and eventually they turn sour, like something rotting deep in the fridge. I have on Ma's body spray, but today it's not enough. Shelly reads my mind, picks out a sparkly tube, and spritzes my neck without asking. I decide to think the very best thoughts about this.

As she applies a fresh coat of everything, I'm surprised to see her put mascara on the droopy eye. I find this strangely inspiring, and my brain grabs on to corny expressions like, *Work with what you got!* and *Beauty is in the eye of the beholder!*

"Di-a-mond," Shelly practices my name, as if it's Swahili.

I know what she's thinking—*It's so Black*—but I was named after my white grandma, Grandma Sylvia, who used to be an amateur ice dancer when she was a teenager. She made her own sparkly costumes; Diamond was her nickname. Her all-state competition dresses have been hanging on my wall since I was little, like art. They're colorful stretchy things soaked in rhinestones with built-in underwear. They sparkle in the dark, my own private stars.

"How old do you think Mr. Jimmy is?" Shelly asks.

"At least twenty-two," I say, deciding it's safest to round down.

"Not even close. He's twenty-nine."

"But he looks so young," I say, thinking about the Van Halen T-shirt he wore today.

Shelly turns on the radio, a shiny Pioneer stereo system that, like everything else inside this old car, is unexpected. The radio is programmed to 97.3, the pop station out of Springfield, and I jump a little as DJ Johnny Jamz blasts into the car, mid–*yo yo yo* as he winds up all the "party people" gearing up to go out later tonight, dancing in front of mirrors or whatever party people do to get in the mood. I listen to him sometimes on the weekend with Ma, who tries to get me to sing along with her to all the songs from the Top 40. I don't remember when, if ever, I've listened to the radio with someone my age. Music makes me feel like all the best things are happening somewhere else.

I look over at Shelly for my cue, to see if I should be bopping my head or tapping something to the beat of the music. She bursts out loud singing Whitesnake's "Is This Love." Her voice isn't bad, but she sings it like it's a Whitney Houston song. I wonder if I'll ever be able to tell her about my harmonizing.

71

"Mr. Jimmy said I'm always the hottest girl in the class." She stops singing and snaps her head my way.

"You've been alone with him?"

"Once or twice." She head-snaps again, with a smile and an eyebrow raise. "He gives me extra help."

I start to get grossed out, but then I remember that thing when a certain kind of grown man says something nice and an unnameable tingle of good feeling and bad feeling creeps through your body like something alive, until another feeling pulses through your head and skin and privates and makes you want to throw up.

This happens sometimes when Ma and me misjudge a car, and I get stuck in the back seat with a jerk who wants to ask me a million questions about school while he's pressed up against me, accidentally brushing hands over my chest, my thighs, sliding fingers under my clothes. I know it's bad news if Ma gets agitated and tells them to pull over and let us out before we get to where we're going, and then she gets mad at me, like, *Why didn't you give me a signal?* And I just can't explain it.

Maybe Shelly likes feeling bad and good at the same time.

"I think you should go for it," I blurt. But it doesn't seem right.

"Di!" she says in sudden horror with her mouth open, and I am so panicked I think about jumping out of the car.

"I like the way you think," she finishes, laughing her face off. Her droopy eye stays in neutral, as confused as I am.

I notice a Betty Boop china figurine Scotch-taped to a corner of the dashboard. Betty is wounded—chipped on the left side of her giant head.

"That's my mom's," Shelly says. "She collects those."

"Is she into cartoons?" I try.

"No. She's into Betty Boop," Shelly says.

"Betty Boop is so cool," I say.

She pulls a photo from beneath the sun visor. It's a photo of young Shelly and her mom at the beach. Shelly has a normal eye, and for the first time I consider that she could have had a different life before something happened, just like me.

"I'm going to live with my mom in Florida as soon as I get my license. She has bad diabetes. I have to make sure someone's giving her her shots," she says. "I was the one who did that. Right in the ass." She lifts up her butt on one side and slaps it.

"Ouch," I say.

"She hates needles." Shelly bites and spits out a cuticle.

"I'm leaving, too," I say. It's the first time I've ever said it out loud.

"Where you goin'?"

"I don't know yet," I say. "Just far away from here."

Shelly looks at me like I'm a new person. "Awesome," she says warmly. "I don't know how anyone stays in this dumbass town."

Is it OK for us to just go? I want to ask.

Carfuls of kids drive up and down Main Street, heads hanging out of windows shouting, *Where's everyone tonight?* The answer is: everyone is everywhere, busy not meeting up in one place. It's a flow I've never been inside of before—looping and hopeful and electric. Everything feels different, looks better, is possible. I've never ridden in a car with just me and a friend. I haven't had a friend since Champei, when I was nine.

We stop by Cumberland Farms to get Hawaiian Punch and Ring Pops.

Right in front of the store, there's a carful of older boys I recognize from school, windows down, blasting Metallica's "Fade to Black." In the dark car, you can only see parts of faces—longish hair and glossy eyes, lit up by the glowing tips of their cigarettes and a haze of florescent store lighting making its way through the glass. Everything in me tightens as their heads turn and follow us, but they say nothing as we pass. Once we're inside, walking through the aisles, it's like we're in a giant, glass-box stage, performing for them.

Shelly drags her fingers across a row of magazines and penny savers on our way to the drinks in the back. The boys move with us, their eyes on Shelly like heat that can't help but overflow onto me, too. The whole world tilts toward us.

I look at all of my favorite foods smiling up at me: Pudding Pies, Cheetos, Hot Pockets. There's a sweet, doughy smell escaping from the rack of twenty-five-cent Ding Dongs and Ho Hos and cinnamon buns; it pokes at me like a nice memory of a place I want to go back to. Shelly buys me a little bag of Cool Ranch Doritos without asking if I like Cool Ranch Doritos. I do.

The boys in the car have moved on to a group of girls, who hang inside of the car windows looking like mutant half people in jean skirts. I'm disappointed; I don't know why.

"Di, look."

In the back of a pickup truck, piled on top of each other like dirty clothes, are two dead deer. I've gotten used to seeing them on the side of the road—the flashes of blood on fur, the twisted antlers—but those black, shiny eyes get me every time. We lean over them, hands covering our noses and mouths to block the musky smell. There's a spill of blood coming out of the side of one's mouth. Both are bleeding from the spots on their sides that were hit by the arrows.

Shelly sticks her finger into the blood pooling underneath them and dabs it once in between her eyebrows.

"Now the hunter is cursed." She reaches back into the blood puddle, and before I can say *Get that nasty finger away*—she dabs me too. It's warm and smells like dirt.

"This is good luck," she says.

"Or, rabies lotion," I say. Shelly laughs. I'm relieved.

The bloody spot on my head feels tingly, like a magic potion is being cooked on my skin. Before I can think that maybe Shelly's on to something, it goes from hot to cool to stinging and itchy. I think about trying to explain a bright, oozy rash circle on my forehead to Ma.

Shelly seems to know where I live without my telling her, so I sit back and wait for my house to appear among the nearly indistinguishable rows of two-story, pastel-colored boxes. My one source of pride: the tree in our front yard. It's an eastern redbud that stands way above the roof and fans its heart-shaped leaves across the length of the entire house. It was never supposed to get this big, but Ma says she put special things in the soil to make it grow. I think she's just trying to take credit for something she couldn't possibly have controlled that turned out way nicer than if she could.

That tree is a fancy-pants dancer, showing off her outfit changes each season: tight pink flowers sprouting from the branches in spring, then wide maroon and green leaves taking their place in the summer before turning sunset red in the fall and dropping in the winter. We're a few more months away from the full red fire—what Grandma Sylvia called our "love umbrella"—and yellow polka dots are just starting to push out the green. Even people who don't notice these things will say, "What a pretty tree!" when they pass our house. Like a beautiful girl standing next to her ugly friend, making the ugly friend disappear.

My dad planted that tree the year I was born.

"That tree is magical," Shelly says on cue as we pull up in front, and I don't even worry about the discarded kitchen set Ma dragged over from the neighbor's trash that's been sitting in our yard for a week, waiting to be hosed off.

"My dad planted it," I say.

"I remember when he disappeared," Shelly says. "That awful picture in the paper of his shoes by the river. The whole mess with the cops and all."

It's unsettling to think she knows so much about my life, that she's thought about me at all. When you have a terrible thing happen that everyone knows about, you can be laid out flat by anyone.

"Is it weird that people still see him? Did you ever see him again?"

I start to say, *No. No. No. He is dead. That is racist bullshit because they don't know what to do with him, with us.* But I just don't know.

"Sorry, never mind, that's nosy." She grabs my hand and tries to squeeze it. It's too big for her to get a grip; she pats it instead, dainty white fingers on animal paws.

Shelly looks down at my arm, where there's a giant bruise shaped like a rabbit head from one of my bike falls.

"I can cover that up if you want."

"It's just my dumb thing. I bruise easy. Here, try. Just pinch me. You'll see." I offer my other arm.

"Di, don't talk crazy. Friends don't hurt each other."

She whips out a compact from another makeup holder under the armrest and dabs at the purple-green blotches until they look like a faded watercolor painting, only a little purple bleeding through the edges.

"Wanna be my partner for the in-car lesson with Mr. Jimmy?" She's not looking at me again. She takes small licks of her Ring Pop; I pray she doesn't notice I've already eaten mine—it didn't fit on my finger.

"Of course," I say. "You shouldn't be alone with him again." My voice has a finger wag in it, which I don't mean.

"Yet . . ." I add dramatically.

"You're funny, Di," she says, laughing again as if there are people watching us. I laugh, too. I bet we look like girls having a ball. I focus on the droopy eye this time and it makes me feel like I'm in on the joke.

"What the hell is that on your head?" Ma says as soon as I walk in the door.

"Deer blood," I say proudly.

"What on earth?" She runs at me, licking her finger and scrubbing it off. Her spit smells stronger than the blood, like an ashtray and cold cuts. I wonder where she got the money for groceries.

"Are you hurting deers?" She stops spit cleaning to look at me. "And why the hell are you so late?"

"I worked overtime," I say, not even attempting a good lie.

Ma huffs. "You better hope that doesn't stain your head." She sniffles with her back to me, but then lets me have four bowls of cereal for dinner without saying anything about it.

"I got a good lead on a job today," she says as she watches me eat at the kitchen table. She waits for me to ask her what it is. I don't. "It'll be a surprise," she says.

I have dirty summer feet, hard and cracked like a sidewalk. I am barefoot almost all the time I'm not working. My feet get so swollen in the summer even my flip-flops slice into me. Ma says the bottoms of my feet are so tough and calloused they're like built-in shoes.

Before bed, she rubs Vaseline into the cracks while I eat cinnamon toast and watch *Dallas*. I think about my dad sitting in between Ma's legs in front of the TV, where she used to separate his Afro into thin sections, greasing each part as she eased dandruff flakes from his scalp into a snowy pile on his shoulders. I thought this was disgusting, and I couldn't imagine ever loving someone that much.

As her veiny hands find all the right spots, she banishes the fluid from the puffy tops of my feet to the rest of my body. She gently wipes some grease on my rashy deer-blood patch.

"Look. It's already fading." She takes a deep breath and then pauses, her eyes flutter.

"Can you tell me where you really were tonight?" she asks.

"I was just out with a friend, Ma. A new friend." I give it to her.

A spark of fear lights up her face, then she laughs. Then she covers her mouth when she sees my hurt face. The laughs leak out through her fingers. "Oh, heavens . . . the deer blood. Were you trying to be blood . . . sisters?"

"I know it's been a while since you had one of those," I say. "Friends."

Rage wells up in me, then Ma's punched-face look traps it somewhere in my throat.

I head to my room and don't come back out again even though *Falcon Crest* is on. Instead, I read the letter Lena sent me again.

And again. And again.

7

September 1, 1915

My Dearest Sweetie,

Today I birthed a white baby with my own hands.

Doctor let me do it, say it was time for me to learn. One minute I'm in the front hall of Toby Manor, scraping summer mud from my boots so I don't mess up that pretty house, the next I'm staring into the honeypot of Mrs. Charles Toby! Doctor say it's coming, and then I reach right inside her to save that baby's life. I feel the cord was in a tangle, a choking-rope around its neck and I yell Ma'am stop pushing. She look at me with such a fright in her face, like I was her brain and she was just a body, What do I do? she say and I move fast and natural, like my fingers have memory. I caught that lump of a child, grey and slick, with a shag of hair so thick could have been a grown man come back from a swim. He was named Charles, after his Daddy. He look like a Charlie to me.

After we were all done and cleaned up, Doctor caught me crying in the kitchen, patted me on the back and say The first time is quite scary and you kept your wits about you. But it wasn't that. I was remembering when you came out of Mama, your whole body in a *shiver, the long hush before that sweet little pout of yours opened up and fill the whole house with caterwauling. And those bright, wet eyes, like black glass marbles, finding me in the back of the room before they could even see. Oh, Sweetie. You come from Mama, but you'll always be mine and don't you forget it.*

I know I was little but I remember. Granny bursting through the door, saying she could smell that Mama's water had already broken— smell—like it was right after a spring rain. Mama's bobcat yowls, how she pulled me close to touch her belly as you worked your way down, how you shot out like a cannonball. Granny caught you, and in one sweep cleared out your nose and mouth, held you up high before sliding you onto Mama's chest like I did baby Charlie today. Sweetie, it just come to me what need to be done before Doctor had to say. Now I wish I'd paid more attention to Granny, watched what herbs she soaked the rags in, asked her how she knew when to help move Mama from one position to the next, like a dance come down from the ancestors. What was it she tucked under Mama's tongue that made her cry from relief? Why did she rub rosewater on special spots on ankles and hands and toes and knees? What comfort was she whispering in Mama's ear that made Mama hum, hummmm. It gonna be OK.

Doctor say I have a special talent. He say he hasn't lost a single baby since I started coming with him on visits instead of Miss Rose but don't go and tell her that. He say a wife like to think she bringing all the things to make her husband shine, Miss Rose especially. He call me his lucky piece. I tell him no sir I don't want no parts of luck when it come to white folks and their babies luck runs out let's just say talent and I'll thank you kindly for the compliment. He laugh and laugh. I wish Mama and Daddy were alive to see me doctoring, catching babies. I wish you could see it, too.

Doctor and me were so puffed up with the glory of God's new creation and worn out from the day, we took the short route and

*rode right through the center of town. Past the Post Office and
Hattie's Bakery, right on by the Railway Boys playing cards outside
of Fletcher's and the mill girls comin' from sodas at Perkins. Yes, we
still riding the buggy. Since we make calls all out in them backwoods,
Doctor say an automobile not nearly as trusty as Charliehorse,
especially after a rain. Even though he surely could afford one of them
Cadillac motorcars with all that money his daddy leave him. He's just
old fashioned. But you know I can't drive a buggy or even ride a horse
straight, so Doctor held the reins like he was old Rudy and me next to
him like I was Miss Rose, too delicate to dirty her white gloves. I kept
my head down best I could but heard all the hollerin', who does she
think she is and what makes her so good she didn't have to leave town
with the rest of 'em? Daddy used to say always look at what's in white
folk's hands, but I couldn't see nothin' with my head down, and I could
only hear Doctor breathin' all hard and fast next to me. That's the
thing that made my hands tremble.*

    *By the time we got back to the house, ugly ole Dog-Face Tuttle and
his posse were all there waiting. This time they brought Sheriff. Dog-
Face ask why is Doctor out there showing off his help when everybody
hurting so badly without their niggers? Doctor remind him that he is
saving lives and bringing new souls into the world and he has special
permission from the town council to keep me on since Miss Rose had
taken sick, and don't they want all the helping hands they can get if their
people are in need? Doctor tell them I mostly stay at home tending to
Miss Rose and helping in the clinic. Sheriff says OK but Doctor shouldn't
be driving me like I was a white lady, that a colored girl of eighteen
should learn how to do the horse driving. Sheriff says I have to follow the
new laws about colored people, that it would be a terrible thing if I was
caught anywhere after dark without Doctor or Miss Rose. They made the
dark itself a boogeyman. Made me scared in my own sleep.*

    Sweetie, they stood there scolding and all I could think about was how after everything they did to us the night of The Leaving, Dog-Face had the nerve to take our milking cow and the chickens. Please tell Robert that one time last week, early, before Rooster starts in, I went by Dog-Face's coop and took all of Henny's eggs, like it was still one of my chores. You can't call it stealin' cause they were stolen from us! That's it, I swear I won't do it again. I know you think I get too mad and forget to be afraid, but I don't want you to worry. I know when to keep my eyes down on my boots, nodding yessir yessum until my head bobbles off. I know how to smile with all of my teeth and say a kindness that could make anyone get shy. I just think about my arrangement with Doctor and I can keep on going.

It won't surprise you to hear that I'm teaching myself how to do the Doctor's account books. I'll be running this whole place soon! I make a record of each patient, what ails them, and what Doctor say is wrong. How they were treated and did they get better. I tally up who pays and who owes in the ledger, how much supplies cost and when new orders are needed. I fill up the capsules, roll the pills, and measure out calomel. I scrub down the clinic every day, boil the instruments because anything not clean can make someone sick. The busier I keep the less time I have to be with my thoughts.

I still carry on with all of my regular chores in Doctor and Miss Rose's house, but it feels different now because I also live here. Miss Rose don't leave her room at all anymore, and if Doctor's not out on a call or seeing a patient, he keep to his office, sometimes up to bed and counting sheep before the sun sets. I can wander this house free as a bird, sipping tea from Miss Rose's tinkly bone china, trying out the velvet parlor room chairs, even the ones no backside has ever touched. Reading reading reading, a library full of stories and learning, the whole world in those books. Can you see my words and penmanship got better? It's strange to think that a place that used to make me so scared, with its echoey halls and chilly corners, filled with things that can break every time you move an arm. This is the only place I feel safe now.

Last night I come downstairs in my nightclothes to eat some blackberry pie, and I catch a look at myself in the window all wild haired and purple lipped. I stuck out my tongue and crossed my eyes—that what always made you giggle. Oh, what a happy thing it is to have a good laugh at yourself! And then I think what would Robert say and what face would you make back and how long will it be before we're all doing googly eyes at each other again? I didn't know there could be such a lonely laugh. I got to wondering, who is a person without their people? How am I Clumsy Clara, silly and stubborn Clara, Clara with her head in the clouds—how am I that girl without anyone who loves me saying it, seeing me?

I think, maybe I am a ghost. Maybe I died with the others.

I watch the sun all day. Even inside I know exactly where it is in the sky. I feel the dark creeping up on me until it pounces, blacking out my freedom. My face hasn't felt starlit air in five months, not since you left. I don't know what's out there in the night, but it ain't for me. The signs are up everywhere. This one right near the mill.

NIGGER, DON'T LET THE SUN GO DOWN ON YOU IN SWIFT RIVER

Everybody gone.

Gone, Sweetie. Gone.

Remember the man they call Pa Bell? The handyman who ran around town delivering white folks news so fast he got there before the operator could track down the person needing the message? Doctor used to use him sometimes like he was a human telephone. Running, running, for pennies a time. I heard he made it all the way to Florida. He's working out on a shrimping boat. I like to picture him strolling at his own leisure to work, squinting out into the ocean for hours, pulling up his nets when they get to being full. No white folks telling him go faster, faster. Go go go.

And here's some news oughta make you scratch your head. Folks are worried about the mill, there aren't enough workers to keep it running much longer. Well what did they expect. White girls are either on their farms or at the paper mill. It pays more, and paper is an easier day than textile, even if the smells make your head ache bout the same. Last time Dog-Face come out here to Doctor's he tried to say I have to work a few shifts. Doctor say slavery against the law last he checked and to go get one of his own daughters to take on extra work. There's talk of a man up north in Canada buying the mill and bringing down his people to do the work—women and men. Doctor say they all speak like people from France. Canucks they call them. That would be something wouldn't it? Frenchie or no, ain't nobody ever going to run it like we did.

Has anybody heard from Gerald who worked at the butcher shop? Doctor is angry at Miss Rose all the time now because of him. She's barely spoken more than a few sentences since The Leaving. They say Gerald out in the woods somewhere waiting for her to come to him. Sheriff and the men go out looking for him. Doctor say if she doesn't snap out of the Melancholia, it will look like they have a weakness for Negroes and we all will be made to leave or worse. He threaten to send her to Manchester for a calming treatment. Sweetie, her sadness is something awful—thick and heavy with its own sour smell. It fill up the whole room, sometimes the whole house. He may call it Melancholia but I call it Heartbreak.

If Gerald's not out there, that means I'm the only living colored person in all of Swift River.

It's past nine o'clock in the evening and I'm up reading in my room. I can keep the lamp burning for as long as I please. It's a book called Gray's Anatomy. Doctor tell me I'll need it for medical school at Howard University. He's gonna give me all of his old books, that way I won't have to pay for anything at all. He keep reminding me—if I give him two good years of work here, he's gonna give me a ticket to Washington in the District of Columbia and pay for all my four years of medical schooling. I come out the other side a doctor. He say they need him to vouch for my good moral character, make sure I know Latin and

Math and English. Doctor Clara Newberry. I know I can do anything for a time if it means I can get to Woodville with everything I need to take care of you, to take care of everyone.

I fight off sleep for as long as I can. Otherwise That Night comes back to me, over and over.

Remember how we used to run and jump in the bed, scared the wild hogs were under there waiting to eat us whole? Don't laugh, but I do that here in my new room. Run and leap like I'm a little girl. Like all of the terrors of the day are hiding under there, waiting to grab at my ankles and pull me under.

It's still strange to be in a bed and not to have your skinny legs wrapped around me, your knobby knees and big ole boat feet knockin' at me like weapons. I wake myself from dreams because I think it's you next to me, talkin' in your sleep.

Come listen to me, Sweetie. Listen. See, I'm pretending to tell you a story like we used to do together. Remember your favorite? The love story about the stable boy and the baker's daughter? Make up a new ending for it when you write me back. In your letter also include a better description of the new house. Is Uncle Henry and Auntie Josephine making it nice, treating you good? And say if Robert is being his rascally self? And can you tell me, was it right for me to stay behind?

You are my whole heart, beating on the outside, probably fillin' up all of Woodville, Georgia with your love and fire.

(One more thing—I woke up in the middle of the night yelling, OK, NOW. PUSH. PUUUUSSHHH! You would have been hollerin'.)

Your devoted sister,
Clara Newberry

ESSIE CHAMBERS

September 30, 1915

Sweetie my Sweetie,

*Miss Rose is gone. Doctor and me find out when we come back from
a three day trip to Ashfield, where we were tending to a very difficult
birthing. Three days. We get back and all of Miss Rose things are still
here, but no Miss Rose. Room to room we went, calling her name,
lookin' every which where, even in strange places—behind furniture,
inside closets—like she might be playing a hiding game. The marital
bed was made, not as good and tight as I do it, but wasn't any rush
about it. She was trying to leave the place tidy and hopeful.*

*Doctor asks is there a note anywhere, but I can't find a scribble.
He say maybe she went to see her cousin Mabel in Boston, now he
remembers that she got a letter saying Mabel was unwell. Sweetie, I
know right then he will never go looking for her.*

*Miss Rose been in a bad way for weeks before we left, more bad than
regular bad. Could barely sit up in bed with her heavy head and floppy
neck. She was so still and blank. Remember that year we found the
frozen wood frog at Miller's Pond? Its little legs stiff and straight, like
the cold caught him mid-leap, his hands and arms all covered in spiky
ice crystals. You say he look like a froggy wizard shooting lightning from
his fingertips. We got to thinking he need a proper burial, so we bring
him home and put him in a matchbox you painted black. Remember
how the melting water soaked the box and we rub his wet, slimy skin
one last time to pay our respects and that darn thing blink and then
quack like a baby duck and we scream as if Jesus just paid us a visit?
Mr. Frog come back to life.*

*That day we were leaving for Ashfield, Miss Rose come back to life.
Her hazy ghost eyes caught a spark and melted. She could see me, see
Doctor. She got up and sat in her reading chair, looked out her bedroom*

window with her hands on her knees, leaning forward like she was waiting for her mama to come home. There was a pink in her cheeks. Doctor kiss her on her dimples—happy, welcome back to the world I missed you kisses. She even smile a little.

I don't so much miss her as I am scared of what her leaving is going to mean for me, for Doctor. Truth be told, the whole house feels lighter without her here. Curtains open, sun finding its way into all the corners. The quiet sound like quiet, not like someone holding their breath. The sour odor is gone. Now there's a sweet, mournful smell, like end of summer strawberries before they turn. I bet she's lighter too, wherever she is. I wonder what it's like to have the kind of love that make you leave your whole life.

A feeling come over me that I need to air the place out. I open every window, every door, and the gusts blow the curtains, make any slight thing wave in the breeze. Doctor say what on earth am I doing, making it so all the critters and creatures of the town can come in and trample us. I say this house wants the wind to make it new again. We both stand in the doorway. Well then, he say, but then nothing else. We stand there a long time.

Something is weighing heavy on my mind, Sweetie.

You know how white folks sometimes tell a colored person their most private business? Shocking things, mean things, sad things, secrets that could ruin a life—with no shame? When I was a child, I remember I didn't know what to do with the things I was told. And I couldn't put together why. Was it me or them? I thought, maybe Miss So and So see me as her little friend? Maybe Mr. Who and Such think I'm smart? Maybe there is something in my wide-open face make 'em want to confide? Do they feel my big heart, my good-ness? Then I grow up and know it's the opposite—they don't see me at all. I'm an empty bucket to pour themselves into. They can talk into the deep black well of me and their secrets will never come out.

Sweetie, I thought you was too young to know before but now I confess it. Miss Rose tell me things.

Even though I been with her and Doctor for four years, it was a few months ago she start speaking to me like I just then come alive, like we are friends and colored folks are what we have in common. She say Gerald make her feel things she never felt with Doctor. She never knew that people could walk around having these feelings without floating off into the clouds. She ask me private things, have I ever had relations with a man, what's it like to be with a colored man, what do they like and how do you take care of them? I just say I wouldn't know I ain't been touched, Ma'am. I don't say, how will I ever know what it's like to love a colored man when ain't no colored men in sight? It don't even cross her mind, there is no one to come calling for me. By the time I'm a doctor, I'll be too old to take on a husband, have a family. She don't know she don't care.

I do think she love him, but I also think why can't she keep it to herself. It's one thing to tell her own secrets, but another thing to tell Gerald's secrets, too. He belong to us. She will get him killed.

Miss Rose tell me she is leaving, that she love Gerald too much. Gerald sent word he would come for her soon and then they go to a place called Mexico where a colored man and white woman can be together. She don't want to hurt Doctor and can't stand the thought of breaking his heart. Well that's just what you're going to do I say to her. I was feeling bold. She tell me take care of Doctor. And then weeks pass and her head get heavy and I think maybe Gerald changed his mind. Decided their love wasn't worth the trouble. I was wrong.

Since Miss Rose leave, Sheriff come to the house a few times asking how is she feeling. Finally, Doctor tell him she all better, she gone to Boston to take care of her cousin Mabel, who has the putrid fever. Sheriff look suspicious then test him with questions. Doctor tells the story in such a way that it sounds like truth, even to me who know it's a lie. He say it so much, that's where I picture her, now—in Boston, at Mabel's bedside, wiping her brow with a cool rag. Gerald is painted out of that picture. I forget that he's gone, too.

I keep thinking Doctor will hate me now, like the white boys who chase me home from the store throwing rocks, coloring me every Negro they've ever known, no one else to blame for their sorrows but my skinny behind. I'm colored, and the man who took Doctor's wife is colored, too. But Doctor come to me last night and say now he know what I must feel like, losing all of the things I love in the world. We both cry together.

My Sweetie. Missing you is like a toothache, always right there, sore and buzzing under everything, even when happy things happen. Every now and again the pain stings so sharp make me jump up and howl. It don't ever get better, I just get used to it.

I hope you don't miss me at all, I hope your Woodville life is so easy breezy, you don't feel a lick of sorrow. You had enough of that.

Your loving sister,
Clara Newberry

8

1980

The summer my pop disappears, I am not allowed to play in the front yard anymore. Ma says it's because of the heat, but it's really about the police cars that circle our house like sharks.

The cruisers slow-crawl down our street a few times a week at first, then twice a day after Pop loses his job at the mill. Soon it becomes as regular as my TV shows. I press my face to the window during commercial breaks from *Gilligan's Island*, hoping to catch a peek of a white, meaty arm dangling on a car door, a dark uniform— neck bulging over the collar like a big belly, sparks of silver badge and pins. As they go by, the cops flick their head between our house and the road in front of them. They don't wave back.

Some things I need to know: Is it the same car and the same two cops going round and round, or do they take turns with other cops? Do they take a break to talk about the clues they've found to whatever mystery we're a part of? What is the mystery? When will they stop?

One day when Ma is at work and Pop is fixing something in the basement, I decide to follow the cops on my purple Huffy. I wait for thirty minutes by the door until I hear radio static and the *pop pop* of tires chewing gravel.

I don't show off my new peddling-no-handed skills, because they are driving very slowly—I have to stay far enough behind to not look suspicious. Together, we're a slow parade of mystery chasers.

The street is twisty and shaded by tall trees—they stand straight like soldiers on both sides, the wind bending them down for me as I pass. I pretend that the shadows they make on the ground keep me hidden; I can only be seen in the sunny patches. The seed fuzz in the air joins us, swirling around my head like a cocoon. My heart thumps so hard I can feel it in my whole body. I am a heartbeat.

At the end of each street, the cop car makes a left turn; soon we are on the other end of my block, where the sprinkling of trees on one side becomes thick woods, where long driveways lead to hidden houses with no lawn chairs or broken toys in yards. The car stops in the middle of the road at the end of the street and the engine cuts off. These are the kind of police who don't even need to pull over to the side. I realize I have also stopped in the middle of the street, in a sunny patch, so I turn around and ride straight into the woods like that's what I meant to do all along.

I ditch my bike, then crouch down behind trees nearest the car, where I'm hidden by tall weeds and curling ferns. The cops are smoking now, laughing loudly as they wait for something. The radio spits out loud, fuzzy voices I can't understand. The lights flash for a second and the siren whoops loudly, just once, like a scream. It scares me so badly I pee myself. I won't cry.

"Where'd that little colored girl go?" One of them gets out of the car and looks into the woods, right at the ferns that cover me. He's fat and gray-skinned; his no-lip mouth draws a straight line across his face.

"Come on, don't fuck with her," the one still in the car calls out through the open window.

"You following us, girlie?" No-lip says, ignoring him.

The seed fuzz is everywhere now, a whirl of summertime snow. The cop swats it away from his head.

I squeeze a cottony puff tight in my hand.

"It's against the law to hide from an officer when you're called."

He reaches into his pocket and tosses a coin into the brush behind me.

"If I have to come and find you I'm not gonna be happy about it."

"Here I am!" I say, popping up from the weeds like we're all just playing hide-and-seek.

I get my bike and go stand in front of him, using it to hide the pee spot on my shorts. I feel hot all over, except where the damp cloth touches my skin, cool like something to calm a fever.

"That your bike?"

"Yes."

"You sure you don't have sticky fingers like your daddy?"

"Oh, for Christsakes, quit it," the one in the car says through the open window.

"Well, yes I do, sir," I say, looking at the sticky seed puff smushed in my hand.

They both laugh.

"Who gave you that bike?" No-lip asks.

"My Grandma Sylvia."

"Your daddy can't afford to buy you a bike?"

I know he's saying something mean. It lands somewhere in my body and digs a hole.

"Why are you driving in circles around my house?" I ask. I am a detective. The wind bends the trees for me. I belong to my father.

Seed fuzz swirls around his head, making him sneeze, over and over.

"Ask your dad," he says, wiping his nose on a sleeve before getting back in the car.

I start to go home, back to my seat at the window, but instead—I ride around the cop car once, twice, three times; a human lasso. It works. They just sit there and watch. On the end of the last loop, I skid out, just as I've seen the neighborhood boys do. My tires spray street dust and gravel.

"Eat my dirt," I yell, and peel out before the cops can arrest me.

That night, I ask Pop why the cops are after us.

"Nobody is after us!" He shouts it at me, right up close in my face like a roaring lion. I stay very still. Hot, cherry cough-drop breath pushes into my nose, mentholated spit sprays my cheeks. I close my eyes as the sound rattles through my whole body. I can't think about anything other than wiping the droplets off my face, like they might burn clear through flesh to the bony shield of my teeth.

"Stop hollering at her like that!" Ma yells back. "I swear to god if you don't cut that shit out . . ."

"Then be a mother and get her away from that damn window." His voice goes low, like a growl. "She should be playing with friends, doing kid things. Invite 'em over here—look at all these toys," he says, sweeping his arms across the living room, pointing to my blocks corner, my Care Bear collection, my Baby Alive in a little crib. All things I'm too old to play with.

The next morning, Ma asks me if I did something bad to Champei. Champei is my best friend, but she has just told her mother that she doesn't want to come over my house anymore. *Leah sin houwy, Champei*, I think to myself. I'm sad, but not surprised. "Leah sin houwy" is how you say goodbye to a friend in the Khmer language.

Last year, my teacher, Mrs. Kelly, held up a picture of a small brown girl with shiny black hair holding a soccer ball and told us that the Allens, who live down the street from me, were adopting a Cambodian refugee from a war. We learned that this meant Champei had no parents, and that the fighting all around her meant she had no home.

"This is your new home," I said, holding her face and kissing her cheek when she got scared during dodgeball.

Until then, Pop had been the only other person in Swift River besides me with brown skin. Everyone else I knew was white and pink, including Ma. Because Champei was brown, too, I knew we would be just like sisters. Except she couldn't understand a word I said. So I asked Ma if we could learn how to speak to her in her language. After school, Ma and me would spend hours in the library reading about Cambodia—the monks and temples, Kampot and the Cardamom Mountains. I learned "Welcome!" "How are you?" "I love you!" "I am going to school!" "Where is the toilet?" and even how to count from one to ten.

Lately, when Champei has come over, we've had fights that lead to me crying, and then to me screaming. The screaming is new; it comes when I feel so bad the words get stuck. I don't know how to stop it once it starts. Something that needs to leave my body is leaking out of me; I scream until I'm empty. Then I'm back to me, until it fills up again.

"If you scream one more time, I never come back here," Champei said to me last week.

"Leah sin houwy, Champei," I said to her. I can't give up the screaming.

I should have added *Knhom srolanh neak, Champei*, which is "I love you, Champei." Maybe she would have forgiven me; I could have had both.

After Ma tells me Champei won't come over, I scream. And scream. Champei is gone.

Pop runs from the kitchen, grabs me by the arm and twists.

"Owwwie! Pop, my sunburn!!"

It feels like my skin has been lit on fire.

"You're hurting my sunburn!!!"

The neighborhood kids don't believe that my kind of skin can get sunburns. Now I could finally show them the giant white bubbles, the curling rolls that peel off in long strips. They leave behind the outline of island shapes surrounded by ocean. The kids peel each other for fun; I want to be peeled, too.

"Stop it! You're twisting off my skin!" I yell, and then go back to screaming.

"How about you stop that, OK, baby?" he asks sweetly with a smile I've never seen. He doesn't raise his voice.

For my whole life, I've only had time-outs. Ma and Pop both got beaten for being bad when they were kids, but I heard them tell Grandma Sylvia they'd never hit me. They made a promise to each other. *It's not 1950*, they said. Grandma is always saying I need a good spanking. Pop says *Lessons should be taught with words, not violence.*

Pop is breaking his promise.

He squeezes my arm even harder and smiles bigger. It's the pain and weird sweetness together that scare me enough to stop screaming. Then he grabs me and holds me so tight I can't breathe, like a time-out pretending to be a hug.

"There will be plenty of kids for you to play with at the barbecue," Pop tells me the following Saturday. "You can make some new friends."

All week, Ma and Pop have been talking about this important barbecue party at Mindy and Tom Campbell's house. We don't get invited places very often, so this is special. The Campbells have leftover fireworks from a 4th of July party last year, and Pop says I can hold a sparkler. Tom is a man Pop used to work with at the paper mill. Mindy is his wife who sells makeup and drives a pink car.

I don't like that the barbecue is interrupting our regular weekend plans. Saturday mornings we have our thing: Pop and me make breakfast, watch *Jonny Quest*, and then sweep the kitchen while Ma stays in bed smoking cigarettes and painting her nails with the radio blasting. Sometimes we hear thumps, like she's jumping or dancing—most likely practicing routines to teach her students at The Creative Talent Dance Studio. It's hard not to go inside that room, knowing how much fun is being had without us.

This morning, Pop makes me fried onions, peppers, and tomatoes for breakfast, and says that instead of cleaning up and cartoons, we have to go outside to get salad makings in the garden.

When Pop was still working, he took night classes at a college an hour from our house. *Plant Propagation* and *Introduction to Plant Pathology* were the names he'd read me from the covers of his books. Two times a week he'd burst through the door with new things he'd learned, holding baby plants peeking through the tops of tiny containers.

"I'm happiest in the dirt, sweet pea, always have been," he said. "I'm filling my head up with what my hands already knew how to do."

He planted ferns and coral bells around the eastern redbud in our front yard. In the side yard, he made eight rows of vegetables into a rainbow: bright red tomatoes, bushy carrot tops with the orange root poking out of the dirt, yellow turnips, green bell peppers, a blueberry bush, and baby eggplants—fat and shiny, like purple dragon eggs hanging off of their branches. He poked holes into a hose and built a watering system, hung a mesh screen around the delicate herbs to keep them from being bossed around by the wind.

"Look at this, sweet pea." He swept his arms out, holding all eight rows between his hands. "I can always feed my family. Always."

Ma called Pop "Farmer Rob" and Grandma Sylvia said he should sell his plants on the side of the road to make some money.

He had to quit his classes when he lost his job, so he doubled up on the planting, adding three new summertime rows of cucumbers, peas, and spinach.

We are in the garden, picking our barbecue salad.

"These motherfuckers are doing it on purpose!" Pop yells, lifting the neighbor boy's basketball off a now squished section of lettuce. He never says the f-word in front of me.

"Took me a whole year to get this romaine growing good."

He holds the ball in his hand for a moment before throwing it, hard, over the fence back into their yard. This is the third time this week the ball has appeared, an orange bomb leaving behind crushed flowers and broken stalks.

"Why don't you just keep the ball, Pop, so they can't do it again?" I ask.

He looks at the fence, then back at me. And again at the fence.

He knocks himself in the head with a fist.

"How'd you get so damn smart?"

"Pop, no!" I say, but he's already climbing the fence, flinging his long, skinny body over to the other side.

"You'll get in trouble!" I say when I don't see him for a few minutes. It's all my fault. "Hurry!"

The ball flies back over the fence, crushing all new things when it lands.

His dark hands peek over the top first, then he straddles it and drops down, landing on his feet.

"I'm the daddy. Don't you worry about trouble," he says.

He picks up garden shears and stabs the ball, smiling as the air oozes out. He looks toward his bedroom window, where sometimes

Ma watches us. I can't tell if he wants her to see, or if he's afraid she already has. He pauses a minute, considering his options, then throws the ball back over the fence.

"They're on notice," Pop says.

"So we can't even bring chips. Nothing?" Ma says, frowning at the pretty bowl of salad she's carrying: our lovingly picked lettuce, tomatoes, carrots, cucumbers, and radishes. I put three of the wild yellow dandelion flowers that grow everywhere in the summer right on top. You can eat those, too.

"There has to be change lying around the car, enough for chips," she says.

"Annabelle, they'll appreciate a fresh salad," Pop says.

"Car's out of gas?" Ma asks. Pop nods toward me, then glares at her until she looks away.

We're walking along the side of the road next to the riverbank, on our way to the Campbells' house.

"Cigarettes are almost gone, too," Ma says. She makes a face that says this is a good enough reason to turn around and go home.

"You know how important this is, Annabelle. Get it together."

Ma is beautiful.

She is wearing her best summer outfit—a blue-and-white flowered sundress. I am wearing a matching one that covers the bruises on the tops of my arms from Pop's squeezing. She is sharing her prettiness with me. Her long hair is still wet from a shower; she sprinkles us with flowery-smelling water whenever she turns her head. Her skin is shiny with lotion, and the freckles that cover her face and body are so summer-dark, she's almost as brown as me. She has on the bright pink lipstick that, by the end of the day, stains her teeth like berry juice. Pop looks handsome too. He is wearing jeans and a white shirt that shows off his arm muscles. His Afro is newly cut short, and he's wearing the spicy cologne that pulls all the air in a room to him.

"You know Mindy's gonna corner me to buy makeup and that butt-ugly jewelry she sells," Ma says to Pop.

"Tell her you don't need that stuff to look good," Pop says.

He presses up against her from behind, putting his arms around her waist, resting his chin on her shoulder as she walks. She stops, standing perfectly frozen until he lets go.

"That's a ridiculous answer," she says.

"I'm happy to be walking, Pop. I'm glad we're not driving," I say to be helpful.

He grabs my hand and squeezes it. I squeeze back.

"Me too, baby. Feel that breeze? The river's like a natural fan."

We walk single file on the path whenever we hear a car coming or a biker whistle. A few cars honk at us. Kids in backs of cars smush their faces into the window. The cops go by two times, three times, four. Pop waves at them like they're friends, except without a smile.

"We're pirates, Pop," I say, whipping at everything I see with a branch I find on the side of the path.

"Just don't throw me off the plank," he says, sounding distracted.

"Cattails!" Pop points to the plants along the riverbank that look like hot dogs on sticks. He tells me how when he was a little boy in Georgia, there were no streetlights on his road. At night, the kids lit cattails from the swamp—they called them mosquito pumps—and caught fireflies in jars. He and his cousin Lena would go from porch to porch, watching all the grown-up bodies moving around in the moonlight. Talking. Laughing. The kids sat at the edges, getting "snapped at and slapped at, and loved up," his aunt used to say.

Pop's mother was from Woodville, but she died while he was being born. His father thought there would be a better life for them in Swift River, where they would both come to live with his Aunt

Clara. She would help him raise Pop; she would be Pop's new mother. They would be the only Black people in town. Pop was seven years old, just two years younger than me. I asked him, what did he mean "a better life"? Better how?

"He thought it would be less hard up here," Pop said. "More opportunity."

"Less hard how?" I asked. His face puckered and he fell into the place of "down South," and lost family.

"This is shameful, why doesn't the town clear this out?" Pop is disgusted. He says the same thing each time we pass by the small, abandoned house where he lived with his aunt and father. It's missing most of its roof shingles, and the grayed wood siding is being overtaken by something green and mossy. The yard is just dirt with a few tree stumps. It's the worst off in a clump of identical small houses, like a rotting tooth. "My aunt is rolling over in her grave right now," he says.

"Doing cartwheels in her grave!" I add, to be helpful.

The mill houses are in bunches throughout town. There's one here, and another where we live in Grandma Sylvia's old house. It's a twenty-minute walk in between the two, with an abandoned church and a one-room schoolhouse in the middle. I ask Pop why they called it The Delta, and he tells me a delta is a triangle of land at the mouth of a river, the in-between spot before the river splits into branches and heads off to a different place, like the ocean. A long time ago, a man who traveled from far away said "The Quarters" reminded him of Southern river country—the shape of it, the fertile soil, and the ways of the Black people who lived there, how it was separate from the rest of the town. When I ask Pop where all those Black people went, he tells me, "Out West, back home down South. Long time ago, before I was even born. Aunt Clara was the only one stayed." He always says the same thing. I ask why, and he'll only say,

"To deliver babies." Ma says Pop misses Aunt Clara, and that she is a sore spot we should try not to touch.

"Thank god we never moved over here," Ma says, pointing to the rundown mill, almost directly across the street from the Campbells' house. "I give it a few more months before it shuts down for good. We would be looking at that thing every day."

Unlike the other mills and factory buildings in town, which are ugly and brick and filled with rows of square glass windows, this one looks like a giant house and a barn. The barn part is connected to a covered bridge that straddles both sides of the river. I used to visit Pop on his lunch break; we'd head out to the middle of the bridge and look down to where the water smashed over rocks, headed angrily toward a waterfall. We made paper boats and threw them out to their deaths, hoping they'd make it to the peaceful patch of river where the current slowed and the top of the water was unbroken, right before the drop. "Go, little boat!" we'd cheer, as it coasted off the edge into nowhere.

A dam further upstream used to power all the mills and factories, but most of them closed before I was born. "Someone needs to burn them to the ground," Ma always says. "We don't need an everyday reminder there aren't any jobs."

The Campbells live in a two-story house, set apart from the others, with a huge deck and a fixed-up basement. Pop says it was a mill owner's house—the kind that's passed from father to son, father to son. Ma jokes that it looked like the boss of the other houses, just like its bossy owners.

"Tom and his toys," Mindy calls out to us as she answers the door. We are standing in the driveway, crammed in between a bright yellow sports car, two motorcycles, a truck with giant wheels towing a big boat, and Mindy's pink car with a license plate that says *LIPSTIK4U*.

"How are they so rich?" I ask. Ma and Pop talk to each other with their eyes; something is not fit for my ears.

"Ugly jewelry sales?" Pop smiles and grabs Ma's hand.

"Get in here!" Mindy waves us inside. Her face is bright red with white cutouts around her eyes where her sunglasses once sat. She wears a fancy necklace that looks like something from my princess play sets. It's thick and silver with rows of big blue and red stones. She has on jean shorts and a pink T-shirt, as ratty as if she were a servant who took the queen's jewels and ran.

"Look at you health nuts. Making us all look bad." Mindy takes the salad from Ma and grabs both of our hands, pulling us through the kitchen toward the back sliding door. The deck is as big as our entire house. We climb down stairs that seem like they'll never end, to a yard where Tom and his brother, Kenny, sit in the far corner around big coolers and a grill. They have the same red faces and white cutout eyes, like a pack of raccoons.

"A whole family could live under there," Ma whispers to Pop, looking back at all that wood hanging over a small hill, long stilt legs holding it up. Another set of stairs on the side leads to two smaller decks, one with a bathtub in it.

"I'll give you a tour later," Mindy says, pointing back at it. "This was supposed to be a New-Deck celebration, but someone got in a fight with the manager at the lumber yard." Mindy nods dramatically toward Tom. "Put the guy in the hospital," she whispers above my head.

"It's an Almost-New-Deck celebration!" Ma says.

"Why do you have it so big?" I ask, pointing up at it. Mindy doesn't hear me, and Pop gently holds his hand over my mouth.

Ma lights up a cigarette; her hands are shaking a little. Pop puts his arm around her waist and pulls her closer. Her head finds its spot under his neck for a second before pulling away, remembering to be mad.

"Can I bum one?" Mindy says as we head for the food table. "You're so lucky. Tom won't let me buy them anymore."

"B.R.! Get over here and grab a cold one," Tom calls to Pop, slapping an open lawn chair next to his. B.R. is short for Black Rob, which is what his friends from school used to call him for a nickname. Pop hates it.

"Let them get a plate first," Mindy says. "Diamond, look, the kids are all playing freeze tag over in the field," she says, pointing to the sea of tall weeds and grass next to their yard.

"Is it safe in there?" Ma says. "Are there snakes or anything?"

"If there were snakes, the kids would have scared 'em off long ago," Mindy says.

I shake my head *no* as soon as I hear Ma say "snakes." I move away from her and hold on to Pop's shirt.

"It's OK," he says. "We'll let her settle in first, get something to eat."

There is a long table of food; it makes me think of the words "royal feast," from one of my fairy-tale books. There are many bowls of delicious-looking white and brown mushy things: potato salad, tuna salad, egg salad, two kinds of pasta salad, macaroni and cheese. There are hot dogs, hamburgers, corn on the cob, three different bags of chips, pudding with M&Ms on top, Rice Krispie treats. And now, our salad—a bright can of paint thrown on the table.

"Can we take some with us?" I whisper to Ma, who is filling her plate with small spoonfuls from each bowl. She glares at me and mouths, *No.* Pop's plate is spilling over, and he's eating before we even sit down. Ma glares at him, too.

"How do you two stay looking like goddamn teenagers?" Kenny says to Ma and Pop when we sit down in the lawn chairs. He rests his plate on his pot belly, using it like a table, pointing and laughing at his joke. Ma says people have always been jealous of her and Pop;

how good they look together, how well they get along—like two best friends who are also a boy and a girl.

"That deck is a beauty," Pop says, opening a beer. "You did all that work by yourself?"

"Nah, the fellas helped out, too. On the weekends."

"If you need any help finishing that railing, let me know," Pop says.

"I'll take you up on that, bro," Tom says. "I might have some work for you up at the cabin on Mohawk, too. I know you've had it rough, lately." He looks at Ma when he says the last part, but Pop doesn't notice.

"Thanks, man, I appreciate it." He's nodding like crazy.

Tom reaches behind the cooler and pulls out a jug of a strong-smelling, brown-colored drink, pouring Ma and Pop big jars full of it.

There is boring talk about boats, cars, recipes, and the mill. Kenny puts a cassette tape into the boom box. Guitars that sound like they're crying and men with scratchy voices yelling make them all remember things. They drink more brown juice from jars and their voices get wavy. No one notices when I go to sit under the food table, right at the edge, so I can listen to what they're saying without getting shooed away. I have a few paper plates and a pen from Ma's purse; when anyone looks my way I pretend to be coloring.

"Hey, you." Mindy slides up to the table where Pop is scooping up the last of the macaroni and cheese. I'm still invisible. She bumps him with her hip as she sweeps empty cups and plates from the table into a black garbage bag. I notice she keeps pulling at the front of her T-shirt, puffing it out to hide her lumpy stomach. She smiles in Pop's face, touching the jewels on her necklace. She has corn in her teeth.

"I like your necklace," he says in a way I've heard him talk to Ma when he's trying to keep her happy.

"Oh, thank you! I made it myself. These are semiprecious stones."

She leans in close and says something I can't hear, then drops a Rice Krispie treat onto his plate. Pop steps back, looking uncomfortable.

"Peekaboo!" She pops her head underneath the table. I jump.

"Aren't you a unique one," she says, smiling.

"Thank you," I say and pretend to be concentrating on my plate drawing.

A slower guitar song comes on the boom box and everyone gets quiet. Tom has put the grill fire out, and it feels like we're all being held together inside a smoky meat cloud. The grown-ups sing along to the song with a happy kind of sadness, *And she's baaaa-ying a stairway to heavooooon.*

"This music is gonna put me to sleep." Ma is up and at the boom box. She pokes through the pile of tapes on the table, pulls one out and hands it to Mindy; they both smile. I recognize The Rolling Stones' "Honky Tonk Women," a song Ma plays in the kitchen while she's cooking. Mindy and Ma start dancing together.

I'm not surprised that Ma is better than Mindy—she is a dance teacher, after all. Mindy is all jerky moves; Ma is wild but smooth.

"Anna's looking good," Kenny says to Pop loud enough for everyone to hear it.

"Yes, she is," Pop says with a dead voice.

Ma's hair is damp and stuck to her face; she leaves it there, in her eyes, in her mouth. There is a wet spot on the back of her dress, in the hollow part right above her butt. The front of her dress is wet, too; you can see two pink nipples peeking through the thin fabric. She is doing something that is making everyone's head sway; no one can take their eyes off of her. I imagine that this is the Ma behind her bedroom door on Saturday mornings. It's too much of something. It's not dancing meant for other people.

Mindy stumbles; no one moves to make sure she's OK. She sits down, mumbling to herself. The grown-ups are somewhere else, far away, each at their own private party with a bunch of ghosts.

Pop comes out of his trance and punches the side of his head, three times. *Shit Shit Shit*, he says to himself.

He leans in and says something close to Tom's ear that I can't hear.

"Oh, I don't really care about all that," Tom says loudly.

"I could use your help, man, you could talk to Smitty and the others," Pop says louder, but still leaning in to make it private. "You know it wasn't me." His voice is high and whiny; he sounds like a young boy. "I don't steal. I wasn't raised like that."

"Let's just keep the past in the past," Tom says.

"But see, that's just the point—"

"Listen, I'll throw you some work."

"I appreciate that, I really do, I need it, but—"

"Let me think about it," Tom says, turning away from him to face the food table. He points at me. "Your kid under there?"

Pop looks at me, like he's just remembered I'm alive.

"It's grown-up time," Pop says, taking me by the arm and pulling me toward the field. Ma gives me a little wave but doesn't stop dancing.

"Anna. Come over here and dance with me," I hear Tom say to Ma as we walk away.

When we get to the edge, Pop bends down to talk to my face.

"No screaming. OK, sweet pea?"

I part the weeds at the entrance to the field; the grass is nearly up to my chest. It thins out quickly in a zigzaggy path, beaten down by the kids' playing. Ahead, I can see them flickering in shadowy, almost-dinnertime light. I look back and Pop is still watching me, the grass now swallowing him up to his waist. He looks like he wants to run in after me and bring me back to the grown-ups and their sad ghost party. I blink a picture of his face like this, so I can remember it when he's mean or gone.

There are four kids in the field—Tom and Mindy's three sons, and Kenny's daughter, all of them around the same age as me. I know them, but they've never spoken to me before. Two boys are frozen, arms out like robots, while the "it" boy chases the girl in wide circles. She is fast, he is clumsy.

"Run!" she yells to me, and I'm off.

We're more than he can handle. We whiz by him in opposite directions, quickly tiring him out. When he stumbles and falls, she grabs my hand and pulls me to the ground, giggling. We're hidden by the grass.

"No fair!" he yells when he's back standing and can't see us. "They're hiding together!"

We lie there, curled in toward each other, still holding hands. We stay like this, our faces a few inches apart, breath pushing our chests out in rhythm. She is the kind of smiley that makes me smile, too, just like Champei. I wonder if the secret to friendship might be in here somewhere, in her face as my mirror and mine as hers. She puts an arm around me; it will keep us invisible. I close my eyes and pretend she *is* Champei.

"Cheaters! I quit," the clumsy "it" boy yells, his voice far from us.

In a minute, the frozen boys are standing above us.

"You suck, Tommy. Look. They were right in front of you."

"They cheated!" Tommy shows up behind them.

"Naw, you're just too dumb to find a bunch of girls three feet in front of you."

We're all standing now. Tommy steps forward to look me up and down.

"What are you?" he asks.

"I'm a pirate!" I say.

Before I can make even one pirate joke, he shoves me in my chest, so hard I fall straight back, like a knock-out punch from a cartoon. I suck in air, desperately—it feels like all of it has left my body at once.

It's almost dark. The clouds are black against the sky. I don't realize I'm screaming until I see most of the kids running from me. There isn't any sound at all, until Pop.

"What happened?" he says, looking all over my body for hurt parts. He has red eyes and breath like dragon fire.

"Tommy shoved me on the ground on purpose." I'm crying now.

"She said she was a pirate, so I had to kill her." He shrugs. "And she cheated."

In the distance, you can hear the other kids calling to their parents.

Tommy won't look at me or Pop. He just stands there, yanking out grass and weeds from the root and throwing them, spraying us all with dirt.

"You need to apologize, Tommy," Pop says. "You hurt her."

"I don't have to listen to you," he says, still without looking at us.

Another dirt shower; some of it hits Pop's white, white shirt.

Pop walks over and bends down to Tommy's level, grabbing his wrist to prevent him from throwing another weed hunk. Tommy shakes his hand free, looks at Pop, and throws it over into his pile, daring Pop to stop the flow.

I know what's next.

Pop grabs the top of Tommy's arm and squeezes. He lifts him up, legs kicking in the air, until he's dangling at eye level.

"You doing some gardening for your dad?" Pop says with a smile.

"I was just chucking grass and stuff . . ." Tommy looks at me, panicked.

Pop shakes him, hard and fast—like something wet he's drying

109

out. You can hear the sound of Tommy's lips flapping, his breath caught. As Pop lets him down slowly, Tommy looks around frantically, like he doubts there's still ground beneath him.

"Sorry I pushed you," Tommy says as soon as he touches down. Then he takes off.

Pop has my hand as he leads me back through the grass maze to the party.

Shit Shit Shit Shit, he says it over and over again, until I think he may have forgotten words.

"We're so sorry," Mindy gushes, running over to meet us at the edge of the yard. "I heard what happened from the other kids. Tommy Jr. is so sorry."

Tommy is up on the deck with his dad, who is yelling. Tommy is limp and crying.

"It's just kid stuff. It happens," Pop says, nervous. Ma looks at him, confused, waiting for a signal. She comes over to hug my head.

"It's getting late, anyway. We should go," Pop says.

"You'll have to come out on the boat with us sometime," Mindy says.

Tom comes down from the deck, handing Pop another jar filled with brown juice. "For the ride home." He slaps Pop on the back. "Sorry about all this. Let's talk tomorrow. I can help you out."

There is a blur of goodbyes. Tommy Jr. comes up to me and whispers, "I'm gonna tell on your dad."

The girl from tag hands me two Skittles. I want to ask her to come play with me and Champei sometime; I think maybe if I bring this girl, Champei will take me back. We will be three friends. But Ma grabs the bowl of wilted, untouched salad, like a thief, and we're gone.

* * *

The breeze along the riverbank is perfect, and therefore it's terrible—
the sweetness smacking up against our misery. Pop is all the way under
now, stumbling and mumbling and singing to himself. The streetlights
are spread out, so in the gaps of darkness it's just us and the reflections
off the other side of the river. And the fireflies. They're everywhere.

"We didn't get to do the sparklers," I say softly.

"You're right, sweet pea." Pop stops. Something catches his eye.
"I have something better."

He points toward the edge of the river at the bottom of a small hill.

"We're gonna catch fireflies," he says. "Down there."

He chugs the rest of his brown liquor drink and holds up the
empty jar—the perfect firefly holder.

"Have you lost your mind?" Ma says. "Haven't we had enough
for the night?"

"We most definitely have not had enough. It's time for some fun."

He grabs on to Ma's arm and does the squeezing thing. She
makes a hurt, shocked face and yanks away from him.

"Come on, sweet pea, let's do what crazy Daddy says."

She grabs my hand and pulls me down the muddy hill toward
the river's edge. She trips once but catches herself. She pulls me in
close to her at the bottom.

Pop follows after us; he slips and falls roughly down the rest of
the hill, landing close to our feet. We don't move.

His arms and legs are spread wide.

"Am I still alive, Annabelle?"

Ma doesn't answer.

He lies there like that for a minute. Eyes staring straight up at
the sky. A high-pitched sound *eek*s out of him, a whimper like a hurt
dog, or a balloon losing air.

"I'm OK, nobody worry." He jumps up suddenly, laughing hys-
terically.

"Show her how to do it. She's never done this before." Ma stands with her arms crossed.

"You just grab them. Cup them in your hands and bring them to me." Pop shows me, grabbing one easily and letting it go into the air like a magic trick. "Then we put them in the jar," he says.

I look back and forth between Ma and Pop.

"Let's go, baby, start grabbing," Ma says to me. Even in the blue darkness, I can see splatters of mud on her dress. She looks scared.

We run up and down a small patch of the riverside, reaching up, out, everywhere. Pop whoops each time we bring him one, but otherwise it's just crickets, cicadas, frogs, and our heavy breathing. He holds his hand over the jar, a mini world of blinking light.

"Please, Rob, it's late. She has to get to bed. Do you have enough fireflies?"

"Yes, this will do," he says, looking over his firefly prison. "It was an important thing for her to learn, Annabelle. A good memory. Right, baby?"

He crouches down in front of me, unsteadily, holding the jar of fireflies between us, the twinkles bouncing off our faces. His breath still smells sharp, but sweet.

"God you are such a beauty," he says.

I look to Ma.

"Say thank you," she whispers and nods. Her face has mud on it, too. Tears have cut two clear streams down the middle of her face.

"Thank you."

Pop flicks his hand at Ma, *no*, that's not what he wants.

"I don't want to hear that screaming ever again, OK, baby?" He doesn't lay a hand on me.

My eyes are itchy with salty powder from old tears, but I keep them focused on his face. My mouth clicks open and closed, something like a yes but without the sound. Chomping down on a promise.

112

9

July 25, 1987

Hello my kin,

I've never heard Casey Kasem's Top 40 on the radio, but I will give it a try if you say it's good. I don't listen to the radio much, except for my friend Tilly's news programs. I make cassette tapes of my favorite songs so that I can have the music I want, when I want it. I love me some Earth Wind & Fire, the Gap Band, the Ohio Players. I tell Tilly I want "September" playing on a loop at my funeral. I was born on the 21st night of September which, if you know the lyrics, makes it like the song is just for me. I would very much enjoy hearing you sing. Could you send me one of your recordings?

How nice it must be to have a new friend. Shelly sounds fun, like a good distraction from all that mess going on with the death certificate. I'm happy to help with the letter you requested for the lawyer. I can certainly vouch for the fact that your daddy hasn't called at Christmas or come to visit or asked to borrow money. I'm sure all of this is very confusing.

You are correct, they passed an actual law saying no "Negroes" were allowed to live in Swift River. That's what they called Black people if they were being nice. I bet you that law is still in the books, even if no one talks about it.

That town of yours is something else. A whole community of Black folks up and left and nobody there talks about it? Thank goodness your mama and daddy at least told you they existed, lived a life. To be honest I never had the full story about that night myself. I guess we're all guilty of looking the other way when something is too sad or shameful to speak on. When I first found out, I was same as you—didn't know what to do with that anger. I can't imagine what it must be like to live there, laying your head down at night on top of a graveyard built by the folks who did the killing. But I guess that's everywhere, really.

This is what I know: It started because a group of our people with jobs at the textile mill were asking for better wages. Mill work was dangerous—there was a good chance you'd get lung disease or lose a limb in a machine or both. The owners paid the Black workers half what they paid the whites, even though there were twice as many of us. We were basically running the whole thing. They could get away with it because they were the only mill that would hire Black people to work the main floor, versus just sweeping in basements like the rest. This was a time when the newspapers were filled with stories of white laborers all over the country joining unions and organizing strikes. The Swift River mill bosses didn't want our people thinking they had that kind of power. Got all the white folks in town riled up, too— *Know your place, Negroes* type of thing. First they *cut* pay and bumped up the rent on the mill houses. Soon after, they passed laws saying Black people couldn't own property, found ways to take back whatever land belonged to us. Mama said they banned us from the shops in town. And our men were getting thrown in the county jail for made-up reasons, like a game for the Sheriff and his men.

In the weeks before The Leaving, they shot two Black men accused of stealing from the mill as they ran for their lives. There were no hangings in a town square, like you'd see in the South, but there might as well have been. There are many ways to take a person's life, Diamond. Mama and them each had a different story about the final, dreadful thing that sparked the plan to go. The only real choice they had was *how* they would leave, not whether or not to stay. Some would go west, others further east, but most of our family headed for Woodville. Stories had been passed down about how to break that land for the most bountiful harvest, the taste of fried blue catfish from the Chattahoochee Lake, foggy mornings and green winters with no heavy coats. They still had family there. It was *roots* home.

All the Black people in Swift River decided to go on a night when they knew all the white people would be in town at a celebration. It was spring, and the days were longer, so that meant the mills didn't have to use kerosene lamps to light half the workday. The party was called a "blow out," to mark the extinguishing of the lamps, the arrival of more sun. Mama said there was always a lot of food and dancing, and folks came from all over.

The planning had started the week before, so on that day, Mama said it felt like they were about to have their own party, except everyone moved around with single-mindedness, cooking and cleaning and packing in total silence; you know, that kind of quiet with only a pulse in your ear like a ticking clock.

Somehow the white people got word and showed up with those oil lamps, smashing them and setting fire to the blacksmith's place and the barbershop. It was one of our cousins who put out the garden fires before they could spread to the houses, where we waited. He was shot in front of his granny's porch, in front of his granny.

By the time our people were on the road, there was a trail of angry white folks behind them, trying to snatch people off wagons, grab whatever animals they could. Like a foot to the butt kicking you out the door while clutching onto your arm, *don't go*. And especially don't go on your own terms. To have that kind of hatred for people you also can't live without? Mind you, at the time, Southern Black folk were pouring into the North, running from the horrors of the South. Our people went in reverse, back to make an old home new.

Now that I know Aunt Clara a little better, I try and focus on the courage it took for her to watch them go that night. If you think about it, it's a choice with just as much force and power as a migration. That kind of brave is in our blood, too.

XO Lena

10

1987

I sit in the driver's seat of Ladybug staring at Ma and Pop's wedding day photo. I focus on Aunt Clara, a rain-sogged old lady in a clump of grown-ups, distinguished only as much as her role in that story, in that strange, hole-filled day, which is to say not a lot. She was always the source of Pop quotes that were meant to teach me something, a strong and wise woman but never a girl, a *young girl*. I have always looked at this picture and seen myself there in Ma's long eyelashes, Pop's smile that took up half his face, Grandma Sylvia's big forehead. But for the first time, I see me inside the twin pits in Aunt Clara's cheeks, *like God poked his finger in dough and the hole stayed*, Pop would say as he tweaked my dimples. Me in *her*. How had I missed this?

We live in a house full of Ma's family heirlooms: feathery yellowed papers announcing ancient births and deaths and marriages, diaries of war generals, antique wedding chests, lacy baptism dresses. Grandma Sylvia hated for nice things to stay locked up in trunks, so we used to have fashion shows and put on Irish skits in Irish accents with whatever wasn't in danger of turning to dust. It was like frolicking with the ancestors.

With Pop, it was as if he sprang up from the ground like one of his plants; there was no evidence he ever had parents, of Aunt Clara having raised him; nothing from family that you could hold in your hand. I'd heard about "down-South kin," but those were just words for the hole in Pop, not real people.

Until Lena sent Aunt Clara's letters. These letters are real. They're like the best book I ever read, but *I'm* in there somewhere, too, the beginnings of me. We are two Black girls with dimples, looking out a window at sundown in Swift River. *Sundown*. The start of a daily prison sentence for Aunt Clara. She was just a few years older than me! *Sunset*, a warning shot. Get inside, or get killed. I wonder if it changed colors in her mind—turned hazy stripes of red into a knife blade, made orange a fist. Like Lena said, I've been sleeping on top of a graveyard. My whole life I'm strolling through the very place once filled with the smoke and fire of that night. It's messing with my head. I don't know this town at all, I don't know anything about anything.

Except that Aunt Clara and Lena are mine. I won't share them with Ma.

They don't belong here in the world of Ma and me, of bills and bank notices, back pain and pills and pills and dead deer being dumped on our lawn furniture, propped up and flopped over like they're having a drunken tea party. I don't want them to live in this heavy house with us. I keep all the letters in the car, where I know Ma will never go, where I can visit.

Ma barely notices how much time I spend in the car or out of the house. We are separate like this, now. Before, we huddled together in rooms, even if in silence, doing our own things—close—as if sitting by a crackling fire in a cold house. Now we keep to our own spaces. Sometimes I hear her stop outside my bedroom door, a long inhale of her cigarette before the smell of smoke worms inside, before she shuffles off to dig inside boxes of papers behind the couch.

We are as broke as ever and our court date is next month. A week ago Ma had to put a notice in the *Swift River Valley Register* telling Pop about the hearing. Like, *If you're alive, come out come out wherever you are. This is your final chance!* Once a week for four weeks, if he is still around, he will be able to read it in the back of the paper next to the tractor sales and bingo schedule. It's not that we think he's alive somewhere reading the *Swift River Valley Register*; it's because Jerry the ponytail lawyer said we had to, that it's part of the legal process to get a death certificate. It's like sending a letter to nowhere, to no one, but that everyone in the world can see, too.

Word gets out. Then the photos come. Of Black men. All shapes and sizes, blurry and captured at odd angles, out and about in nearby towns, at the Grand Union in Ashfield, the Rock N' Bowl Alley in Conway, an Indian man at CVS.

"Don't even look at them," Ma says. "Throw them right in the garbage."

But we store them away in a scratched-up Tupperware container, for keeps, as if they are long-lost Black uncles. Or clues in a treasure hunt leading to Pop or the reasons why he's gone. I admit, I study those pictures looking for a trace of me in their faces, too. It makes me not trust my own brain.

Shelly says people have been seeing my dad for years, just far enough away to not get caught.

"They think he might finally turn up," she says. "That would be wicked crazy, right?"

We're in her car after class, parked at Cumbies, one of the hangout spots in a rotation where kids come to smoke and drink before they get chased out by cops and on to the next.

"Remember when that Harlem Globetrotter came to town to sign autographs at Bart's Sport Shop?" I ask. It was a highlight; we don't get famous people coming around here, just the circus or actors from the lame soaps, not like, *General Hospital*.

"He was wicked cute," Shelly says.

"Seven feet tall. People would stop us on the street to ask if my dad was back."

"Back from the dead where he learned to twirl a basketball on his finger," Shelly says.

I had begged my ma to take me to get an autograph, for no good reason since I didn't even like basketball. She wouldn't do it, but Grandma Sylvia did.

The line to meet the Globetrotter went almost out the door. When Grandma and me walked in the store, he saw us right away. He was sitting behind a normal-sized table, but it looked like a school lunch tray on his lap. He was from another planet—dark and awkward against all of those happy white and pink people.

He saw me and smiled, and it was a smile that was *just* for me, different than what he was giving all of the white kids crowded around him. They were either so scared they couldn't look him in the face, or so hyper they grabbed at any part of his body they could get their hands on. The little ones crawled under the table to touch his big sneakers, and he shook them off of his feet like they were puppies.

Grandma went right to the front of the line, leaned down and whispered something to him I couldn't hear. He nodded and stood up, and a force, like a strong wind, came with him as he unwound his body and walked over to me. Ma and me and Pop *never* got special treatment like this. We never asked for it. The whole room gasped at his full height, then bitched when he autographed a Bart's flier *for me*. Wrote a special note just *for me*, Diamond the line-cutter, courtesy of Grandma. He bent down and gave me a hug—pulled my head right into his chest. I remember his knuckles were dark and dusty, like they'd been dipped in powder, just like Pop's. I couldn't stop staring at the line on the side of his fingers where the dark brown front skin met the beige underside—it was beautiful. I could smell sneaker rubber and cologne with sweat creeping through.

I started to cry. Grandma was so embarrassed. Yanked me out of there, apologizing, *She's had a really bad day. A very shitty day.* That wasn't true.

I had all this love for Pop left over. I didn't know where to put it.

"That's gross," Shelly says. "People in this town are gross."

I scored a point. But I still wonder if I'll ever stop feeling like it's my job to change people's minds about me, about us, like I'm connected to them by an invisible thread until I can crack the code to their kindness and understanding.

"I like it when we talk about stuff," I say, tugging at the thread.

Jerry the ponytail lawyer also informs us that Ma can't look like she's just "sitting around waiting for the money." She gets and then loses a job as a salesperson at an appliance store, then as a receptionist at Tootsie Roll—where they make custom wheelchairs for handicapped dogs (she's allergic). Then she lands a paper route. Our next-door neighbor, Mrs. Williams, an older lady who had taken over the route after her son joined the army, decided she wanted to sleep in now that her kid was grown.

"These routes are so hard to come by," Ma tells me. She says there are only seven covering all twenty-five square miles of Swift River. I know from kids at school that they're passed along from one generation to the next, like a family inheritance. The lore of the Christmas tip goldmine is known far and wide.

* * *

121

"All you have to do is push the cart and count the money. I'll deliver the papers."

I smell her in my sleep before I hear her voice. Nicotine, cough drops, and damp hair form a vaporous cloud around her. It's the still-dark of a Sunday morning—I'd guess 5:00 a.m.—and she's sitting on my bed, leaning over my face; after-shower sweat and hair-water drips all over me. Around an hour before, I'd been woken up by the sound of the delivery van pulling up in front of our house, rolling open its doors and dropping stacks of uncollated papers onto the ground with a loud *thwap*, like a body getting punched in a kung fu movie.

"Say yes, Diamond."

A pillow over my head is my answer.

"I'm already late and the Sunday papers are so heavy. I'm losing tip money right this very moment."

"Nope."

"My back, it's bad again—" Her breath catches on the words. "That last job, sitting at that desk all day, it did me in. Please, if I lose this, no one else will hire me." I can feel her shaking.

Ma has become like a kaleidoscope of a person; her shape changes depending on the ache and the drug used to squelch it. It shifts fast. I can't think about it for too long or else I start to shake, too.

"I have to work in an hour, Ma."

She sighs, pulling herself up with the resolve to go it alone.

"Maybe, if you want, someday you can have this route?"

She sees my expression and realizes that she has just offered up her same life to me.

"Just for pocket change and exercise, you know. Not your main real job."

"Sure, Ma."

I watch her through the window, dragging those thick paper stacks further into the driveway, where she separates them into piles for each section—comics, sports, news, real estate, travel, *Parade* magazine—before putting them together, one paper at a time. I don't move to help.

This is the best day of my life.

Shelly and me are in the Tee Pee Motel pool. It's three o'clock, just after my shift has ended. My boss, Tim, is at Bible study, so I am free to break the "no employees swimming" rule. I make a deal with my co-worker Dawn—I'll take her shitty night hours for a weekend, and in return she won't tell on me. The pool is empty of guests; it rained earlier today and the stay-indoors feeling lingers for everyone but us. I am full with my new auntie and cousin.

Shelly had come early to help me finish faster, get more pool time. We polished the motel mascot in the lobby—a wooden statue of an Indian chief holding a peace pipe, totem poles on either side of him. We hosed off the plaster teepee on the roof, a confusing thing that looks more like a school art project, a papier-mâché mountain peak. We scooped out the leaves from the pool, swept the area around it, and poured ice water on the blackened gum blobs till they scraped right up like hardened clay.

The motel is all dull oranges and browns with faded tribal prints, everything just shabby enough that guests feel free to carve their initials in a door or bedframe. We sanded off the curse words, mostly on the chief. "It's so disrespectful," Shelly said of the *I suck dix* on his left cheek. I feel relieved that she gets it. People call him my grandpa. "Yeah, this whole thing," I swept my arms around, "is disrespectful." Before the Black people were chased out of Swift River, there was a massacre of hundreds of Native American women and children and elders—it happened while they slept. This ridiculous motel is meant to be some kind of tribute. Tim keeps a fresh supply of pamphlets detailing the history at the front desk. We're all supposed to memorize them so we can recite facts to guests if they ask. No one ever asks.

Next, we made beds, cleaned bathrooms, and vacuumed empty rooms. Shelly threw people's nasty things at me with gloved hands—dirty socks, crusty tissues, a giant gray bra, a condom wrapper. I forgot for a moment that I sometimes eat the food they leave behind—cold, cigarette-scarred pizza, half-eaten Whoppers, melted ice cream. I forgot myself.

Today, all these people are yuck and everything that belongs to them is contaminated, because Shelly is here and she's not, we're not.

"She new?" Dawn asked when she saw Shelly wiping down walls with a bucket full of scummy water and a rag. "Where's her uniform?" Tee Pee employees all wear a despised brown sack, fringed at the bottom; we're meant to look like "Pocahontas."

"She's just helping me," I said.

"For free?" she asked. "Shit, you couldn't drag me here if there wasn't no money. That's a good friend right there."

She is. There is something about seeing Shelly all sweaty, T-shirt streaked with grime, hair pasted to her forehead, bleeding mascara raccooning her eyes. It makes me love her.

"I didn't mind it," Shelly said after we were done. She has a job as a checkout girl at The Colonial Candle, "Home of Scent-sational Souvenirs," *sitting on my ass all day smelling Spicy Pumpkin Patch and Wonderberry*. She likes my job better. "It's kind of like an accomplishment, you know? Making it all clean," she said. I thought about the junk-house she lives in and her sparkling, orderly car.

"Yeah, I don't mind it either," I said. That's only part true. The stuff I've seen, the private stuff, like what people's bodies leave behind—makes me gag. The thing that allows me to clean up after their foulness, put up with their staring, their ice bucket and clean towel demands, is this: Someone has saved up many paychecks to be here. This is someone's first time in a pool. Someone has nowhere else to go. Someone is hiding out from someone else. This is the first time someone has ever seen someone Black.

I told Shelly this.

"You're so, like, nice and understanding," she said, her head tilted. "When you don't have to be."

Don't I?

"I've never met anyone like that."

We float. My body can do that. I'm not fat in water. The heaviest part of me is my long, wet T-shirt, gripping me down to my knees.

Are you nervous about tomorrow?

So nervous.

Do you want to practice on my car first?

Nope. I want tomorrow to be my first time, so I do it right, no offense.

We do water-dance moves in sync, like old-fashioned swim cap ladies.

What's it like to be with a boy?

In the summer they go buck-wild and leave you, then come back in the winter when they want to be warm.

We splash, play Marco Polo. *Marco! Polo!* Summertime words I've heard from behind fences, coming from backyards, always just out of sight.

But what's it like to BE with them be with them?

It feels good. Especially when they go down on you before you do it. Their cum tastes like dirty pennies and sweat.

I think of car rides with dry fingers inside me, pinching my nipples, swirling around my mouth, jagged nails catching my inner lip.

It feels so fucking good, Di.

I want to feel good. Something rises up in me, squeezing my insides.

Do you think there's something wrong with Mr. Jimmy for liking me?

I think, maybe. But you didn't do anything yet, right?

Of course not.

We hang under the diving board, our own underwater cave.

There's something wrong with my ma. I don't know what to do about it.

I know. My dad, too. He just sits in the middle of all that garbage, waiting for my mom to come back. I can't breathe in there.

We do handstands, handstand splits. We fill our cheeks with water and have spit fights.

My great-aunt was brave and delivered babies and my cousin in Georgia is a nurse.

So cool, I don't know anyone who went to college except our teachers.

Who knows maybe one day you'll have a friend in college. Maybe me.

We stay in the pool until our lips are bruise-colored blue and wormy, our eyes red and chlorine-stung. And then we stay some more. Nothing at all is the matter, is how it feels.

Your boss has baptisms in this pool?

We call them the Jesus and Mary Swim Team.

Maybe that's why it feels so good in here. Like, holy.

When we finally pull ourselves from the pool, the sun is disappearing behind the teepee on the roof. We wrap ourselves in scratchy, too-small towels and head to the vending machines—Cheez-Its for me, Doritos and Skittles for Shelly, a couple of Sprites for us both. Then off to Number 7, the nicest room at the Tee Pee, the one Tim saves for his minister. No scratches on the wood, no stains on the green shag carpet. A pastel, quilty bedspread with matching curtains that look like watercolor paintings. Plus, actual watercolor paintings of birds and frogs and streams hang on every wall, as if the whole place wants to be a lily pad.

"Oh my god, this room is awesome," Shelly says. "Like a hotel in France, or Canada."

I feel proud, like I got it just for the two of us. Like my shitty job has some good things. Like my life isn't a total waste. I wonder if Ma could ever be happy for me, sitting here like this, almost normal.

Shelly starts stripping down before I even have a chance to get out of the room and into the bathroom. I change out of my wet suit and T-shirt with the bathroom door closed. I do it fast and sloppy, terrified she might not care enough about closed doors and private things. When I open it she's sitting on the bed naked, waiting to get in. I look away quickly, but not before seeing a flash of surprisingly dark pubes, pale boobs traced by hard tan lines. She has pink nipples, like Ma, like other white girls I've seen in locker rooms. Mine are dark brown, like African women I've seen in magazines.

Shelly takes a long shower. After a while, steam pours from underneath the door, making the whole room dreamy. She finally comes out in a towel looking as happy as I've ever seen her, combing her straight, knot-free wet hair for what seems like ten minutes. She pulls lotion out of her purse, parts the towel at the bottom and puts her foot up on the dresser. She rubs lotion into the same part of her leg until I can't imagine it getting any moister. This ritual is mesmerizing. I can't stand spending that much time with my body. I remember the fact that she's probably living out of her car; this clean-body ceremony might be a rare treat.

We sit in the armchairs by the window and look down at the pool. On the edge of the chain-link fence, five deer of all different sizes, looking like some kind of life-sized toy collection, are staring up at us. There's a meadow and some woods behind the fence; it's from there that deer come pouring into town as if there's an endless supply. Because we feed them cereal every day—which it turns out is like deer crack—I recognize these as "the regulars." There's White Butt, Sad Eyes, Dummy, Second Biggest, and the little one, Baby, who makes a sound like squeaky shoes.

"They look like they know you," Shelly says.

"They're here every day. They just want food."

"What if the big one is like, your dad come back to life?"

I try and make sense of the rush of relief, the total absence of doom I usually feel with outsider Pop talk. Maybe it's because she said he was dead, as a fact, that he's watching over me.

"Goodnight, Pop," I yell in the direction of the deer, and we crack up.

We lie on the bed and watch TV. It's one of my favorite episodes of *Alfred Hitchcock Presents*, the one where a waitress and her boyfriend try to poison this old lady to get her fortune. Then the episode of *CHiPs* where Jon and Ponch confront a gang of dirt bike–riding cattle rustlers.

"I hate this one," Shelly says. "Ponch doesn't make out with anyone."

"I like it when Jon makes out," I say, even though I like Ponch better. I want Shelly to know I can like the white guy.

"Look, Di." Shelly's fingers are covered in orange Dorito dust. She sucks each finger in the way I can only guess she would suck a guy's dick.

"Nice work," is the thing I think to say.

It starts raining again. The sound—like the hiss of a crowd cheering—pulls us off the bed. We sit in the chairs and watch the droplets attack the pool, the surface of the water pinged by tiny darts.

"Does rain make you sad or happy?" Shelly asks.

"Both?" I say. "It makes me sad about some other happy time.

This day will be that other happy time the next time it rains. Make sense?"

"Totally."

On our walk to her car, Shelly pops my bubble. "I think I'd get a job at the Tee Pee if I wasn't getting out of here."

Shelly is leaving Swift River as soon as she gets her license. She acts like a person who is leaving soon. Leaving gives her courage for *fuck yous* and *eat mes* and the rest. When a woman called me *nigger bitch* in Cumbies last week after I bumped her by mistake, Shelly yelled, *Fuck you dumb bitch, she's not like that*, and I wanted to say something, tell Shelly she didn't get it exactly right. But I feel the same force in the opposite direction: I live here. I accept stuff I don't want to. I love people who say terrible things. I want some of her leaving to rub off on me.

Come to Florida.

Maybe.

We can swim in a pool every day! You can go to college. You're too smart not to go to college.

Maybe.

No, the ocean. We'll swim in that. Sail in sailboats. Drive convertibles.

Maybe.

We can live with my mom. In her apartment on the second floor with a trash chute and a dishwasher and a fig tree in the yard.

Maybe. But already I'm filling up with it.

When we pull up to my house, it's dark. The outside light isn't on, and I can see a candle flickering through the living room window.

"Is your mom gettin' it on with some dude in there?" Shelly says.

I laugh at the outlandishness of that idea. It does look romantic, though—the perfect surprise for a person in love just coming home from a hard day's work. I feel a ping of something in my gut; I wish the idea wasn't so ridiculous. Instead, the truth: the electricity has been cut off.

I walk in the house singing out loud; it's a song from the radio that Shelly and me love.

Every-body wants to rule the world. I hear Ma trying to sing along with me before I even see her.

"No," I say, standing over her at the kitchen table. I hold my hand up, *Stop singing.*

She's pill-drunk, neck unhinged, pretending to read a newspaper spread in front of her. By candlelight. It's lucky she hasn't burned the whole house down.

"Someone's in a good mood!" she says and points at me. "Electric is off, so we'll have to camp out in here for a few days."

She says it with glee, like more misery-adventure should bring us even closer together. It cannot.

"Gas is also off, so we can only eat cold things. It's perfect timing, really. Too hot to eat hot food."

"And here's another bonus from my peeeperroute . . . a free peeeper!"

Her head bobs over the front page of the travel section, where there's a photo series of goats on the side of steep, nearly vertical cliffs in the Rocky Mountains. Giant poufy balls of white fur are held up by tiny legs bent in sharp angles, with delicate hooves grabbing on to mere inches of standing room. The space for them to navigate is so impossibly small, they look like they're baked into the side of the mountain. A mile to go in any direction, they are perfectly still, thinking about their next move. What a miracle. I'd read about them in *National Geographic.*

"I didn't want to have to tell you this, but someone's after my route. They're trying to get me in trouble. Saying I'm always late, the paper's crumply, this and that nonsense."

"Look, Ma." I point to the picture of the goats. "It's the wild mountain goats of the majestic Rockies. I think they're so symbolic, don't you?" Sometimes when Ma tries to burst my bubble, I say things I know she won't understand. Or I go sit in Ladybug for hours, where I know she won't come.

Her face freezes. "Oh, yes," she says and nods.

"Did you know that seventy years ago Black people weren't allowed to be seen outside after sundown in this town?"

Her head stutters, her eyes well up. She looks like she's about to nod yes, but changes her mind.

"No, I can't say that I knew that. It's just so . . . I can't find the right words for it."

I take the *F* encyclopedia from the shelf in the living room, grab a flashlight and head to my room. These books were Pop's pride and joy. He made payments to the encyclopedia salesman for a whole year before they belonged to us. He read them like they were novels. He had gotten through *L*.

The common mockingbird (Mimus polyglottos) is the Florida state bird. It is a superb songbird and mimic. Its own song has a pleasant lilting sound and is, at times, both varied and repetitive. Often, the mockingbird sings all night long, especially under bright springtime moonlight.

Aunt Clara. Aunt Sweetie. Lena. Pop. Pop. *Pop.*

* * *

Something is happening. The past is gathering itself together, tak-ing a solid shape somewhere I can't see, like hands on my shoulders from behind.

The lights flutter—on-off and on again with an electric *tzzz*. A mistake, most likely—the bill is still unpaid. But my brain won't remember this until later. In the moment, the sound is singular: both sad and hopeful, like the *swish-click* of counting coins on a kitchen table. Maybe there will be enough. Maybe there won't.

11

October 31, 1915

Dear Sweetie, my stubborn sister who sasses her Aunt Josephine,

*I feel like I'm fifty years old. I didn't know a person could feel so deep
down tired. I may not take care of Miss Rose anymore, but six days a
week I still cook, clean the house, go on house calls, and run the clinic
for Doctor. He won't hire anybody else to replace all the colored folk
used to work here, he's too afraid of somebody finding out Miss Rose
never came back. Probably couldn't find anyone anyway, there are no
extra white girls looking for jobs out here. I put my foot down and tell
him there are not enough hours in the day for me to go to the General
Store too, so I give him a list of things we need and that's his chore. He
tease me saying I'm worse than Miss Rose with the orders and why can't
I just be sweet and agreeable. I wish for the day when I only have to
answer to God and my medical schoolteachers. Doctor say the buildings
at Howard University look like castles and the library is as big as one
hundred houses. They have their own school song, Sweetie! I'll be the
loudest one in every room lifting my voice to sing it.*

Sundays belong to me. Unless we have a bad case that needs tending

*to, on Sundays I get to go back to Little Delta, back to our home.
Doctor say our Delta house wasn't abandoned like the others because
I'm still here, our things still here, and it's mine until the Canucks
arrive. The mill has been sold, so folks are hoping the new workers get
here by first snow. I hope they get lost. If not, I can't come to The Delta
much longer.*

*I take our shortcut through the woods from Doctor's. Every time
I get to the clearing, right before the rows of houses peek through the
trees, I gasp. You never seen a place so empty in your life. Like the
houses themselves have died. No people anywhere, no smell of wood
burning or cornbread baking, no fiddle playing or mamas calling. But
then the maple trees don't care—they're still turning orange and red and
yellow. The gardens keep growing, waiting to be tamed and harvested.
Birds make nests on the rooftops and ground squirrels cover the yards
with their burrow holes. It's like a big graveyard. My voice the only one
saying, We were here. This was our home.*

*I keep the inside of our house spotless, as much as the dust want to be
sneaking in. Everything look just like when y'all left—two chairs next
to the wood stove, one still with the rickety leg, the table in the middle
of the room, decorated with a cup full of dried out lavender flowers
in the center, the stools Uncle Henry made from the elm with the tree
sickness. Our room still papered with the prettiest adverts from the Swift
River Valley Register. Under the bed, a bottle of castor oil Robert hid so
we wouldn't have to line up for winter spoonfuls. I left up the string of
cranberries we looped across the wall for Christmas, our last Christmas.*

*Our beds all neatly made. The rocks we heated to warm them up
still there. I have a good laugh at our quilt. Me and you left that thing
in tatters from all the back and forth yanking, calling each other a
blanket hog. I find your marbles and Robert's broken yo-yos everywhere.
All our rooms put together are still smaller than one room in Doctor's
house. But I miss it, these walls feel like a tight hug to me.*

I bring food from Doctor's house so I don't have to light a fire in the stove. I don't want anyone to see the smoke and get an idea to come hassle me. I make thick slices of bread with bacon and duck fat. I pick tomatoes from the garden and they so good I eat them like apples. Strange to have any food in this house without one of y'all asking for a bite of something. I can see you and Robert standing in the doorway, covered in mill dust chanting we hungry, feed us, and then marching around the house till you got shushed. Barefoot and always getting splinters from the patch of floor near the wash basin. My first doctoring was pulling out wood slivers from little feet.

I fill up the basin from the well, but I can't heat it, so I wash myself with icy water. Sometimes after I grease my legs I don't put my clothes back on. I stay naked. I know I sound like a coo-coo bird but it makes me like feel I'm free. I can pass hours like that sitting in the chair, trying to find my thoughts. I might daydream that I'm a little girl again, and it's one of those Saturdays where we would go meet Mama and Daddy at the edge of Little Delta after work and then walk home with all the mill people. By the time the light was gone, we were singin' and teasin' each other, couldn't see nothin'. I can still feel the love-tug on my plaits. A finger poke from an imp of a cousin. An uncle scooping me up and carrying me on his back the rest of the way home. The light was blue and we were all the same black against it. It was like being hugged by a song in the dark. Did you feel that, too?

It's not safe for me to stay at the house overnight, but before I head back to Doctor's I go to our church. I sit in our usual place in the third row to the right. I sing. Loud. And don't you dare poke fun at my voice, you just jealous of my talents. I sing His Eye Is On The Sparrow and Wade In The Water. I read my Bible out loud. And I pray for you children, for our uncles and aunties, for all of our people spread wide from Woodville to California, for Doctor and Miss Rose, and for Gerald. I pray that I know how to be right, to do right, without anyone to teach me, to show me. It ain't nothing like Pastor Morgan would bring to us each Sunday morning but it's something that keep me going.

You ever think about that last morning in church?

Spring was shoutin' joy into the windows but the mood had a dagger in it. I remember the Spirit tossin' the whole congregation this way and that. With every song, folks sang louder and cried harder. Everybody praying for strength to carry them through the long journey ahead but I was praying for God to help me tell you and Robert I can't go with you. Uncle Henry and Aunt Josephine already knew they'd be taking you in, but I had to be the one to tell you. I couldn't do it while we was all cooking and filling provisions baskets, packing wagons and feeding the animals. And not when I was mending your shoes or washing your little bodies for the last time, Robert with enough dirt behind his ears to grow a patch of corn. In my head I was saying goodbye to you, just for now, and also goodbye to the Clara who belonged to people. And then the white folks got word too soon and come from their celebratin', drunk and raging hearted and then the fires come. You wouldn't let go my hand and I nearly died. No, I did die. I breathed in the sooty air for punishment, rubbed char on my face and soiled my clothes, kept my eyes open so they would burn. I made myself watch the caravan till they were fireflies in the distance. At some point Doctor come for me, wrap me in a blanket and shield me from the kicks of men who had made my head a spittoon. And then I was alone with the only true horror of that night—the look on your face, my Sweetie. I can never be sorry enough.

In your last letter you ask me do I ever cry thinking about all what we lost? I do. I go to the river, to our spot where it gets shallow and the rocks are just the right smooth for swimming and washing without cutting up your feet. I cry and yell until my throat is gone. Yesterday I think I may have screamed the good sense out of my head, because something strange happened, Sweetie. Make me doubt my own mind. I was sitting on the rocks, not caring that I'm getting my dress wet, scaring away the fish and every living thing with my wailing, and I see a black man on the other side of the riverbank, like that was a natural thing. It wasn't Gerald, it wasn't any one of us. He was tall and dressed in fine clothes, like it was Sunday and he was headed to a big city church. Had on fancy trousers and a matching waistcoat, angel-white shirt and a tie. He don't see me at first but when he do, he smile wide, like I was what he come for. He had a big gap in between his front teeth. Sweetie, sometimes I see Mama and Daddy like they still alive so I think this is someone come from the beyond to take me back with him. I scream. I put my face in my hands and when I look up again, he was gone.

See now, what with my naked wanderings in the house, Sunday sermons by myself and now a gap-toothed black ghost, you must think I done gone mad. I may be on my way. But for right now I swear it's still me, your ole sister. Hoping you're being nicer to Auntie Josephine.

November 21, 1915

Sweetie,

Our house is gone. The Canucks are here, they came by the dozens, on foot, by railway, automobile and wagon, and they moved into Little Delta, spreading all through the east side of town. For the first time in fifty years, a family who is not a Newberry is calling our place home. I'm not too sad about it, knew it was coming. Maybe I'm already a steel-hearted woman at eighteen. Or maybe after losing everybody, the house was just like the scab falling off the wound.

Doctor helped me get as much as we could fit into the wagon. I mostly took the things that still had the whiff of you all in it. Like the toolbox with Daddy's initials carved in the side, Mama's old head rag stained with beeswax and violet oil. Now I sleep underneath all of our old quilts, still with your smells, in my bed. I tucked a piece of the head rag in this letter for you. Inhale it, deep and long, and tell me what you remember.

Town is full of people speaking French. It's like I woke up in another country. It seems like they're laughing at us all the time and you can't understand a word that comes out their mouth. In the store they point at what they want and then say Marcie. The regular Swift River white folks don't like it one bit. Say wherever the Frenchies go they make a "Little Canada" so dirty and filled with sickness it's not fit for a dog to live in, and that even colored people are more self-respecting. Say Canucks work for less money and then leave and bring it all back to Canada. The new mill Canucks turned our little church Catholic. Doctor say it's the wrong kind of Christian where they want to eat Jesus and drink his blood. And their men will take any job, even the ones the girls do—spinners and doffers and twisters and even the drawing-in girls' work.

Swift River white folks start to talk to me like I'm one of them or at least I'm not as bad as a Canuck. Make it easier for me to move around town on my own now. Doctor is sending me out by myself on some of the visits he used to make, and people don't put up too much of a fuss once they see I know what I'm doing. If someone starts to hassle me on the streets a mister might come along and say, Leave her be, she's our Negro. She's good and hardworking.

Sweetie, I know white folks don't see me, Clara Newberry, but they do see a person can help them, can save them, who knows things about their bodies that their husbands and wives and children could never guess at. They open their mouths and stick out their tongues, they show me their oozing, bumpy privates, their bellies swollen with secret children. They tell me about their fevers and broken bones and cook fire burns and the last time they made urine without bleeding. They trust me, depend on me even. I don't know how I feel about it, seeing a white person turned inside out like that. Especially ones I remember from that night. I have to cut that part out my mind or I couldn't make it through a day or this life.

Doctor mostly keep to his office now. He say he's doing research all the time but I know he is sad. I think it's the same as Miss Rose in bed with her heavy head, but him in an office chair instead. We don't talk about Miss Rose.

With all of this extra work for me, I beg Doctor to take on a housemaid and a cook, say I can't do it all no more. He finally say OK and he hire a Canuck girl. She look about fifteen and her name is Marion and she ain't dirty like they say about the rest. She has pretty blond hair and blue eyes and a scared look on her face all the time. She don't speak English, but she also don't treat me like I am dirt on church clothes. She won't look at me straight, but as long as she cuts the biscuits with a glass and polishes the banisters the way Doctor likes, I don't care if our eyes ever meet.

The air is the cool of late fall about to turn. Feeling that air used to stir up a worry in me that we wouldn't have enough clothes to stay warm for the coming winter. How was I going to make sure all of you children had coats and extra socks and boots with sturdy soles? Doctor give me Miss Rose's long and heavy wool coat so I'm like a princess who never has to worry about the cold. But not worrying about the cold also makes me feel like I'm forgetting something. And then remembering makes me feel bad even though you're warm and safe in Woodville and don't need a coat or any shoes at all. I guess what I'm saying is the cool air make me feel awful. Does that make sense? Sometimes worries are a comfort, what connect you to another person. What make me feel like your big sister.

Just now a young white fella come running up to the door and say come to the mill, there's a doffer dropped to the floor and now her baby is coming too soon. They just ask for me, don't even ask for Doctor. I'll write more when I get back.

———∿∿∿———

Sweetie, how did I forget? The way that everything in that mill rush in and try to fill up your body. The smell in your nose, the heavy white air, the roar of the looms so loud they blocking out your own thoughts. As soon as I walk in my eyes burned and I scrambled to get a rag around my mouth before the dust get to my lungs. The men at their posts pointed me toward a corner, where a group of women bent over a young girl with no shoes and a medium sized belly. I guess seven months. Blood and waters trickled out from under her dress. Bloody footprints were all around her.

She was dirty like all of them folks work a full mill day. I had sterilized rags all ready in my bag, and got to clearing her face, her legs. I felt her stomach for the baby's position, put my ear to her navel to listen to the bloods and pulse. The women stood around us like a shield blocking the men folk from seeing. I send a few of the nosy boys to get fabric to put underneath her, cushion her from the cold floor. She grab my hand and cry, hollering something in French I can't understand. Her pains were close together so I knew the baby was coming fast.

And then I see him. First through the cracks in between the shield women, then right at the head of the girl, placing a reem of white fabric under her head. The gap-tooth black ghost is a real living man. He remember me as the wailing girl from the river! That day I scare him, too. He tell me he work for the new mill owner and will help me talk to the girl on the floor, take her French words and give them to me in English. That what he do for work! He call himself a translator. A translator is someone who know two languages. He take a word in one language and then speak it in another, so two strangers can understand each other. He speak English in a different way from us—he don't sound like any colored man you ever met. He tell me exactly what the girl say and he tell her what I say. He nod when I say how to breathe and say Respiray and she look at us both like we the same voice, one voice together. He is calm, younger than he look from a distance, maybe twenty or so, but he rub his head and beard like an old man. He don't even seem afraid as the blood and the waters come. His eyes tear up when the strong new baby girl got to yowling, no language yet to speak of where she come from. He call me Doctor and tell me I'm a wonder.

Sweetie, after all this time not seeing a colored man, when I catch a look at his skin near my skin it's like a kind of a looking glass, shining against all of the white skin around us. Something in me open up. What blooms there—Daddy and Robert and Uncle Henry and belly laughing and ashy elbows and big hands that hold on to my hands with care, and care, and combing a tender-headed somebody to make four plaits (that's you). He smell like wood smoke and apples. He is handsome, Sweetie, so very handsome. He stand straight, and his wide shoulders pull at his shirt and waistcoat. His shoes are shiny, like he never set foot outside. I'm wearing one of Miss Rose's day dresses, it have flowers for buttons. We look like we dressed up to play a game called White Folks. Like God took two pretty black dolls and smashed them together—go now, make a life.

12

1980

Ma stayed home from work again today. Pop says she can't ever go back.

A few days after the Campbells' barbecue, a strange guy wearing big black boots and a bandana on his head started hanging around outside the dance studio. Pop said it was someone Tom Campbell sent to scare us. Ma said it was just a regular creep, that she was safe with all of those people around her. "Nobody's gonna mess with me and the girls. Too many witnesses." I imagine them all in their leotards and leg warmers, charging after the man, chopping him with high kicks and jazz hands.

There are two different Mas; this is the brave one. Regular Ma will make me come into the basement with her to hang up wet clothes. I sing my songs for her when we hear scurrying in corners, hold her hand on the way back up the stairs while she digs her nails into me. Brave Ma stands up to Grandma Sylvia whenever she says something bad about Pop, telling her we'd rather be out on the street than disrespected. A few times Brave Ma started packing our things into garbage bags until Grandma said she was sorry.

"We don't have a choice. I have to go back to work," she says to me while making saltine and jelly sandwiches for us. I don't remember the last time she's been home during snack time.

"My job pays for this," she says, pointing to her mouth, full and spraying cracker dust.

"Don't worry, sweet pea, I'm pretty sure that man thinks I'm a friend of his," she adds. "He's just coming to say hi."

I smush a cracker sandwich on my plate; I don't believe her.

Later that night, when I'm supposed to be asleep, I crouch down by their bedroom door and listen.

"You sure it's not mill people? The owners?" Ma says.

Pop laughs like a madman.

"This is funny to you?" Ma says.

"Annabelle. We are arguing over which of the many people out to get me is responsible for sending that jackass."

Ma is quiet.

"It's Tom. I know it," Pop says. "I don't care what he does to me—he's not gonna fuck with my wife." He pounds his fist on something in rhythm to the last few words. Things fall to the floor. "He is sending me a message you could never understand," Pop says.

"Baby, please," Ma says. "Don't do it. It'll ruin everything. We're not even sure Tom knows what happened."

"I put my hands on his kid! That's what happened!"

"Just his arm! You can explain it . . ."

"Who knows how that little piece of shit told the story. It's too late. I shoulda been the one to tell it."

"What about Diamond?" Ma says. I am her weapon and her shield.

"God help us, Tom was about the last person who could have stood up for me," Pop says.

"Tell me how to help you," Ma begs.

"To help *us*, you mean," he says.

I haven't screamed once since the barbecue and the fireflies night, but Champei won't even be around for me to tell. The Allens are moving before school starts; me and Pop will be the only browns again. Now I eat snacks instead of screaming. It doesn't help—this is all my fault. When I close my eyes to sleep, all I can see is Pop dangling Tommy Jr. over the ground, Tommy kicking at the air furiously, looking over his shoulder like he's trying to outrun a monster.

The next morning, Pop and me go out to the garden to pick tomatoes. Yesterday they'd been bright red, hard and soft in just the right way, fat with skins about to split. Pop smelled the stems and said in one day they'd be the perfect sweet and sour for our sauce.

But the garden is wrecked.

Plants are smashed, all of those pretty curves and angles flattened, bright colors mushed into a dull green-brown. A whole bag of trash has been scattered: empty cans of Yoo-hoo, Manwich sauce and Schlitz beer, kitty litter and TV dinner trays—licked clean except for the veggie section, where tiny peas stick to the plastic like green sprinkles. Wads of toilet paper and dirty napkins hang from beanstalks and tomato vines. It's a garbage garden.

Pop bends down to pick up one of our beautiful, perfectly ripe tomatoes lying on the ground, the only thing left that is close to being whole. It looks like someone has taken a bite out of it, then decided they didn't like it. Pop throws it down as if the tomato itself has insulted him.

"You see?" he screams at Ma, but since she's inside, he's yelling at the house.

"Pop, remember you stabbed the neighbor's basketball and threw it back into their yard?" I say. "Maybe you made them mad."

145

I think it might make him feel better to believe it's just that one family—one mom and dad, one teenage boy, and one baby girl—instead of a whole army of people, including a man with a bandana and big stomping boots, out to get him, out to get us. He looks over at the neighbor's house for a long time.

But he doesn't say anything. He just looks at the garbage garden and then walks back to the house.

Since we can't make tomato sauce for dinner, we have spaghetti and margarine with chunks of spam made to look like meatballs, instead. Pop won't look at Ma or me, just his plate. He jabs at the noodles and gets mad at them for sliding off of his fork. Ma keeps staring at him; she tries to touch his hand. He doesn't pull it away, but he stops eating and sits perfectly still until she takes it off. There's a knock at the door and we all jump. I start to run and answer it, like I usually get to, but both Ma and Pop say "Sit!" at the same time.

Pop answers the door. It's a policeman.

"Evening, Rob. I'm sorry to disturb your supper, but I need to talk to you. Can I come in?" He looks friendly but has a hand on the door like he might push it open without permission. The air behind him is the blue-gray of almost night. I can hear the neighborhood kids playing an after-dinner game of Red Light, Green Light. They're all yelling, *Go Go! Go!!!!!!* I wish I was them—full with dinner and ice cream sandwiches and games and nighttime without parents—everything that can be squeezed in between now and bedtime.

"Why?" Pop asks. One hand is on the top of the door, the other taps at the doorknob.

"I need to ask you some questions about a theft at the paper mill."

"Outside," Pop says, and moves past him through the doorway.

When I turn to Ma so she can explain it to me, she focuses on slurping a very long string of spaghetti. She looks up at me and her

146

eyes go wide, flashing something like *help*, like asking for me to explain it all to *her*, like begging me not to ask any questions. It happens in the time it takes for a noodle to be sucked in through her puckered lips, a splash of wet at the end, then gone.

"Everything's fine," Pop says when he comes back inside. He's holding his own head in his hands like it might fall off.

"Stay here and finish your dinner," Ma says, following Pop to the bedroom.

A chewy piece of Spam jiggles a front tooth loose. I've already lost a lot of my baby teeth, but this will be my last front. I think about the cool air rushing into each new hole, how I couldn't stop my tongue from dipping inside, over and over, even though it burned each time. The penny-flavored blood. The dull white ridges of grown-up teeth hiding just beneath the surface. The Tooth Fairy money. *The Tooth Fairy money.*

"Hey!" I say, but then decide to keep it to myself.

After day camp the next day I see the bandana man for myself. While I'm waiting for Ma to pick me up, I lie on top of the metal railing on the YMCA stairs, stomach down, arms and legs dangling on either side. It's hard to balance like this, and I spot the bandana man just as he smiles and nods, like he's impressed. He's leaning up against a car in the nearly empty parking lot; it looks too small to fit his big body.

I'm so scared I can't move.

He waves, in the way a kid would wave, hard and fast. That wave confuses me. Before I can think what to do, I see Ma charging at me from the side. She grabs my arm and nearly drags me to our car. My legs can't keep up with her. "Well if that's a friend of yours, you should say hi back!" I say into her red, red face.

* * *

147

"Why doesn't he just come for *me?*" Pop says to Ma behind their closed bedroom door. Ma is crying.

"What kind of man tries to scare a little—" And here Ma stops herself.

Like me, I bet she sees Tommy Jr. dangling in Pop's hands as he squeezes him to black and blue.

We're going on an adventure down South to Georgia, stopping off along the way to camp and roast marshmallows. Grandma Sylvia is not coming with us; she's going to visit her cousin Eileen in Pittsburgh. She gives me her favorite blue suitcase for the trip—just small enough for me to drag, with a travel set of matching lotion and mouthwash containers that snap onto the inside pocket. She knows I'm crazy about that set. Before she leaves to catch her bus, she hands me two family-sized bags of Starburst candy and tells me, "Don't share with your mom and dad but only eat three a day." It's like a brain twister. "Then there will be enough left for me and you when we're back together, which will damn sure happen, sweetheart." She seems worried and in a hurry to get away from us.

We hit the road while it's still dark out. Ma is scowling and Pop is cheerful in a crazy way, cracking jokes and trying to tickle. This is normal now—one of them happy while the other is sad and then they switch places. They both seem jumpy, like Ma on too many cups of coffee. As we move farther and farther away from Swift River, they start to meet in the middle. We all lean our heads back on our seats. On the radio, country and rock stations crackle in and out, then soul and jazz ghost into their places without us ever touching the dial. *That takes me back*, Pop keeps saying, singing along. We go wherever the songs on the radio take us. Stevie Wonder makes us the happiest.

I'm in the back seat with a bed of blankets, my books, and the Starburst bags. No one pays attention to how many pieces of candy I eat. I decide not to listen to Grandma; I have a mission. I'm making woven bracelets with the colorful Starburst wrappers, just like I've seen kids at the Y wearing. I'm careful to chew with side teeth, so as not to disturb my loose-y.

"Have you ever seen two male peacocks fight over a female peacock?" Pop asks.

We're playing a game.

"Never!" I say.

"Well you will in Woodville," Pop says. "It looks like two feather fans with heads and legs going in circles around each other."

"You ever had a taste of scrapple and eggs?"

"No!" I say.

"Oh, it's outta this world, Diamond."

"Can I get some down South?" I ask.

"That's the place for it," Pop says.

"You ever laid under a weeping willow tree and looked up at the stars on a hot night?"

"We have stars and weeping willows in the North, too," Ma says with a flat voice.

"And hot nights!" I say.

Pop turns up the radio again.

We pull into a rest stop in another state. Ma brought our lunch from home in a bread bag: cheese sandwiches with mayo and mustard. There is a Howard Johnson's restaurant, a store, and some bathrooms all inside a big building next to the gas station. I beg Ma and Pop to buy us even just a snack, like fried clams or chicken pot pie, but they say no. Families sit outside, their picnic tables covered in delicious-looking food that does not come from a bread bag.

Ma takes me inside to use the bathroom; there's a long line that starts near the entrance. In the HoJo's cafeteria, people carry trays filled with hamburgers and soda and colorful Jell-O squares; they sit in comfy-looking booths. I've never in my life seen so many different looking people together in one place, or so many people who look like me and Pop. They stare at Ma and me, but I stare at them, too. Black people, white people, young people, weird people. A white kid covered in puke. Triplet brown girls in matching jumpsuits. An older Black woman in a fancy dress and a hat with a feather. A basketball team in uniform, legs as long as I am tall. Everyone is moving fast, winding through the crowd, darting in between people. Everyone is in the way. Ma's hand on my head makes my stomach feel tight. For the first time ever, it seems like she's more of a stranger in the room than me.

Outside, Pop has found an empty picnic table near a large brown family. They have a radio that plays fast music with trumpets and maracas. I ask Pop what the music is. "Salsa, I think," he says. I'm sitting next to Pop; Ma is across from us. I wonder if people think I belong to him and she is just our friend.

"Go stretch your legs out," Ma says to me, pointing at the kids around us running in circles. A brown girl does cartwheels and roundoff back handsprings on the grass near the tables, yelling, *Watch! Mira!* to her parents, who pause every now and again to clap and whistle.

I go to the edge of the grass and do a backbend—something I've taught myself. I try to kick my legs back over but fall in a heap to the side. I look up and the cartwheel girl is leaning over me, her thick black hair hanging near my face. She smells like shampoo and hot dogs. We look like we could be sisters. I think she might help me up, but instead she flops down next to me.

150

I see Ma and Pop looking over at me in that stupid, hopeful way. Ma's hair is flat and greasy, while Pop's Afro is big and lumpy—he hasn't combed it. Their heads look tiny and giant. Ma is wearing her favorite Rolling Stones T-shirt with the big red lips and a big red tongue sticking out, and Pop has on a white mesh tank top; his brown nipples like two unblinking eyes underneath. They're both slouching. They look like goofy kids, kids who couldn't possibly have their own kid. I don't know why that's what I think about right now. Ma waves.

"Do you take gymnastics?" Cartwheel says to me.

"No. I just mess around by myself," I say.

"I'm on the gymnastics team. Last meet I medaled in two events."

"That's really neat," I say.

"That your mama?" she says, nodding toward Ma.

"Yes."

"She's white," she says.

"Uh-huh." My face prickles.

"Mira!" She smiles, gets up, runs away from me and does the most beautiful flip I've ever seen. She could be a professional. I think with awe that I might see her on TV in the Olympics someday. And then she's gone, heading back over to her family, who are packing up their food and radio and children. She never looks back to see if I liked the flip.

"You made a friend," Ma says in between drags of her cigarette. Pop rubs his hands together like, *This is getting good.*

"Yes," I lie. "We're going to be pen pals. She's going to be a famous gymnast, someday," I say. Smiles crack their faces open.

"Well how about that," Pop says, shaking his head.

Ma stubs out her cigarette. "Let's go. This place is nuts," she says, as a new wave of people come rushing up the walkway, let loose from their cars to eat and pee.

151

* * *

Back on the road, I wake once at a tollbooth to a man giving Pop directions. Then again as we cross a bridge, the *chucka chucka chucka* of tires hitting metal. There's a slow song on the radio and Pop's big hand is wrapped around Ma's little one. They're both squeezing. The next time I open my eyes we're at the Funtimes Campground.

Because it is almost dinnertime, the whole place smells like smoke and barbecue. A ranger in a ranger hut points out the bathrooms and the area that has the most empty campsites. He hands us a map and a list of rules and says, "No, there aren't any bears," even though we didn't ask that question. He talks a lot about trash and noise; Pop nods extra hard as he explains it, making sure the ranger knows we're not rule breakers.

All I can see around us are tall trees, like the woods at home, but the bay is hiding behind them; the ranger says there's a path that opens up to the water. The bay is the ocean without waves. I can smell it—heavy with salt and fish—even though I can't see it.

Our campsite is flat and covered in wood chips; we have our own firepit and picnic table. There are others next to and across from us, but the woods are thick enough that you can hear things but not really see people: a laugh, a stick breaking, someone hocking a loogie. Pop pitches our orange tent and Ma spreads the blankets inside. I get twigs and small branches for our fire. It's like our own little house and yard. Ma sings "This Little Light of Mine" and Pop snaps along. I forget all about Georgia and home. I think maybe we could live here in the middle forever.

It's still early enough for a swim before dinner. Just like the ranger said, the dirt path opens up and the bay is wide and everywhere. Now I understand how the ocean is inside of it—the way the water still comes in and out, small laps at the shore like a promise of big waves somewhere else. There are a few families left on the beach, but most are packing up their coolers and towels for the day. Gray clouds dragging night behind them are just about to push out the orange sky. The three of us stand in our bathing suits, holding hands with me in the middle. We walk out until the water is up to my chest. Ma and Pop hold me—one on each side—as I float. We don't say anything. Just Pop with a low humming that means he's happy. I don't need their help to stay above the calm water, but I let them think I might.

After a dinner of hamburgers and chips, Ma and me take flashlights to pee while Pop builds a fire. We go behind a tree since the bathroom is too far. We squat and listen to the night; it's a dark web of sounds. One thing on the left answers a thing on the right and then behind us, like they're all talking to each other.

"Stay close," Ma says. I move next to her. Our pee makes two streams in the dirt. We splash on each other's feet. Ma puts her hand on my head, runs her fingers down one of my braids.

"Sometimes I wish I was Black like you and Pop," she says.

"Me, too," I say for the first time.

When I see her face get scared, I change it to, "I like your skin how it is, Ma."

I decide to forgive her for having greasy, flat hair today.

"OK," she says.

We drip dry. Then she shows me the kind of leaves you'd use for a number two.

Wind makes the fire catch suddenly, and it jumps up with a *whoooosh*, toward our faces. The flames light up a circle around us. Where the light ends, it's a flat wall of blackness and trees. It's blazing hot inside the circle, but the air on the back of my neck and legs is cool, like I'm in two places at once. Pop looks proud of his fire. Ma looks sad and lost, somewhere else—not with us here at Funtimes Campground. She tells me to go get a book to read by the fire while we roast marshmallows.

I dig through my suitcase, looking for *Nancy Drew: The Secret at Shadow Ranch*, and realize I accidentally brought *A Field Guide to the Birds*, a library book that is now past due. Betty, our librarian, sweet Betty, will be so disappointed in me. I think about our town's little library on the hill, how this is the first year I've been allowed to walk there by myself. I think about Betty teaching me the Dewey decimal system; how the books she picks out for me smell like rain and dust; the Pajama Story Time Grandma Sylvia used to take me to. I think about home.

"Ma!" I say, running out of the tent. "I forgot to return the birds book to the library."

"Oh!" Ma says, looking a little panicked, too. "Well . . ."

"We can send it back once we get to Woodville," Pop says.

"But how will I pay the fine?" I ask.

"We'll put some money in the book," Pop says.

Ma shakes her head. That's not how it works.

"I'm supposed to put it in the library drop box!" I say.

In the firelight, Ma's face droops. She drops her head, and her greasy hair hangs in her eyes. Pop leans in underneath her face to make sure she sees him.

"We are not in Swift River, so we can't put the book in that drop box." He speaks very slowly, looking only at Ma. "We are moving to Woodville. We will send it from there."

"We're *moving*?" I say.

"Not necessarily . . ." Ma begins.

Pop walks over to me, snatches the book out of my hand, and throws it into the fire. The plastic cover crumbles, then there's a brief shimmer of rainbow before it's gone. Black smoke and ash rush up into the sky. It smells terrible. Pop looks back at Ma with his chin way up and his arms out. The smoke and the sparks from the embers make him look like he's on fire, too.

"Why did you do that!" I start to cry.

"Diamond, go in the tent," Ma says.

Inside, I eat cold marshmallows and Starbursts and put a blanket over my head, a tent inside a tent. I try and cover my ears, but I can still hear them.

"That's where *our life* is," Ma says.

"If we go back my life is over," Pop says.

I can't breathe. I rip the blanket off of my head. A Starburst catches my loose tooth and sends a lightning bolt to my head.

"So this is the answer? We hide out in the woods in east bumfuck with Ranger Rick and then go live with strangers?"

One's voice gets loud, and the other one *shhhushes*. Then they trade places.

"SELFISH, SELFISH, SELFISH, Annabelle."

"You're acting like a lunatic. It's like you're not even you anymore. What is happening? This is hard for *everybody*."

Ma and Pop shadows are painted on the tent; they look like cutouts from the night. They are my shadow parents, long and distorted and wild. I pretend that my real parents are somewhere else, doing laundry, aerobics, clipping toenails in front of the TV—normal things. My shadow parents are the babysitters.

"Then we'll go back without you!" Ma yells.

Their voices punch the quiet. We are breaking the ranger's rules.

"Shut the hell up!" someone yells in the distance. Ma and Pop stop talking.

"Fuck off and mind your own business!" Pop yells back.

My stomach hurts, the sugary goop growing inside it like a rotten marshmallow baby. I want to start the screaming but I made a promise to Pop. My tooth aches; I can't stop wiggling it with my tongue. The sweet sludge from the candy sticks to my lips like Ma's lip gloss.

This is all my fault, all of it.

I don't realize I'm holding on to my tooth until the pain explodes in my mouth. The burning is wide and deep and it hurts so much I wonder if I've yanked out *all* of my front teeth. But no, there is just one baby tooth in my hand, hard and white like a tiny seashell. Blood is everywhere, running down my face, dripping onto the blankets.

"Hey!" I yell.

Ma and Pop go from shadows to terrified faces in the opening of the tent.

When I wake up in the middle of the night, Pop is looking down at me.

"Go back to sleep and I'll meet you there, sweet pea," he says.

I do. And like he promised, he's there in my dream. A bear is chasing Ma and me down our block in Swift River. Neighbors come out on their porches to wave, like we're in a race or a parade. They cheer. Soon I realize that Pop is the bear.

It's still night when I wake up again; now it's Ma watching me.

"Are you in pain?" She looks worried.

"Yes," I say. The top of my mouth still burns. It hurts underneath my nose.

"While you were sleeping your father went and got you some frozen peas." Ma wraps the package in a T-shirt and rests it on my top lip.

"That poor tooth wasn't ready to come out yet."

"I forgot to put it under my pillow," I say.

156

"You can save it. We're going home. The Tooth Fairy is going to come there," Ma says.

"How will she know?"

"I told her. I left her a note."

"Where?"

"At home, under your pillow."

"But you didn't even know my tooth was loose."

"Mas know everything."

Pop, with his back to us, lets out a chuckle.

"We're all going together?" I ask.

"Of course," Ma says.

I leave a Starburst under my pillow, a gift for the Tooth Fairy just in case she forgets and comes here instead.

We're going home.

I want to ask about our Georgia adventure, if we'll ever try again, about the peacocks and scrapple and weeping willows at night, if Grandma Sylvia can come with us next time. I want to ask if Ma's fake friend the bandana man will be waiting for us when we get home. I want to know why Ma is more scared of the Georgia family strangers than the stranger with the bandana and stomping boots and an army of invisible enemies.

The tent is lit orange by the sun coming through; it smells like rubber, smoke, and morning breath in here. Ma and Pop are sleeping with arms and legs spread out, all over each other, blankets kicked off. Each like they think they're alone in their own bed.

My head brushes up against paper, and I turn to see a piece of money resting next to me. I've never seen this kind of money before; it looks pretend. It says one hundred dollars. I touch it; it *feels* like real money.

"She didn't listen to you, Ma!"

Ma sits up, squinting. Her eyes are puffy and lined with crust. I hold up the bill in her face.

"The Tooth Fairy! She didn't wait until we got home!" I say.

She looks at it confused, then mad.

"No, she didn't, did she," Ma says.

Pop leans over her, smiles big.

"Is it fake?" I ask.

"Tooth Fairy doesn't do fake," Pop says.

"But last tooth I only got one dollar," I say.

"This means you're a woman now," Pop says, laughing so hard tears come down his cheeks. Ma looks at him like he's lost his mind.

We pack up the car in silence. Pop doesn't bother to fold up the tent into its tiny case—he throws it in the trunk on top of the dirt-covered stakes. We're all nervous as we drive past the ranger hut; we sit up straight and don't move around too much. Luckily the ranger is too busy studying a map to look down at us, even though we stop and drop our bag of trash into the dumpster next to him, as he'd instructed.

In the back seat of the car, I try and make a list of things I want to buy. Nothing feels special enough. This money should make me happy, but it doesn't. I had put it in the trunk, tucked deep in my suitcase, behind the mouthwash, magnified through the see-through plastic container, colored icy blue from the liquid inside. I keep my tooth in my shorts pocket, wrapped in a leaf. I feel around for it every few minutes, comforted when the sharp edges prick my finger.

"Why don't you write to your gymnast friend?" Ma says.

"I'm going to pay for the library book with my one-hundred-dollar bill," I say. This feels right.

Ma and Pop look at each other, then me.

"No," they both say at the same time, back on the same team again for a few seconds.

I put aside the list for now and focus on my Starburst bracelets. From a distance, each link looks like a bright, square jewel. I finish one for each of us.

"You can't take these off," I instruct Ma and Pop.

"We won't," they say.

But they fall apart in just a few hours, colorful trash on the car floor.

13

1987

I have to get up in an hour," Ma whispers from behind me. At some point in the night she's come into my room, my little bed, and is now curled up around me, her front to my back—the position they find old couples in when they die together.

This is the last time we'd lie here, snuggled up like this.

"I hate getting up when it's still dark out," she says. "It's not natural."

I'm pissed at myself for not waking up when she crawled into bed. And I'm pissed at the part of me who, even in sleep, accepts this as normal: Ma's phlegmy breathing at my neck, her smell—like bread and sweat. I don't want to know her smells in the dark. She feels me changing, knows something big is about to happen. She knows I have Lena and Aunt Clara without knowing how to name them.

The flashlight from last night sits on my bedside table, a weak beam still shining in the hazy dark. Ma must have turned it on when she came in.

A memory comes:

You're scared of the dark. You're going to need it.

Ma's voice from the hallway closet, talking to five-year-old me.

I am running away from home. I don't remember my five-year-old reasons. Just that I tell Ma in advance. She is helping me pack. She hands me a flashlight.

I'd thought that people who ran away did it like hobos from the movies—hopping trains with all their life's possessions in a hanky tied to a stick slung over their shoulder. I get a stick from the yard and go to the kitchen to stuff a dishtowel. Ma helps me fill it with carrot sticks, a raisin snack box, my Barbie, and the flashlight. She ties it all in tight with a piece of yarn.

I stand on the porch, looking out over the neighborhood. Already it looks different—prettier, brighter, no longer belonging to me.

"I'll really miss you if you leave," Ma says, "but I understand."

I insist. I have to go.

"Well you better be on your way before it gets dark," she says.

I'll admit it. Looking back at this Ma, I admire the flat-out kookiness of it all, the possibly bad mother-ness, her clear-headed confidence in the power of her love to bring me back. She knew I wouldn't make it far. If she was scared I'd be snatched by a perv, or hit by a car, or mauled by wild dogs before deciding to come back— she didn't show it. I looked back at her waving to me from the porch and her face was wide open and trusting. Like she'd be standing right there in case I decided to return.

Unless it was something else?

Unless it was the beginnings of her giving in to the part of herself that was already tired, already worn thin?

I only make it to the end of the block, never out of her sight, nor she out of mine.

I feel Ma's stomach gurgle into my back. Something rustles at the window across from my bed. The blinds are up just high enough to frame a deer head looking in at me, at us. Two glassy deer eyes, big and familiar, stare without blinking.

I'm embarrassed at the thought of this deer catching Ma and me spooning, then embarrassed at being embarrassed in front of a damn deer. But I don't question why it's here, watching us.

When Ma gets up to go to the bathroom she scares the deer away. Luckily, she doesn't see it. She'd be terrified. I lock my bedroom door behind her. She rattles it for a good minute before shuffling back to her room.

It's the height of slow-motion summer, when it's so hot most folks can only drag themselves from house to car, car to work, work to car and home again. This is usually the hardest time of year for Ma and me to find rides. When Shelly picks me up for driver's ed for practice test day, the streets are so bare it looks like they've been re-claimed by packs of animals. Ghostly clouds of gnats form phantom shapes. A freakishly large group of squirrels gathers acorns in front of the trees along Oak Street under the lazy watch of neighborhood cats. Dogs drink from Mrs. Wolinski's water-spitting lawn gnome. Ducks walk in single file along the side of the road leading to Dog-fish Pond. Pitch-black lawn jockeys hold birdbath trays overflowing with sparrows and warblers.

"It's so empty! Where are all of these losers?" Shelly calls Swift River people losers a lot, lately.

"They're smart and inside or at the beach," I say.

"That's where we'll be every day when we get to Florida!" Shelly says. She has turned my "maybe" to a "yes" overnight, even though I haven't decided.

The air-conditioned Get In Gear! Driving School classroom is like a vacation. We've been coming for over a month. This is the last day in the classroom and the first of our in-car lessons with Mr. Jimmy. All twenty of us have paired up; Shelly and me are scheduled to go out with him after class today. I have to focus hard not to look like I'm smiling at nothing—or worse, at someone. I squeeze my lips so tight my jaw starts to hurt.

Even though it's the middle of summer, everything has an end-of-school-year, high-energy vibe, with the other kids bonded and the goof-offs competing for laughs. Mr. Jimmy is everyone's best bud, so the class is rowdy and not easily brought back from disruptions.

"If Danielle has her car's gear in reverse," Mr. Jimmy points to a long-nosed girl with short hair in the front row, "and turns her wheel to the right, what direction will the car go in?"

The day plus the easy question gives me a shot of courage. I raise my hand.

"Forward!" someone yells. Five people wave their arms, but he calls on me.

"The car would go to the right," I say.

"That's cause *you're* sitting in the passenger seat!" a wrestler named Danny says. Danny is sitting on the other side of Shelly. She crumples up a piece of paper and beams it off of his head. He laughs it off, like it's a fun game between them. "Nice one!"

"Diamond, you are correct. I would trust you driving me any day," Mr. Jimmy says.

I start to get red, to feel complimented, but then I see him flick his eyes at Shelly. He's being nice because of her.

I look around the room at these dopes and can't help but think about the fact that Aunt Clara is probably responsible for half of their lives, if you do the math. I walk around thinking about this all the time now—her pulling out babies who gave birth to other babies who then became these meanies. It's so intimate and thrilling and awful; a strange new thread that ties me to them.

* * *

By the time class ends, my legs tingle from being crushed under a puny desk for so long; I pray for the bigger of the two driver's ed cars, the one with four doors and a giant sunroof, instead of the one with two doors and a massive *Get In Gear! I'm a Student Driver!* sign on top. Crawling into the back seat of a two-door car is a nightmare for me—seat shifting as far forward as it can go, breath held in, hips at just the right angle, and still sometimes I get wedged in.

"You girls are gonna be stoked," Mr. Jimmy says, ushering us over to the four-door slice of heaven in the parking lot. A yellow *Student Driver* magnet sticks to the driver's side door like an afterthought— more *In case you'd like to know* than *Stay back if you'd like to live.* Otherwise it's a normal car, and we could be three normal friends going for a ride.

"Who's first?" Mr. Jimmy looks at Shelly and smiles.

She shrieks and does a skip leap, pony style, toward the driver's side in answer, forgetting to look over at me until she is already opening the door. Even though she's driven before, Shelly is as excited as I am.

"It's fucking hellfire in here!" she screams and thrusts her hips into the air, her short jean skirt exposing most of her legs above the hot vinyl seat. I have on leggings and Mr. Jimmy has on his regular khakis, so we feel heat but not fire as our legs touch down. Mr. Jimmy whips off his outer long-sleeved shirt—fingers a crazy flutter on each button—and spreads it underneath Shelly's butt, careful not to touch her in the process, as she presses her pelvis into the steering wheel. He does this so fast, it's not until he sees Shelly eying the curly black hair-garden sprouting from the V in his yellowed undershirt that his face seems to register many uncomfortable things at once.

"I'm a chivalrous dude, what can I say?"

Shelly settles into the nest of Mr. Jimmy's shirt around her bare

165

legs and smiles back at me. The shirt looks like Mr. Jimmy probably washed and ironed it, and I don't know what to feel about that, other than it seems wrong to be sitting on it. Shelly doesn't seem to mind. She adjusts the rearview mirror and turns on the air-conditioning. She's reaching for the radio when Mr. Jimmy stops her.

"Wait! Wait—I'm supposed to ask you questions before we start. First, adjust your seat so you're comfortable, and then what comes next?"

"You drive?"

"Try again."

After a few seconds, Shelly looks embarrassed.

"A nap?" I offer from the back. Shelly smiles at me gratefully in the rearview mirror. Mr. Jimmy looks annoyed.

"Seat belt?" I say, apologetically.

"One at a time, Diamond. Let's give Shelly a shot."

"Seat belt?" Shelly says.

"Bingo. Let's roll."

Since Shelly already drives regularly, she is more stumped by Mr. Jimmy's questions than she is challenged by the road. She parallel parks with one-handed ease but can't answer *When would you use your hazard lights?* She handles winding roads like a race-car driver (so says Mr. Jimmy) but doesn't know where her blind spot is.

I sit in the back, playing with garbage someone left behind. The whole car smells like old, bad food. Like the ghosts of a thousand sandwich bits that fell into crevices; Shelly and Mr. Jimmy don't seem to notice. I tie together two empty Skittles wrappers and twist them into a rope, like I used to do when I was little. I make a ring out of Hershey's Kiss foil. I gather it all and make an efficient pile inside an orange peel, placing it in the corner behind the passenger seat, so it will be easier to throw out later. I scan the rest of the car for more, treating this like it's my actual job here today, trash gathering.

Mr. Jimmy looks relaxed and happy, like he's responsible for Shelly's driving skills. He snaps his finger and points in the direction he wants her to go. He stretches his arm across the back of her headrest. He turns around to smile at me.

"Didn't I used to see you riding a bike around town?" he asks.

"I outgrew it," I say, quickly. I heard Ma give this answer to one of the neighbors who asked where it went. I feel like I betrayed a person, not just a piece of metal and plastic.

"It was a beautiful bike," he says.

"Thank you. I liked it."

"It looked real fast."

"It was more for a kid, you know. That's all."

He takes the hint, rolls down the window, and sticks his head out. "Do you mind, girls? I like my air natural."

The breeze drifting in through the window feels warm but nice, like good breath. It's around six thirty, and people are starting to come out on their porches. The long day's banishment is over. Mr. Jimmy looks bright and young with his head leaning on the edge of the window, the wind holding his smile. Except for his mustache and the dark stubble that covers the bottom half of his face, he could almost be our age. He is midsummer tan, and for the first time I wonder if he's something other than Italian. It's strange seeing him in his undershirt—even though it's still just a T-shirt, it looks like home clothes. Like private things. His black curly chest hair clearly shares a pathway to his pubes, so it's like seeing inside things outside. He's softer, eager to please, with only flashes of cocky. I want to break up the heavy air around us with jokes. I think about asking their opinion on deer riding, but instead:

"Where are you from, Mr. Jimmy?"

Terror jumps across his face, a look so familiar we practically have a whole conversation inside the twitch of his cheek. I have asked the exact wrong thing, of course, but it's also the one thing I really want to know.

"Good question. All over the place, man," he says. "I've lived everywhere. Connecticut, Vermont, New Mexico, all over."

"You're Mexican?" Shelly asks.

"No. I'm a good ole American boy."

"'Cause with your tan you look like you could be Diamond's father," Shelly says, making me cringe at the mention of my dad. "And I could be her mom," she says in a cutesy way.

"Haha—Diamond is our little baby." Mr. Jimmy jumps on the weirdness.

"Goo goo ga ga?" It's the best I can do. This is awesome and lame at the same time.

"Isn't Diamond hilarious?" Shelly says.

I decide I don't like the way she is around him, around men in general.

Shelly tries to turn on the radio again.

"Not while we're driving," Mr. Jimmy says, stern. "And not in front of the baby." He tries to lighten it up.

"Whatever, dude," she says.

Shelly pulls over to the side of the road and it hits me that I'm moments away from being in the driver's seat. She's taken way more than her allotted thirty minutes—closer to an hour—so we're all the way at the edge of town close to the farm stands and covered bridges. Over here you're just as likely to hit a dirt road as a paved one.

"You ready, Diamond?" Shelly asks.

I nod. Words are balled up in my chest.

"Is this your first time driving?" Mr. Jimmy asks.

"Oh, yes," I say. I can't help thinking about Ma. I am overcome with a flash of memory: Her dopey smile. When she looks at me, proud. The way she brags about me to anyone who will listen. *But she is my ma* pops into my brain. Nothing comes before or after that. Something is breaking open inside of me.

Shelly gets out and runs over to open my door, grabbing my hand to help me out of the back seat. She gives it a squeeze as I pull myself out. I try to make it look as effortless as possible, scattering my little trash pile in the process. She kisses me on the cheek and I love her again.

Before I turn the engine on, Mr. Jimmy asks his questions, and I do everything I've seen Shelly do, except that I know the answers. I give just enough of a pause so as not to make it look too easy.

My first touch of the pedal on the gas makes the car buck, so I slam on the brakes and we all fly forward with an "Oh!"

"It's OK, Diamond," Mr. Jimmy says reassuringly. "Get a feel for it. Try again."

Deep breath.

I go slower this time, with smaller bucks, finding the right amount of pressure for the right amount of speed. I can't believe my own foot is doing this. I am connected to the wheels and to the ground. The gravel from the road is vibrating throughout my whole body. When a stray rock kicks up into the underside of the car I feel it. I turn the wheel and we all turn. I make the car go faster or stop, all of us in this big metal box that I control and it seems like a miracle. How is it even possible that people do this every day without pausing to think about the magic of it all? It's a goddamn excellent feeling, is what I mean.

I'm driving.

"Look at our baby go!" Mr. Jimmy shouts. Shelly slides off her seat belt and leans into the front seat.

"Go, baby, go!" she's yelling, almost directly into my ear.

"Your baby's going!" says someone who sounds just like me.

"Hey, hey. Safety first," Mr. Jimmy says playfully, pantomiming a seat belt for Shelly.

We reach the covered bridge that straddles Ruggle's Creek and I look at Mr. Jimmy. I know that driving over it requires the wheels of the car to stay precisely in the center of the two narrow planks that sit on top of the gravel, almost like a train track. Missing them wouldn't send you into the creek below, but might mean bumping into the rickety walls of the bridge that hug your car with only a foot or so to spare on either side. Only one car can pass over the bridge at a time, and you have to crane your neck to see through to the end of the tunnel to make sure you're clear. In other words, you need skills.

"Well?" I ask.

He looks at Shelly. They scrunch their faces for a minute and then both nod.

I honk the horn in final warning. *I'm coming through.* I hit the grooves perfectly, and we enter the darkness. It feels like the tires want to move on their own, pulling to get off the planks, so I hold the steering wheel tightly. Cracks of light from the gaps in the old boards on the roof pass over us like we're driving into another dimension. We look at one another—dark faces, white teeth and wild eyes in the light show. As we come out on the other side, I see Shelly make a move toward the sunroof, and before my eyes have even adjusted to the light again, she pokes her head through the top. She is screaming with full-on Shelly-joy.

"Fuck yeah, motherfuckers!"

The road turns from gravel to smooth pavement. A relief.

Mr. Jimmy is turned so his back is up against the door. He looks up at Shelly with panic, and then something else takes over his face. He undoes his seat belt and kneels on his seat to get closer to her. He grips her waist with both hands. Shelly slides more of her body through the sunroof opening.

"You shouldn't be doing this, Shelly," he says, holding on to her as if she were slippery.

"It's dangerous," he yells into the wind. The car sways slightly, and I assume she is moving her arms around in the air.

I don't slow down.

Shelly's knee now rests on the front seat partition. Her tummy is at my face level, blocking Mr. Jimmy from my view; I can see the pucker of her belly button peeking from under her shirt. As I look back and forth between Shelly and the long, straight road ahead of us, Mr. Jimmy's hands shift to get a better grip on her waist. The hand he thinks I can't see moves slowly down past her hips, and disappears under the edge of her jean skirt, just below the curve of her butt. I feel Shelly's body tense and then relax, the quick arch of her back pressing her closer into me. In the mirror, a flash of pink underwear with white lacy trim. Goose bumps on thighs. Fine blonde hairs standing on end like an alarm. The digital clock on the dashboard says 7:57 p.m. The car is still swaying with the force of her arm waving, so I take this as my cue not to stop. Oh Jesus, should I be stopping? I feel hot and overwhelmed with the bad and good feeling. We drive like this for another five minutes, until it comes out of my mouth:

"Can I go next?"

Shame hot is a different kind of hot. I am on fire.

"Time to come in, Shelly." Mr. Jimmy's hands are moving down quickly.

"That's it for today, girls. Diamond, I'm going to take over the wheel now. You did a great job. You both did."

Shelly falls into the back seat, breathing hard. The wind has reshaped her hair into a stiff mound—a rat's nest, as Ma would say. I try to catch her eye in the rearview mirror, but she looks spaced out. The nest quivers a little, and I can't tell if it's her head or the car that's shaking it.

I pull over on the side of the road, and we all get out to switch seats, like musical chairs. Road dust sticks to our sweaty skin and collects in our creases, forming black lines in our neck, arm, and leg folds.

"We are one dirty family," Shelly says, wiping her face with Mr. Jimmy's shirt. She hands it to me and I do the same. I climb into the back seat again. Shelly gets in front. Mr. Jimmy takes the wheel. He does not look at me.

We continue on the endlessly flat road past the tobacco fields and the llama farm. Mr. Jimmy steers with his knees. It's late, almost sundown. A ball of orange fire is dipping behind black cutout mountains, while pink hazy light is making everything way more beautiful than it should be. This light breaks my heart.

"This is my favorite time of day," Mr. Jimmy says wistfully. "They call it 'the gloaming.' "

"Oh yeah, I've heard that before," says Shelly.

"I haven't," I say quietly. I can only think about sundown. The end of a day will never feel the same again to me.

Near downtown, we see someone walking on the side of the road. The figure is coming up a hill from the other side, so we see the head before the body. It hits me in my gut first, before my brain recognizes the big head and wispy blonde hair, the skinny arms and legs. *She walks faster without me*, is my first thought. It's strange to imagine her as a person who exists alone in the world, too. This is nowhere near her route. Where is she coming from? What is she thinking about, head down and hands in the pockets of her gym shorts? I duck down fast when I realize she could see me.

"Hey, isn't that your mom, Diamond?" Shelly says. "Shouldn't we pick her up or something?"

"No no. She likes to walk. For exercise."

My head is wedged in between the driver's seat and mine, facing the floor. I sniff in deeply, hoping the stink of smelly feet and rotten food below will erase Ma's wispy head.

"I remember when you were little, Diamond," Shelly says nostalgically, out of the blue. I don't say anything, not wanting to know if she's in character or real life. I stay on the floor for the rest of the ride back.

As Mr. Jimmy pulls up in front of my house, I gather the re-scattered trash before I get out of the car. It feels important not to leave it behind.

"When can you do it again?" Shelly leans across Mr. Jimmy, yelling through his open window. She seems fully recovered. I am wrecked.

"Maybe Wednesday?" I say.

Shelly looks at Mr. Jimmy and he gives the thumbs-up.

"You're a good driver, Diamond," he says, looking at me directly for the first time since I asked my question.

"And a good daughter!" Shelly adds.

"G'nite, daughter," Mr. Jimmy says sheepishly as they pull off.

Ma's not back yet, so I go outside to sit in Ladybug. It's totally dark, except for a corner of the dashboard that's caught in the streetlamp glow. I feel around like a blind person for all my dad's things. It's comforting to know a place without having to see it. I push in the cigarette lighter and wait for it to pop back out, like an old habit. The hot coil died years ago with the battery. I adjust the red, stained seat-cover he wished was leather. I fish around under the cup holder and touch the cherry Chapstick, the half-eaten peppermint patty (I lick it, to see if it's still good, and yes—it is), the fifty-cent coin, *No Nukes Now* metal pin, an Afro pick. My hand drifts to the sun visor:

one cigarette burn, two cigarette burns—plastic pimples on the smooth vinyl surface. My second-grade class picture bleached and crusty—tucked inside. These are no longer things that mark the tiny mysteries of my dad's life; they stand on their own now.

I haven't talked directly to my dad in here for years, no *I miss you* or any of that crap. I used to say things out loud to shock him in case he was listening. When I was little I would say stupid stuff like, *I snapped Barbie's head off and threw it in the toilet* or *I ate a whole bag of cookies* or *I hit a boy at school who called me crazy* or *I made Ma cry.* Tonight I say, *I am fat. So fat. I want to be a slut. Ma is sick. I can drive.*

I can drive. This makes me happy.

Were you the one who sent Lena to me? Lena wants me to be happy. Ma doesn't want me to be happy. I am leaving.

I haven't eaten, but I feel swollen with something else. My skin is two sizes too small.

I am leaving. I am going to Florida.

14

August 9, 1987

Dear Diamond,

Thank you for the cassette of you singing. I can't believe someone
in our family has a voice like that! I can't carry a tune in a bucket.
I've played it going on ten times now—you're really something.
Your pop would be so proud. What a beautiful young woman
you've grown into.

You have a traveler's heart, I can tell. Florida is a marvelous
place for you to visit. It's right next to Georgia. And you're learning
to drive! What a blessing it will be to get your own self from A to
B, and all the freedom that comes with it. Be safe, now.

I appreciate you asking about me. I do love a good adventure.
In addition to being a nurse, I happen to be a world traveler myself.
I don't have any kids. You might wonder, how will a woman of
(over)ripe childbearing age ever settle down and have children if
she's dashing all over the globe? But I say, how can I dash all over
the globe with a pack of slobbering, pooping, whining children
underfoot? My traveling companion, Tilly, thinks I'll change my

mind someday. Tilly is an optimist, whereas I am what you call a realist. These two things work well together when you're trying to find a bathroom in the Redwood Forest! We've also been to Chicago, Niagara Falls, Paris, and the Scranton Jazz Festival. One year we took a cruise to the Panama Canal. This fall, we're planning a trip to the Mayan Ruins of Mexico. We're waiting for a few things to fall into place before buying tickets and such. One being how long I have to stay in Woodville. I am living back in Mama's old house, looking after my father's sister, my aunt Willa Mae, as she's fallen ill. My siblings and I are taking turns looking after her, and it's my turn. I am currently negotiating when it will be someone else's turn.

The store in Woodville is a lot of responsibility, what with the quilting workshops and knitting groups and keeping on top of the inventory. Diamond, I'll admit I won't shed a single tear if I never see a bolt of jersey knit again in this life. Tilly always says patience is bitter, but its fruit is sweet. This is the same person who can't even wait for hot coffee to cool down! She pours a splash into her saucer and sips it like she's a damn cat. Dainty about it, too. It's very cute to watch. Tilly is proper, in an endearing way. She owns her own house in Atlanta. The truth is she's been encouraging me to reach out to you. FOR YEARS. I let her say "I told you so" now that she sees how happy I am being in touch with you. She's good at that sort of thing, staying connected to people. Sends out thank you notes, Christmas cards, writes down everyone's important dates in her little black book. It can be annoying at times, but mostly I hope to be more like that. We had good friends who died this year. We're holding everyone a little tighter.

I wanted to share with you that before Mama passed, she asked for your dad. Every day. She was a little cuckoo at the end, so every-damn-body was Robbie. *Did Robbie bring my medicine today?*

Tell Robbie put his face close to mine, Robbie, come hold my hand.
She had a special bond with him. The day they handed him over to
her—the day he was born—he took right to her breast like it was
his own mama. She swore they made a promise to each other, right
there, as he looked up from her nipple. She said to him, *Your mama
is gone, so we belong to each other, now.* And he said to her with his
baby eyes, *For always.* It made folks cry when Mama told that story,
knowing that, in fact, it wasn't "for always." It was only for seven
years. I remind people that I brought the milk that fed Robbie;
Mama had it because she was nursing me, too. I was born a month
before Robbie. Sometimes we each had a breast, kicking at each
other for lap space. I have the fuzziest memory of seeing his little
pear head tucked behind the mountain of her chest, blending into
her beautiful brown skin, our toes touching.

I'm delighted you're enjoying the letters from your Aunt Clara.
I feel like we're honoring our family and honoring your daddy by
knowing her story. I was telling Tilly what a difference it makes
to have someone else to remember with (no offense, Tilly)! What a
difference it makes to know Diamond.

With Love,
Lena

15

December 19, 1915

*Come listen to me, Sweetie. Listen. Let me tell you the story of The
Midwife and The Frenchman.*

    *One day after many long days and a terrible night, The Frenchman
travels from a far-away place to the land of Swift Rivers, what she calls
home. He comes from a land with more people than you ever seen,
living up in tall houses, on streets full of motor cars and giant poles
with telephone wires. He shows her on a map and his finger trace a
line down, across rivers and lakes, through mountains and towns, to
her town. She puts her finger on that map and trace a line way down
south, to a land called Georgia, where she say her heart live now. The
Frenchman say she is en deuil, in mourning. She know the English
word, it means a time of sadness after you lose someone you love. She
like that it also sounds like the other kind of morning, the start of a
day, the end of a long night. He say they sisters, these words. One comes
after the other. He teach her French and she give him Latin, her new
language. Latin helps describe the body and what happens to it in a life,
how to mend it. They play with words together, like splashing around in
water.*

The Frenchman try to court The Midwife in a proper way, but there were no porches to sit on or elders to keep watch so's no parts touched that weren't supposed to be touching. And they couldn't much be seen together because they the only two that look like each other, and the town scared that two together bring trouble. So they meet in secret in a cold, empty stable every Sunday afternoon, making a table and chairs out of bales of hay. The Frenchman say he wish The Midwife had a Mama and Daddy alive to ask for permission to come calling. Instead he ask their Spirits, I would like to spend time with your beautiful daughter, would that be alright? and wait for a sign that they approve. They decide that when an Old Black Rooster wander into the stable, staring and chuck chucking at them, that means yes.

The Midwife tell The Frenchman how The Moon and The Stars had been stolen from her by evil men who threatened her very life if she was seen after The Sun went down. Can you imagine, taking the night from a person? The Frenchman say that's like taking air, or fire—it can't never belong to people. The Moon belong to The Sun. He tell her a story his father tell him, about where he come from in Africa. There, The Moon is called Mawu and is married to Liza, The Sun. Mawu bring the night and coolness. Coolness bring wisdom. Liza bring day and heat and strength. Together they are the creators of everything, like God, but cut in two. You can't have one without the other or everything die. When they come together and make love, that is when you can see The Moon cover The Sun. It look like a perfect black circle with a ring of fire behind it.

One Saturday afternoon, The Frenchman comes in a buggy to The Midwife's house and tells her boss, The Doctor, that a young French gal from his land was losing an early baby, and can he take The Midwife fast to help save the girl. He give the boss ten dollars, and so even though the boss don't like the idea of his help riding off with this Negro dressed up like a white man, he let her go. Anyway, he don't much care for

180

*French people, and was too sad and drunk to go himself. Be off the road
by nightfall, the boss say, and The Frenchman tells him they will.*

*It was the first big snow of the year, and The Frenchman place a
blanket over The Midwife's lap to keep her warm. They ride for a few
hours and end up in a faraway town, where they stop off at a small
white house in the woods at the end of a narrow road. He tell her this
place belong to his friend, a white man. He and the man both come
from the same land Up North. He say the house is empty and they can
use it to get warm, the stable just fine for the horse to feed and rest.
The Midwife worry about the mama in trouble and say can't they keep
on going a little ways more? The Frenchman say he have to confess,
there ain't no mama, no early baby, and do she trust him? At first The
Midwife was mad as the Devil that the lie would get them in trouble.
But she do trust him, and she do like the fire he build. Her fingertips
were icicles by then. She was scared and excited at the same time, and
glad for the cold to use as a reason for her shaking.*

*She unpack the chicken, greens, and cornbread she made for the
journey and heat them up on the cookstove. They eat proper, at a table
with silverware and a candle in the middle. He bring out a bottle of
brandy and she have her first taste. It was sweet and strong, it warmed
her belly and made her giggle.*

*Come, he say, I have something to show you outside. It was dark,
and the outside was forbidden to them. Nobody around here for miles,
he say, it is just us. They bundle up and step into the cold. The snow had
stopped and their frosty breath was like night clouds hanging all around
them. They walk up the road to a clearing in the trees.*

Look, he say and point. La Lune.

*There was The Moon, her old friend she hadn't seen like this in so
very long. The branches on the trees around them, heavy with snow,
bent toward the light, like knights bowing down to their king. She was
safe with The Frenchman. Right there they have their first kiss. His*

lips were soft and sweet with brandy fruit. He hold her head in his big hands.

When she look up, the snowflakes come down from nowhere, from everywhere. The white was lit up against the darkness, and it look like The Moon was breaking itself into little twinkles of light, or maybe giving them The Stars as a gift. They open their whole faces and swallow all of it. She look over at his wide, gap-tooth smile and white frosted eyelashes, and it feel like the first snow of her life.

See, Sweetie, I'm telling you a love story, just the way you like. 'Cept for it's my story. Can you believe it? But also, it's the story of moonlight and starlight. How they came back to me.

16

1980

We make one last stop.

A few hours away from the campgrounds, just as we cross over into Connecticut, we start to see the billboards. Pop reads each one out loud.

All the action you can handle.

Family fun for all.

So much to do, so much to see. Just off Exit 31.

There are pictures of white boys packed into roller coasters, their daredevil arms straight in the air; white girls in colorful bathing suits on water slides; white families eating ice cream cones, laughing at private ice cream jokes.

Pop hums the jingle we've heard on the commercials. *Come to Adventureland, for the greatest day of your liiiiiiife.* He laughs for a long time; it's not a funny song. Nothing about him matches up with right-now things that are happening.

He turns around to smile at me, his head nodding, full of a plan.

"No," Ma says. The first word she's spoken the whole ride.

"What are you saying no to?" Pop asks.

"I don't know. Just no."

"Listen to me." He makes a fist and places it on her hand. "This is gonna be a rough couple of months. Years. Please give her this."

"You sure it's not for you?" she says quietly.

Come to Adventureland, for the greatest day of your liiiiiife. He sings even louder.

"This is insane," Ma says. "We have no money. None."

"Diamond." He's grinning at me like a kid. "You can use your Tooth Fairy money, baby."

"Maybe you can just give her another hundr—" Ma says, clamping her hand over her mouth before she finishes.

Pop punches the steering wheel three times; the car jerks. It's scary.

"Enough," he says.

Pop opens the trunk in the parking lot so I can get the one-hundred-dollar bill from my suitcase. I put it in my shorts pocket, crumpled. I do not treat it with care. This money feels like Adventureland—something happy and good that does not make me feel happy and good. It's something that means I will have to pretend for Pop. It's Ma when she makes the best of things with a wide smile that doesn't match her leaking eyes. It's when she swipes at her wet cheeks like there's something pesky on them, and her hands are shaking.

"How will we ever find our way back to Ladybug?" I ask Pop, looking across the sea of cars, our little Volkswagen already swallowed up.

"Stop worrying so much," Pop says. "You see what you're doing?" he says to Ma.

"Let's go, Adventureland," Ma says like a cheerleader. She grabs my hand and squeezes too hard.

* * *

As soon as we pass through the welcome arch, I realize I won't have to pretend. I forget everything bad. It's late afternoon, but the crowd has not died down, as Pop had predicted. It is buzzing and wild: flashing lights, happy screams, a roller coaster that roars by us like a rocket ship taking off. A haze that is both dirty and bright holds inside it more people than I've ever seen. They stand in line for rides that fling them in circles, lines for food, lines for tickets; they puke in bathroom lines too long to hold it in. Everyone rushes from place to place like walking is not allowed here. The families are all different colors, but not mixed like us. They look and dress like somewhere far away from Swift River. We three are the only people who seem like we don't know what to do, standing still in river rapids. *Look over there*, Pop keeps saying in every direction.

Everything is loud—music and voices and *beeps* and *boops*; the noises change with each step, like when I twirl the radio dial through the channels and Ma says, *Go slow*.

I breathe in and my nose and lungs fill up with fried things. The smell is so strong it takes over my ears; it has a sound.

We eat everything we want: hot dogs on sticks, French fries with drippy yellow cheese, cotton candy, and the soft, creamy ice cream from the billboard, it's really just the best. Pop says yes to everything. No one has asked me for my one hundred dollars, but I decide to keep it in my hand just in case.

He takes me on the Tilt-A-Whirl and the Devil's Wheel, as Ma watches from the side. On the bumper cars, I make it my job *not* to bump into anyone. A kid with a black eye comes fast at me and I cut to the side at the last moment; he bounces into the sidewall. "Nice maneuvering!" Pop yells. When we come back out, Ma is standing next to a short, muscly man with blond feathered hair. He is trying to talk to her, offering her some of his nachos. She won't look at him. *I said no thank you*, she says over and over. Pop rushes up to them, wraps his arm around Ma's neck, *You need something?* The man looks at Pop, keeps eating nachos. Then he looks at me, nods, and walks away, like I am what makes him go.

Everyone stares at us—their eyes swinging down our line—Pop to me to Ma. But they stay on Ma. She has on the same old T-shirt and cutoff jeans, her lips bright red from the slushie we all shared; but they can see she's beautiful even when she's not dressed up. Pop stares back at everyone who looks in Ma's direction. He used to smile and puff up, all proud. Now he frowns, like each look might break him. I want Ma to be invisible.

"I wish we had a camera," Pop says as he practically drags me to the merry-go-round line. The merry-go-round looks boring—it's for little kids—but I think I might break his heart if I don't go on it. "We *have* to get a camera when we get back," he says to Ma, who scrunches up her face like she doesn't recognize him.

Through the speakers in the center, the tinkly merry-go-round song comes out slowed down and sharp, like a music box that needs cranking. Next to me, a rowdy teenager bounces up and down on his horse, yeehawing to his friend. My stomach flutters each time I pass by Ma and Pop. They stand in front of a fence, straight as boards, not touching. Everything around them blinks and whirls. They smile and wave when our faces catch each other, then freeze and frown when they think I can't see. Like someone is pushing their on and off buttons. Like *I* am their on and off button, their power source. Something about this moment makes me know we are in very bad trouble. I am too little to be everything that holds us up.

When nighttime comes, the "ice cold ones" start. That's what Pop calls beer. He always says you're not supposed to have alcohol drinks before it's dark; he learned that from his father. All around us is the

whitest light I've ever seen, so white it hums. It's only in the far distance that I can see blue-blackness and stars, like we're sitting on the
sun looking out into the galaxy.

The little kids start to clear out, teenagers pour in, and grown
men's eyes pass over me in that way that makes my stomach flip.
Pop goes quiet and holds Ma and me close. We walk awkwardly, our
heads pressed into his sides.

Then Pop mumbles and melts into the crowd. The weight of his
arm is gone from on top of me, my head is cool. Ma holds me in place
so he can find us when he comes back. People bump into us but we
stand firm.

A long time later, Pop returns with half-eaten fried dough and
more beer, powder around his lips. He finishes the beer in one long
gulp, hands me the fried dough, and puts us back in the arm crush.
In a few minutes he's gone again. "I'm not hungry anymore, Pop," I
yell after him. It's the holding us so tight that makes his leaving feel
scary. The sudden cool on my head.

"Where's he going?" I ask Ma.

She opens her mouth to say something, then changes her mind.
"I don't know, baby."

"What's going to happen?"

"Everything will be fine," she says.

I want to go home. Pop wants to win me a prize.

He points to the big yellow Tweety Bird stuffed animal at the
booth where you throw darts at balloons. "You want that?" he says.
Before I can say *No, I hate Tweety Bird's voice and I hate Tweety Bird*,
he is slapping down dollars onto the counter. A white man with a
beard and a rattail of hair snaking out from under a baseball cap
scoops it up. He shows off by throwing three darts, popping each
balloon with ease.

"Man, you're good. Give me some of that magic." Pop smiles at the dart man. "I want to win for my girl."

"Three darts for a dollar. Three darts in a row gets you anything you want." Dart man looks only at Ma. Pop doesn't seem to notice. I want to grab that man by the cheeks and pull his eyes over to Pop, like when Ma makes me look at her; I want to make that man take in all of Pop's friendliness, his love.

Pop tries to stand up straight, then stumbles to the side. He leans on the counter, holding his own arm to steady it. He pops two balloons and misses the third. Ma claps like this should be the end of it, but he ignores her. More money slaps down. This time he only gets one. The third time he doesn't get any; the darts hit nothing or bounce weakly off the rubber. Again and again without any.

"I think that's enough," Ma says. "Diamond doesn't need more toys."

"You should listen to your lady." Dart man chuckles. "You can't play for shit."

The dart man takes a drag of a cigarette with one hand and throws a dart with the other, hitting a balloon with a loud crack.

"I don't know who you think you're talking to," Pop says.

"I don't think you want me to answer that, in front of your lady and all," the man says, bored. Pop gets up close in the dart man's face but the man doesn't move.

"I want us all to go on the Ferris wheel together," Ma says, putting her whole body in between Pop and the dart man, her face in Pop's face. "We're making good memories, remember, baby?" She holds his cheeks in her hands, strokes them with her fingers. They stand like this for a minute with Pop breathing hard. He leans his forehead onto hers, eyes closed, a triangle of space between them.

"OK. OK, OK, Annabelle."

* * *

A Black man is in charge of the Ferris wheel. It makes it feel like everything will be all right.

He is tall, with beautiful vines of hair flowing down his back. I ask Ma and she tells me they're called dreadlocks. When he moves they move in slow motion, heavy but graceful. Before he collects our tickets, he takes off the thick glasses he's wearing and cleans them on his dirty T-shirt. His eyes looked tiny behind the glasses, but without them they are big and dead, wandering off at weird angles, in opposite directions, like the glasses are the only thing holding those eyeballs straight inside his head.

"Make sure she don't put her arms up," he says to Pop. "She'll get 'em chopped off."

He snaps a bar over us, locking us into place, me in the middle.

The one-hundred-dollar bill is mashed and wet in my hand. I smooth it out, hold it in the wind to dry it off.

"Put that away," Ma says. But I don't.

Pop goes quiet again.

As we begin to move up into the air, our seat rocks back and forth, threatening to spill us. Ma sucks in her breath and clutches the bar. Pop doesn't try and comfort her; he's looking up and off into the sky. That's where I look, too. We are being lifted out of the screaming lights into the blackness of the galaxy.

"All those people down there look like ants," Ma says.

We reach the top and then pause. We're not a part of this world anymore.

"I want to go *there*." Pop points up at the stars.

We dive back into the lights and the noise, our stomachs dropping and the wind in our cheeks. We whip by the man with the glasses. He smiles and his tiny eyes twinkle; he knows the secrets of this wheel, of being up in space.

On the way back up again, we slow down and the whole thing

rattles, shaking all of the soft parts on Ma's and Pop's faces. They look blurry and scared.

I see other people in their seat cars looking around, *What's happening?*

I see all of the cars around us buck and stop, our seats swinging wildly, like rocking chairs, like we might spin all the way around until we're upside down.

I see the hundred-dollar bill floating away from us.

I have to look into my empty hand to know for sure that it's mine, that it doesn't belong to someone else who has dropped one hundred dollars from a Ferris wheel.

It gets caught in a pocket of air and freezes, waiting for me to fix my mistake, to jump down and grab it. For a second this makes sense, more sense than anything else that is happening to us.

We buck forward, flying fast again, and the bill is behind us, fluttering to the ground.

Ma grabs my face to link our eyes.

"What was that?"

I show her my empty hands and she knows.

"Please, man, we're broke. Don't make me beg," Pop says to the glasses man. He wants him to stop the ride while we look underneath and around it.

"That's not a couple nickels fell out our pockets. That's food for the month. Please, man."

"You got two minutes," he says. "Not even." He hands Pop a flashlight.

"Was I supposed to buy our food for the month?" I ask Ma. She shushes me.

"I'm sorry, Ma."

It's a strange thing when you go from walking around looking out at people and things, to down, everything down; down is the beginning and end of the world. Feet and trash and filthy treasures. Lights pass over unused tickets still attached to each other, a pocket comb, keys, a stick of gum. Someone's painted toenails in flip-flops run by me. I pick up a green plastic back scratcher and hear Ma yell, *Put that down.*

"I'm sorry, Ma."

I look up and people have stopped rushing around. They stand and watch us, pointing. "Look under that thing over there!" They try to be helpful. Some start to look with us. A teenager yells, "Yo, somebody dropped something!" His friends rush over to join in the search. I think they might keep it for themselves if they find it.

"What an idea giving a kid that kind of money," I hear Ma say to Pop. "What the fuck were you thinking?" He just keeps looking, lifting up a piece of paper, a candy wrapper, just in case, just in case.

"If you wanted to punish me, I can name ten other ways you're already good at," Ma says.

He stops what he's doing and looks at me. Stares, his eyes red and wet. He winks. Then stumbles, as if the wink had force, was too heavy.

"It's in someone's pocket by now," Ma says.

"I'm sorry, Ma. I'm sorry, Pop."

"Time's up!" the glasses man yells.

Ma runs over to talk to him. She is saying things softly that I can't hear. He smiles, fast, like she just told a joke. Pop comes up behind her. He points in the man's face.

"Get your eyes off my wife's chest," Pop yells.

"Fuck outta my face with that," the man says. "I don't want your white woman."

He turns back to the people still underneath looking.

"Everyone out now, or this thing will chop you in half. I'm starting it up in thirty seconds."

"You probably took that money yourself," Pop says. "Empty your pockets, motherfucker."

The man laughs and pulls the crank; the cars jolt forward. Everyone on them from top to bottom is bent over their bars, watching Pop and the man, not outer space and lights and small ant people on the ground.

"He wasn't looking at Ma's chest, Pop! He can't even see!" I yell. *Oh, Pop. I'm sorry, Pop.*

Dreadlock vines fly through the air, like waving arms. Pop is punching the man in the face. The man punches Pop. Heads snap back.

"Stop!" Ma screams, trying to pull the man off of Pop. She falls backward onto the ground. The man gets Pop by the neck and holds him there in the crook of his arm. Pop punches the air. The man is missing his glasses, his googly eyes move in circles.

"Quit it. I'm not trying to fight you," he says to Pop. They both are huffing, like they can't find their breath, snot and blood everywhere.

"Listen to him, please, Rob," Ma screams from behind him. Red dribbles down from her nose into her mouth.

"OK," Pop says, and the man lets him go.

It's a trick—Pop is back punching, tired and punching. His hands aren't hitting anything anymore. The man just watches Pop like he's doing some sad, strange dance; a toy, winding down to nothing.

Pop wobbles, then falls into the man's arms.

They stand there like this until Pop stops punching and they are only in a hug. They could be family, brothers, back together after a long time apart. I've never seen Pop hug a man like that. It looks like they're shaking, two big earthquaking men.

Until I realize that Pop is crying. Hard, heaving cries.

"All right, man. It's all right."

I pick the man's glasses up from the ground and hold them up to my eyes. I look at the crowd gathered around us—they are miniature, like they're inside my viewfinder, and smudged—a ruined painting. Sharp, loud voices come from the blurred tiny people. Some cheer, some tell Pop to keep punching.

Ma is suddenly holding me like I'm a baby, my long spider legs dangling over her arms. I'm too big for her to carry. I breathe into her neck. I touch the blood on her cheek, her lip. I want to taste it. There is no Tooth Fairy. Pop is the Tooth Fairy. There is a yellow light pulsing on Ma's neck. Like when I hold a buttercup flower under her chin; if it casts a golden light it means she loves butter. She does. Love butter.

The yellow light turns to red and I realize it's flashing and there are cops who are dragging Pop and the man away, putting them into the back seat of a police car. There is a police car in the middle of the park.

Ma is screaming. She pushes my head into her chest. Again, we are still. A bunch of river rocks in the churning, cold, cold water.

The truth: I let go. On purpose. I let that money go.

That's what I remember.

17

1987

It has barely rained in weeks; the Swift River is low and creepy quiet. Downed trees and ridges on the bumpy rock riverbed poke through the water like hungry ribs through skin. Ducks, finding no food in mud-puddle ponds, are flying south early, fanning out in Vs across town. "Getting the fuck out, just like us," I say to Shelly, who looks at me with a blank face.

It's the last week of Pop's notice in the paper; he's a low hum in the background of everything. People yapping their nonsense about seeing him here and there. I feel a jittery buzz all the time now, like something I want badly is fighting it out with something I want gone.

Town gossip is weirder than usual: someone saw Homeless Richard riding a deer in the woods; Deb Bednarski found a human finger near the dumpster behind the Thirsty Moose; Mr. Hill, the high school janitor, moved away suddenly—people say he joined the cult of Billy Graham, and now chases tent sermons from one town to the next. I can only imagine what they'll say when me and Shelly don't turn up for school next month.

For the first time in my life I don't care. I have Lena. I have Aunt Clara—a family army, or at least enough for a family band. Pop would say I have the wind at my back. There is something in this feeling I could chase down for the rest of my life. As soon as I decide to leave Ma, the whole world feels like *Go go go*. I worry that once I start moving I may never stop again.

Now when me and Shelly drive past my favorite houses in Swift River—the ones with the wide and shiny painted porches, flowering plants dangling like delicate earrings over white wicker chairs, surrounded by oceans of grass pulsing green and capped with boxy hedges—instead of gagging on my own jealousy: Nothing, I feel nothing. Except maybe a little *Oh, that's a nice bush*. Now I dream of orange trees and summer all the time, college and Disney World, *real* ocean, whose tides always come back in, not like a river that can carry away a person for good.

And Black people. *And Black people.* Not secret ones.

Even the Elks don't stress me out anymore. Shelly and me are sitting in their parking lot, waiting for Mr. Jimmy to show up for the first of our final two lessons. Through the open windows, we can hear them singing some kind of army song. They're getting all worked up. It sounds like *rat-a-tat, boom, fight fight fight!* Shelly sings along whenever she can make out a word, but in her R&B way.

"Siesta Key Beach has the finest, whitest sand in the world," I tell her. I feel we're close enough now to interrupt the singing.

"Who says?" Shelly asks.

I pull out the *F* volume of the World Book Encyclopedia I stole from the shelf in our living room, holding it far enough away that she won't put her Cheeto-dusted hands on the shiny pages. I'm not supposed to take the books out of the house.

"No matter where you go, you are never more than sixty miles from the ocean," I point to the picture of the blue, blue water with *Florida* spelled out in the sand.

"You're such a nerd girl," she says, licking her fingers. "I love it."

Shelly's mom lives in St. Petersburg on the second floor of the Legend Oaks Apartment Complex, a forty-five-minute walk to the beach. I ask Shelly if there are oak trees or legends about oak trees and she doesn't have any answers. We'll be sleeping on a pull-out couch. This makes me nervous; I have nightmares about collapsing it, sending both of us to the ground with a *crash* that wakes up her mom. I will probably make up a reason I have to sleep on the floor. The plan is to leave in three weeks, after we have our licenses, after Ma's court date is over. I don't tell Shelly about Pop's insurance money.

"Lila says she'll get us both a job on the boat. I told her we're good at cleaning and singing," Shelly said.

Lila is Shelly's mom, who works as a waitress on a dinner cruise. Shelly decided to get her GED, not go back to school with me. I try not to be worried for her, but I have Pop in my head. *Education is the bridge to your future. It's power no one can take from you. It's freedom.*

"It'll be awesome, just like *Love Boat*!"

"How will I register for school?"

"Lila is good at that stuff. She went to FCC for two semesters."

"She doesn't care you're dropping out?"

"Di, you're going to remember this moment when I ask you to be in my first music video for MTV."

"How's our kid today?" Mr. Jimmy says to me after I buckle into my favorite student driver car—the one with the sunroof and longer seat belts. Shelly and Mr. Jimmy are still playing that gross game where they pretend they're the parents and I'm the child. At first, it gave them permission to kiss hello and goodbye on the mouth and call each other "honey," and me, "sweetheart." After a few times, it gave them permission to make out in the back seat while I chauffeured them around. We never spoke about what happened that first drive. It always starts with Mr. Jimmy sitting next to me in the passenger seat, as my driver's ed teacher; then once we're a few towns away, he asks me to pull over next to a field or the woods while he takes a leak. I put the hazards on, and me and Shelly watch the back of him, his square butt in faded Levi's, hips thrust forward. He doesn't hold his thing while he goes, just looks down at it while it shoots out sparkling yellow into the sunshine. Shelly says not holding it means he's either got a really big one or a teeny-tiny one. They haven't had sex yet. I don't know how it matters either way, but I get a rush every time he tucks it back in, still zipping when he turns around. Back at the car, he knocks on Shelly's backseat window, *Can I come in?* Sometimes he has a daisy or a black-eyed Susan in his hand. Once he tried to give her a bouquet of poison hemlock and I had to tell him, "That's how they killed Socrates." He does not appreciate my wisdom.

One time Mr. Jimmy let me drive on the highway and we nearly made it to Boston. They were in the back coiled around each other snoozing, his head on her shoulder, not even looking out the window as the woods on either side of us changed to cities, two lanes turned to four, the cars around us filled with white and Black and brown people. Sometimes I think they need my eyes on them to feel like what they are doing isn't wrong; so they can sleep like babies. I can't get Shelly to talk about how weird all of this is; to her—anything can happen in the space before leaving. That's where we are.

I'll admit it, I'm a creep, too. I like being called "sweetheart" and "my baby." It stirs up a close feeling that I imagine normal people carry with them all the time.

Plus I like to watch them.

Today, Mr. Jimmy kisses Shelly hello like it's been two months, not two days since we last saw him. I do not—will not—call him "Daddy." His hair is still wet from a shower and he has it slicked back, curling around his ears; he's growing it long. New to his face: No mustache; he's shaved it off since the last time we saw him. The space above his upper lip is ghostly white against the rest of his skin, and moist. I see now that he sweats there when he's nervous.

"It looks kinda weird," Shelly says. "You should grow it back."

He laughs like she's joking, but we all understand, not. He looks like his own younger, less attractive brother.

We're barely out of Swift River when he tells me to pull over. This time he doesn't bother to piss, just climbs into the back seat, his bony hip knocking into me on the way. Even with the radio on, the sound of wet smacking fills the car. In the rearview mirror, I see tongues plunge in and out of mouths, Mr. Jimmy's hand rubbing and squeezing Shelly's boobs in circles that seem more and more important the harder he breathes. By the time he tries to go down her shorts, he's making the same noises I make when I eat after being hungry for too long. Like it tastes good, but I'm still mad remembering my empty stomach; like I might never be full again. I can't help but think of Aunt Clara and her Frenchman, their kiss under the moonlight. I feel embarrassed for all of us. No fairy-tale romance happening around here.

Shelly looks up at me in the rearview mirror, winks with her good eye, and plucks his hand out from between her legs, nodding in my direction when he looks at her like, *What the hell?* I'm her permission to make him stop.

"Shoulder rub?" Mr. Jimmy offers. That's his other move.

"God, no," Shelly says. "Can you get back in the front?" She wipes her mouth like she suddenly caught a case of cooties. "I need a Diet Coke."

It's hard to read Shelly. She can be hot and cold, ping-ponging a light meanness between me and Mr. Jimmy. Like she can't love more than one of us at the same time. Right now, she loves me.

"Shelly, your turn to drive." Mr. Jimmy rubs at his ghost-stache, annoyed, as if it's the source of his problems.

"Diamond, pull over at this next corner." He snaps his fingers and points. "Remember to signal and then put your hazards on."

In the back seat again, with all of the driving adrenaline gone, I feel the sting of the grooves carved into my chest by the seat belt. At the same time, my body feels weightless, like I've just stepped off a roller coaster. The car suddenly smells like Shelly's "Confess" Designer Imposters Body Spray, a copy of Obsession; she's done a quick re-spritz. Mr. Jimmy will think it's for him, but really it's because we're about to stop at the store. Shelly fiddles with the radio, going from station to station, not happy with any of the songs she lands on. Mr. Jimmy's arm is casually wrapped around her headrest. This is our routine together. It's nice.

I forget who I am, forget my body, forget what has already happened to me in back seats of cars. I imagine myself back here, braided into a boy who circles my boobs (more softly than Mr. Jimmy) and makes those sounds, me with the power to say *Yes, more*, or *That's enough for the day*.

When Shelly pulls into the parking lot of The Snack Stop, the front tires crunch a can and we all jump (last week a kid in our class hit a dog and now everyone is paranoid). Shelly parks in the back of the lot; she likes to give herself a lot of runway. Mr. Jimmy's eyes are pinned on her ass until she disappears into the store. We've stopped here before on our way back from long drives to get Diet Coke for Shelly, Dr. Pepper for me, and Welch's Grape Soda for Mr. Jimmy; we share Cheetos or Cheddar Guppies. This town is about forty-five minutes from home, but it still feels like Swift River, just with different faces and names I don't know, long strings of family gossip a mystery. In this parallel-universe parking lot, there are the same mustachioed men and stiff-hairspray-haired women. The same pickup trucks towing the same John Deere lawn mowers. The same shirtless white boys, their back pockets bulging with T-shirts that dangle like ass-flags, bottom lips swollen with tobacco dip, spitting brown juice into beer cans. These boys have the same smell as our boys—weed and river water and sweat. They are frightening, white boys with dip in their mouths. I hold my breath waiting to either be invisible, or a target of their terror. There is nothing in between.

"You look like you're losing weight." Mr. Jimmy turns around from the front seat. People think this is the best compliment you can give a fat person, even if it's obviously not true. Except this time he might be right. I haven't stepped on the scale since it stopped registering me, but my shorts have felt a little looser, even after a wash. With all this out-and-about-with-Shelly, I go for longer periods without eating.

"Uh-huh," I say.

"What's up with Shelly?" he asks. His cheek twitches, an almost-wink.

I feel the tiniest bit bad that he has no idea we're leaving. But also, I like having this big thing he's not in on.

"Up with her, how?"

"Does she like me?"

I know from TV that this is how teens talk to each other. I had no idea grown men spoke like this, too.

"What's not to like?" I don't sound very convincing. Mr. Jimmy laughs hard, throwing his head back. For the first time, I notice he's missing most of the teeth in the back of his mouth, like something terrible happened just out of sight. He sees me staring and his lips crumble over the black holes, the shame of those holes seemingly greater than his shame of being an adult man trying to date a teenager.

"I got somebody for you, too," he says.

Before I can respond, Shelly comes bouncing out of the store. She looks into the small blue car parked in front of the entrance and her eyes go wide; she stops suddenly in front of it, squints at whatever she sees, and then keeps going, faster, faster, until she's nearly running back to us.

"Did you see who's in that car?" she asks, out of breath. "I just got the chilly bumps."

Me and Mr. Jimmy strain to get a look, but the sun turns their back windshield into a mirror, just us and sky and clouds.

"Shadow Man?" I say.

A dark-skinned arm lets itself dangle from the driver's side window.

"See!" she says.

My heart flips, but this is always its response to Blackness. I'm ashamed that my breath can be taken by a Black man's arm.

That arm is the same shade as Pop's.

"Don't take this the wrong way, but is that your dad?"

"Jesus, Shelly. Just because he's Black?"

"You know I'm not like that. From the front he sort of looks like you. Same eyes, same nose. And he looks like he's super nice, just like you."

"You could tell that in two seconds?" Mr. Jimmy says.

The arm raises in a wave to someone inside the store. The reflection of the clouds moving quickly through the back windshield makes it seem like that car could be flying. The arm, a wing.

A young Black girl comes out of the store, holding what I can see is a Reese's Peanut Butter Cup, my favorite candy. She's six or seven, wearing one of those cute matching short and T-shirt sets, frills at all the edges. She holds the orange-and-brown-wrapped treat with both hands, palms up, like she's carrying something precious, breakable. She walks in exaggerated careful steps, giggling, amused with herself. She has the lightness of a kid with no adult troubles bleeding all over her little life. She doesn't *not* look like she could be related to Pop.

And then I am not me, but instead someone outside of me who is amazed. Amazed at the concept of Pop here in this parallel universe, living with a parallel-universe daughter. Amazed at the thought of him starting over, so close to where he stopped his old life. But I guess that is how parallel universes work? Existing within a few breaths of each other but unable to touch? I hadn't really ever considered the *idea* of starting over, what it might be like; that it could look so normal. That there could be trips to the store, silliness, and Reese's Peanut Butter Cups, my favorite candy. In Swift River, everyone is doomed to go in one straight line for the rest of their lives, no zigzagging. No fresh starts. But isn't that just what I'm about to do? Quit my life with Ma and start a new one in Florida?

"Let's follow him!" Shelly says.

"No fucking way," I say.

"Only if you go the speed limit," Mr. Jimmy says. He is practically inhaling Shelly's excitement.

"Come on, Di, please?" She doesn't even bother to come up with a reason.

The man's car starts, and the silhouette of the little girl grabs his neck and kisses his cheek. Lots of little kisses. She puts something in his mouth, probably a peanut butter cup. Pop used to eat them in one big bite.

I stay quiet, giving my answer over to them. I can't be the one to give permission.

And so we follow them.

We all put our heads down as he pulls out of the parking lot.

"Stay at least two car lengths behind him," Mr. Jimmy says.

The man is a careful driver, always using turn signals, never speeding. He's easy to follow.

"Did you get a look at his face?" Shelly asks.

"Nothing. Only that one arm," I say.

We go through the tiny downtown and past a sprawling grocery store; it's bigger and better than our A&P. Then we're in a neighborhood like mine, with identical rectangular houses, all trying to outdo each other with American flags, fences, and lawn ornaments. Mr. Jimmy and Shelly are both leaning forward, alive with spying.

The houses thin out and we pass a giant, painted billboard for Putt-A-Round Mini Golf—a city of fake grass, mini waterfalls, volcanos, and rock mountains cut out of the middle of a cornfield. I've seen local commercials for it—there's a corn maze and everything. A few hours ago I might have gotten excited—I never had a friend to do anything like that with. But here we are chasing after a Black man's arm that doesn't belong to my pop. The Putt-A-Round seems like a happy thing that will always be in some close but too-distant cornfield. I feel stupid, bad. I imagine what Lena and Aunt Clara would think of me and I want to melt into the seat.

We're back to a neighborhood again. At a stop sign, the little girl throws a piece of trash out the window. I bet it's the Reese's wrapper. The man immediately pulls the car to the side of the road and puts his hazards on. The passenger-side door cracks open sheepishly and the little girl gets out, head down, in-trouble face on, to collect the wrapper. That's something Pop would make me do, too. He hated litterbugs.

"Go! We can't just sit here. Drive past them!" Mr. Jimmy says.

"We'll lose them," Shelly says.

"Drive, Shelly!" Mr. Jimmy is frantic.

"Only if you stop shouting!" Shelly shouts. "Diamond, duck down." We drive slowly around them.

Shelly makes a right at the next street, and we go around the block, hoping to catch them. She goes over the speed limit. They're gone.

For the next few minutes we drive straight down the road he was on, pausing to look down every side street. I feel relieved. Maybe we could even go back to Putt-A-Round.

"There's the car!" Shelly yells.

It's in the driveway of a small one-story house with shutters, which instantly impresses me. Shutters are for people with money. There is a fence, and the lawn is freshly mowed; I can smell it. By the time we're in front, the man and the little girl are already at the door, ready to go inside; we can only see the backs of them. The little girl is on his shoulders, they're friends again. Both of his large hands hold her tightly at her waist. A Black woman opens the door, smiling. She kisses him before they go inside.

My eyes take in all of the clues at once: Are those Pop's hands, his muscly arms? Were his shoulders wider, his legs longer? But my brain has made him as flat as his photos. I try and force him out of the picture in the pumpkin patch, or the one at the beach with Ma in his lap, or doing the dishes with Grandma, or holding me upside down next to a jungle gym. I don't remember the day, only the photo.

It comes with force: I don't want Pop to be alive. I want him to be dead. I imagine his body floating down the river like a log and I don't feel anything. I feel it so strongly I almost make it a memory. I cover my face with my hands.

"What's the matter?" Shelly pulls a hand and kisses it. "Do you think it was him?"

"I don't know."

"Want to come back again?"

I don't answer her, but my answer is yes. I want to come back. I want to see the little girl. I want to see that family.

18

August 17, 1987

Hello my kin,

I ask myself the same kinds of *what if?* questions as you. I used to wonder would Robbie have been better off if he had stayed in Woodville? But now I understand, no, because then he would never have had you. Of course you want to know why did they take him back to Swift River, and the simple answer is they were looking for somewhere he'd be safe. Sometimes worry can be its own kind of terror.

The baseball inside this box, it's something I've been holding on to since I was seven years old. Doesn't seem right anymore; it should be with you now. This ball is part of the reason you're alive, with your particular mama and daddy, living in that particular town. It's part of the story of why they sent him to live with Aunt Clara.

It starts two weeks before your daddy left Woodville for Swift River. I never saw him again after that.

On that particular day, I remember Robbie ran inside the house, his whole body the color of Georgia dirt. He sat in Mama's lap while she spit-cleaned his face, smiling through the red dust. She always scrubbed faces too hard, but he loved every second being that close to her. We all did. She was the favorite auntie to my cousins—the one who told the wildest, funniest bedtime stories, who made the best fried chicken and dumplings, who got down on the floor to play checkers with you while dinner was cooking. The girl cousins left their own houses, their own mamas, and would line up for her to do their plaits; she took extra care with the tender-headed. Even when she was scolding, she snuck in kisses on your face and neck, tickling you. Especially with Robbie. Your daddy's own mother died in labor, as you know, so that he could be born. All of the aunties from both sides of the family stepped in to fill the hole she left. Between them, the women had fourteen children to look after. Those ladies were a swirl of skirts against our small bodies, running back and forth across the street to each other's houses to help with the cooking, to sweep up a missing child, or just to share gossip and keep company. Your Aunt Clara was the sister living up north in Swift River. She spoke French and everybody thought she was fancy.

My mama was pregnant at the time. Robbie'd gotten shy around her ever since her belly got big, especially when I tried to make him feel that great big bump, wait for it to move. To be honest he didn't care a whit about that baby—he was scared for Mama. She was older than most women having babies, and we both felt the worry she carried, even though she tried to hide it. Robbie'd already asked if the baby might kill her, like he'd killed his own mother. She promised him this would never happen. He wasn't convinced. Neither was I, but I didn't say it out loud. Mama tried to make Robbie feel better by asking him to help name the baby. He'd offered up "Stormy," the name of her favorite song about the weather (that was before we knew who Her Majesty Lena Horne was). Also because Robbie thought the baby was a dark cloud over our lives. Mama laughed at first, but the name stuck.

"When Stormy is born I'll take care of him so you can put your feet up all the time," Robbie said, always a kiss-up. Mama's feet were swollen the size of two cantaloupes.

Mama's response was to cry. She did that a lot, now that I think back to those last few weeks, especially when she looked at Robbie.

The cousins were running around us like lunatics that day. They were always so loud. It was hard to find peace for yourself in that house. They all liked to be around each other, but I preferred the calm of small groups, of being inside my own head. Maybe that's why I liked your daddy's company so much. Robbie had a temper when you got him going, but on most days you could knock him over with a feather. He was kind and fragile and in any room we were in, he bent himself toward me.

"Can me and Robbie go watch a baseball game, Mama?" I shouted.

"Ask your brother to take you, and come back before your fathers get home." She barely moved her head she was so tired.

Robbie and me first caught sight of the baseball team practicing a few weeks before on our way to a church supper. Robbie's daddy had slowed the car as we passed the field, reading aloud the sign hanging on the fence: *Greenville County Small Fry Baseball*. We watched as a little white boy in a crisp white uniform cracked the ball over everyone's heads. Another player ran backward and leapt into the air, catching the ball in his glove before his feet hit the ground. I remember the white folks lost their damn minds cheering.

Robbie's daddy was in awe. "Those little white boys can *play some baseball*." Now this is a man who didn't throw around compliments easy, so that was a lot. He was the kind of man you looked around for whenever you did something good, like helping a little cousin or an auntie without being asked. You hoped he'd catch you and give you a smile or a nod. He once told me, "You look pretty as a picture," when I came into church wearing my new Easter dress. I just about fell out with joy. If he thought those little white boys were special, then they were as good as princes to me and Robbie.

After that day me and Robbie were obsessed. We had never seen white folks look so happy. And while we'd played catch with the big cousins before, we'd never seen a ball go so far in the air just from being hit with a stick. We guessed at some kind of magic but were determined to see how it was really done.

The baseball field was in an area of town where Black people were allowed to walk through, but getting there could be tricky. On most streets you had to keep your head down so as not to look any white folks in the eye by mistake. Other streets were to be avoided altogether. Any person with good sense used the well-worn shortcuts through the woods instead. We had taken these shortcuts dozens of times, but always with our big brothers and cousins.

Me and your daddy went everywhere together. In the summertime we slept outside in the same sleeping bag. Chewed on pine needles. Counted owl hoots and mosquito bumps. *Two peas in a pod*, Mama said, laughing when she saw our heads sprouting from the red flannel cocoon. Diamond, have you ever seen white moths in moonlight? They glow like fairies. We thought they came out just for us.

Because Robbie and me had each other, there was the assumption that we were safe enough to come and go as we pleased, as long as we didn't go so far that we couldn't hear our names being called or one of the aunties banging on a pot for mealtime. We'd been known to disappear for hours behind the bushes in the yard, where we created an alternate universe out of broken toys, empty containers, pine cones, and twine. We were ankle grabbers, hiding under couches and porches, waiting for just the right moment to frighten someone near to wetting themselves. We were right there in plain sight, and then we were ghosts.

So no one paid much attention when two seven-year-olds holding hands made their way down Chester Road, heading in the direction of the Greenville County Baseball Field. We disobeyed Mama and went it alone.

Robbie wore his red cowboy hat for the journey. He was crazy about cowboys and horses. His daddy had bought it for him at Cullum's when he was in Augusta looking after one of our fabric stores. Most of the way we played One Hop Two Hops, a game we had invented, until the route called for climbing over fences and making our way through the dense woods to the other side where the road was safe to pick up again. This was the way the big kids had taken us. In the thickest part where the light came through like long white fingers, we played monsters; Robbie and me turned into monsters when we were afraid. Roaring, stomping, eating little children for dinner and using their legs as toothpicks to clean our teeth—this was comforting. The other things that could hurt us weren't as easy to recognize or understand. "White folks" was a tight feeling in our stomach, but it was confusing when it came to real people.

When we got there, I ran right up to the fence behind the Small Fry Baseball sign. The bright green field was buzzing and electric through the chain-link grid pattern. A coach and his team were huddled in the middle. I crouched down in the dirt so no one would notice. Robbie was still standing on the road.

"What are you, scared to come closer?" I don't know why I said it. Of course he was.

But I kept on teasing him.

Robbie and me had overheard stories about how fancy Aunt Clara up North wasn't afraid of white folks. No one ever said it outright, but their tone of voice always conveyed *she ain't got no sense at all* when it came to white folks. She wasn't more than knee-high when she was running up to them on the street, drooling on their dresses and grabbing at their pant legs. And when she was old enough to go to work for them, she got fired for defending cooks and housemen she didn't even like. I always got the sense that Black folks were in awe, maybe even a little scared of Aunt Clara. The more time that passed after they left her behind, the less like a real person she was, the more like a warning, maybe even a thing to feel a touch of guilt about. *I can't believe she's still there*, I once heard Mama say.

Aunt Clara moved through the world like she had a white-folks force field around her.

Robbie and me wanted that force field, too. We learned French words to protect us.

"Mer-ci!" I called to Robbie, summoning up her bravery.

He shuffled to the fence. We stood off to the side of the sign so we could get a better look at the action.

The coach was pitching the ball to the same player, over and over again. The kid kept swinging and missing. The coach got angry, yelling and waving his hands all around.

"This is dumb," I told Robbie, rattling the fence with my hands. And then just as he fixed his face to tell me to be still, the coach stopped mid-pitch, whipping his head in our direction. He shielded his eyes from the sun to get a better look, then laughed.

"Hey, you," he shouted. "Come over here."

We froze. And I mean, we were like statues of little Black children by a baseball field. Frozen like freezie pops.

"Hey, cowboy. I just want to ask you something, is all," he said, more gently.

Before I could yell, *Run away!* Robbie was off running. *Toward* the coach. Something surged in him. Maybe he thought of our French auntie. Maybe he thought of my teasing. Maybe he thought about Mama's poor puffed-up ankles.

Diamond, I've never felt so scared.

I yelled for him to come back, then followed after him, standing at the edge near home base.

"What's your name, boy?" the coach asked.

Robbie knew to keep his head down. I couldn't think straight—I looked right at the coach, who was tall and freckled with red fuzzy hair peeking out from beneath his baseball cap. He stood like the cowboys from Western movies we loved.

"Robert Vernon Newberry, sir," Robbie said, his eyes still on the ground.

"That boy over there forgot how to hit a ball," the coach said, loud enough for the rest of the team to hear. He pointed at the no-hit kid. "So I figure maybe you can show him what to do."

"No, sir, I don't play baseball," Robbie said.

"Now you do."

The coach held Robbie by the shoulder and walked him to the batter's box. Robbie looked back at me desperately, and then nodded, like anything could happen. I could be a witness if he hit that ball up into the air, high enough and far enough to make his father say *That boy can play some baseball!*

"There's no such thing as a niggra cowboy," the no-hit kid said as he held out a bat half Robbie's size. Robbie ignored him.

"Shut your trap," the coach yelled. "Looks like somebody's scared a niggra cowboy is gonna whup his behind."

The coach took a few seconds showing him how to position his arms. How to bend his legs. Where to put his eyes.

"Give it to him soft and low," the coach yelled out to the pitcher. The first time Robbie dropped the bat in the middle of a swing. "You ain't ready for the niggra league, that's for sure," the coach said, laughing. The next few times Robbie managed to swing the bat and keep his eye on the ball. "All right now, keep your head up," the coach said. "Look that pitcher in the eye like you mean business."

The next thing I remember was hearing a pop, and then Robbie flew up and back like there was an invisible hand yanking him to the ground. Then I was on top of him, crying into his face. Blood poured down his head like it had been split in two. His eyes were closed and he wasn't moving. There was no sound as my tears carved squiggles through the red blood. Then the volume turned on and the coach was yelling at the pitcher for throwing the ball too hard. I was just screaming. Robbie looked dead.

"Aw Christ." The coach leaned over Robbie.

"You're gonna be OK, son. I've taken more than one ball to the head in my day." The coach knocked himself on the side of the head for emphasis. "Let me give you a ride home."

"You leave us be," I yelled at him, wiping my snotty, teary face on Robbie's shirt.

"Poor things," he said. "Come on, let's go."

Robbie sat up and looked around for his cowboy hat. He was obviously dizzy. Blood melted down his face and onto his clothes.

"We kin hurt you if we want, mister," I said to him in my most convincing growl. I must have been out of my daggone mind, Diamond. That kind of sass could have gotten us killed.

By some miracle, the coach just laughed.

"He killed his mama, you know. He can kill you, too," I said, grabbing the baseball and holding it like a weapon.

The coach stood up quickly and dusted himself off, looking down at us with the same disgusted look he'd given the no-hit boy. He spit on the ground, helped Robbie to his feet, and handed him his bright red cowboy hat without another word spoken.

It was nearly dark; a southern kind of dusk with heavy air that took the light and divided it into stripes of gray and orange across the sky. It was a sad kind of beautiful, Diamond. The moon was already out. Robbie and me walked down the dirt road heading toward the orchard, kicking up dust and rocks. We didn't look at each other.

"What did you say that about my mama for?" Robbie asked me, finally.

"I was just trying to scare them away," I told him. I'm not sure if that's true, even to this day.

Robbie didn't look convinced.

"Stormy's gonna kill your mama, too," he said.

Diamond, I know in my heart he regretted it as soon as it came out his mouth. I ran up ahead of him and stopped just far enough to put some distance between us.

"Wait! I take it back," Robbie said. But it was already out.

We continued on like this, marching home ten feet apart, a couple of sorry-looking seven-year-olds. We didn't bother with the shortcuts. We didn't keep our heads down. A monster had already cleaned its teeth with us.

We passed by white folks on rickety porches who came to the edges to yell, "You lost?"

A skinny old white man on a bicycle said, "Hey now, what's this?"

When we were ten minutes from home, a police car pulled up beside us.

"I've been looking all over town for a cowboy and his cowgirl," he said to us through the open window.

"Your people are real worried." He got out of his car to help us. Robbie's face still looked a mess. The cop tried to touch it, but Robbie pulled away like a hurt animal.

We got into the cop car and Robbie looked over at me with bug eyes; I looked straight ahead, pretending I was still mad. Truth is, I didn't know how I felt. It was too many things.

As we pulled up to the house, Robbie's father stood on the porch with Mama, Uncle Henry, and Uncle Idas. They were huddled in a worried clump, not speaking. A coil of smoke drifted out from an uncle's pipe into the darkness.

After the doctor bandaged up Robbie's head, I snuck back downstairs to spy on the grown-ups while he lay in his bed. From inside the front closet, I could hear everything they said.

"I'm not blaming you, Sweetie, but you have too much on your plate. They could have been killed. The boy needs his own mama," Robbie's daddy said. "Clara raised up both of us! I want him to know her. *I* want to know her, again."

"I don't want to hear nothing about Clara being a mother, Robert." Mama was crying. "She chose that place over us and now you're doing the same thing."

"It's safer. And there are good jobs, a house—" His daddy's voice softened. "Sweetie, I can never thank you enough for what y'all have been to him, but you know it's time. I want him to be a man someday. A man who gets respect."

"Please don't take my baby." Mama's voice was low and raw, like she was raking it over the words. "He belongs to all of us."

"Leavin' is a part of lovin'," he said.

"That's a bunch of horseshit," she said back.

Later that night, I crawled into bed with Robbie. I placed that baseball on top of the covers.

"I took it for you," I said. "I put it in my pocket. There's still blood and everything."

"Wow." I knew he couldn't wait to show it to the big cousins.

"You flew up in the air, just like the ball. Like magic," I told him. "I was scared."

"Wow," Robbie said again. He looked so grateful that I'd forgiven him, like he didn't want to say anything to ruin it.

"You can keep it," he said, handing the baseball back to me. "It's OK."

"You and your daddy are going to live with the fancy French auntie up North." I rested my head on his chest. "She's gonna be your new mama."

"No we're not," Robbie said. "I'll hide in the woods so he can't find me."

"I'll go to North with you. Mama won't mind," I said. I decided I would give Mama up if I could keep Robbie. She had all the other cousins; he had no one but his daddy. Mama belonged to everyone. Robbie belonged to me.

Then Robbie got quiet, but he looked like he was considering the idea.

"I know a word we're gonna need for the new auntie," I told him. "I learned it for us."

I wrapped my arm around his neck.

"Bone-jar." I sounded it out slowly. "It's French. It means, 'Hello Auntie Mama, I love you very much.' "

I heard Robbie practicing before he fell asleep. *Bone-jar.*

In the morning, he would hold Mama's head and whisper it in her ear.

It turns out that your daddy and me worried over the wrong person. Mama didn't die in labor. It was Stormy who didn't make it. His little body came out purple, umbilical cord wrapped around

217

his neck. We buried him in the backyard behind the pine trees, which I didn't like one bit. That was where me and Robbie played! I didn't want to be running into Stormy's ghost all the time.

Diamond, I have to admit I never cried for Stormy, and wasn't sorry, that I can remember. Does that make me a terrible person? Now your daddy—for him I cried. I'll cry over Robbie for the rest of my days.

There are a few new Aunt Clara letters here, along with the letter you requested for your court date. They can try to make liars out of y'all, but it won't work as long as I'm around. Also, I hope it's OK that I've tucked some money in here, for a bus ticket if you ever decide to come visit us. If you're not ready yet, you can save it for a rainy day.

Love,
Lena

19

June 7, 1916

Ma Chérie,

Did you hear me screaming all the way down in Georgia? I hollered so loud when I saw the newspaper cutting Uncle Henry sent, I scare myself! A Newberry textile mill! Ain't that something and a half? I was telling Jacques how when our people first came to Swift River, black folks weren't even allowed to work the machines. Say we were too dumb. Only reason they brought us up from the basement was because all their white workers got killed off by the brown lung, like it was a fire swept through the place. Now, only two years gone from this wretched mill, and we go head and make our own. My chest is so puffed up with pride it could float right off my body.

   You'll be happy to know me and Jacques not a secret anymore. It's a relief not to have to keep lying about people being sick that wasn't sick so we could meet. Felt like bad luck. All of the Frenchies love Jacques, and now the Swift River whites think of me as their Midwife Granny. But Jacques' boss treat him different than Doctor treats me. Give him respect. Call him Monsieur Da Costa, that is his name with a mister in *front. The boss knew Jacques' daddy, too. The daddy was an educated man, also a translator like Jacques, who spoke so many languages he helped the Indians trade with all of the white folks coming from Europe. You studying your maps and your countries yet? The daddy was killed by a white man from Spain. The daddy ask for the money he is owed, the man refuse to pay and killed the daddy for asking twice. Jacques inherited his father's land. It's too hilly to plant, but the hunting and the fishing are good. He rent it out to some lumber men. He make enough to pay off all the taxes.*

Jacques' boss gave him a mill house, the one closest to the end, with the oak tree that has all of those beautiful roots look like arms with long fingers. Every good doctor and midwife keep a garden just for medicine. I like to keep mine at his house instead of Doctor's house. When Jacques comes outside to help me tend to the plants, he says it feels like I'm his wife, out here gathering greens for dinner, and when can we make it real and start having babies? And before you can even ask, no we have not had relations. Not until we husband and wife.

Truth be told, Sweetie, I don't know how much longer we can wait to get married. Jacques say he want go with me to Washington next year when the arrangement with Doctor is over. He say he'd get a job as a translator there while I finish my medical schooling. Then we can go to Woodville and open up a clinic, and then Canada where the land is waiting. Can you imagine? It makes me want to scoop y'all up and take you around the whole of the world with us. What a glorious time we could have.

What make me worry—the closer I get to Jacques, the angrier Doctor get.

Last Saturday Doctor got drunk and fight with Jacques for doing Doctor a kindness and fixing a wheel on the buggy! What are you doing to my property? he keep saying. After Jacques calm him down and leave, Doctor tell me, You're an unmarried woman carrying on like a common Negro whore. Sweetie, I never hear him speak like this or raise his voice to me, and I want to say it's the whiskey speaking through him, but the whiskey is always in him now so the real truth is it's just Doctor speaking through the whiskey. I swear it, I almost turn around and run after Jacques. But then Jacques might knock Doctor clear out his boots, and I think about this whole beautiful life we laying out in a plan, and I think I can do this one more day, one more year.

Later Doctor come to me and say he sorry, that he is scared I'm going to do him like Miss Rose. I can't even look at him. I say, But Miss Rose was your wife. He don't like to hear that. He remind me that he's the one has to write the letter about my good moral character in order for me to attend medical school. He say You need to start showing me that. Later he feel sorry and try to make things good again with a new Doctor bag, but I won't take it.

Then my whole life change in a day.

It started with Jacques walking me back home to Doctor's last Sunday after supper, the one meal we can eat together each week. We had a late start. I had been sewing up some of his torn trousers, hanging up his white shirts to dry in the summer sun, them shirts that make me so proud. You know what early summer like here, it's that thing you feel you earn after a long winter, the prize for walking straight into icy wind for four months. I was dawdling, wanting to take in every warm breezy moment I could. I ask him to do this and that chore for me so I can watch him. He fix the fence around the garden and the third step off the porch. I talk to him so it won't seem like I'm just gawking while he work. Don't nobody like to be watched while they working if the watcher ain't doing a thing. My thing is talking. Daddy used to say I could talk the hide off a cow! By the time we got ready to go, it was too late to take our normal route through the woods from The Delta. It was that almost evening air where everything look hazy and your shadows get long, and every step we took I knew we should have left sooner, just *knew that it was my fault, typical Clara foolishness. Not even halfway along, right as the sun was setting, we hear the crackling of fast, heavy shoes snapping a path through brush, then a dog barking like it got the scent of a meal, and then what sound like the cock of a gun. Jacques grab my hand and we take off running.*

We jump off the beat down trail into the thick of the trees. It's like the sound turn on and off in my ears. I only get snatches of heavy breath and the smack of branches Jacques break to make way for me. Fear trying to shut down my brain. We so nerved up and we run so hard and far I don't know where we are when we stop, how much time has passed. Could be Maine the next day for all I know. It start to rain and Jacques pulls us under the roots of a fallen tree, the pit in the earth so deep, it made a small cave. It's dark and I can barely make out his face, but his eyes look scared, his breath sound scared.

We have to stay put, he says. It's safer to be here for the night, with the bears and bobcats, than out there on the streets with white folks. He angry, very angry. I don't know what I feel, but it's the thing after fear burn a hot hole into your gut. Empty and sore.

We hold each other, only moving to brush off the tiny beetles that drop from the stringy tips of the roots onto our heads and our shoulders, until we don't notice it no more. We fall asleep sitting up. When we wake the rain has stopped. Everything is lit up by the moon. For the first time we notice that there are trees torn up from their roots all around us. Like a giant came through, mad at God and having hisself a tantrum, ripping up pine trees like they daisies. Lightning storm, Jacques says. I ain't never seen a lightning storm do that but ain't nothing else to make sense of it. Angry giant, I say back and he laugh. Sweetie, this the magic part—everywhere there wasn't a tree was covered in a thick, soft moss. Even in the moonlight it was the greenest green I've ever seen.

Take your boots off, Jacques say and we feel that cool wetness with our bare feet, like stepping in someone's hair that just been washed. We giggling like a bunch of babies who fell into a nighttime storybook, walking for the first time on the moon.

Jacques points to the moss and say it mean water is nearby, which is good because we thirsty. Sure enough, we follow the moss up a hill, and there's a creek almost dried up but still moving and safe to drink. I wash my face and shake the dirt and bugs off me.

We come back down and find a patch of moss that's not wet because it's covered up by the branches of a weeping willow over it. We lay down, sinking into it, it curls around us and I can hear it in my ears. Isn't that marvelous? I never knew moss have a sound, a voice. I feel around for Jacques' hand, and we lay there like that, under the night clouds, green in our noses, ears, and mouths. Sweetie, I'm telling all of these little things because I want you to hear the moss and feel the coolness and see the willow dropping little flower petals on our faces when the wind blows because I can't tell you what happened next, you ain't grown enough. Someday. Maybe when you sixteen.

In the morning, Jacques is quiet, and I get scared he's mad at me for getting us in this predicament. Or mad about what happen last night. Did I do something wrong? You still sore about me making us late? I ask him. He say, No no mon amour, I'm sore because I have to walk my wife through a forest to a house that's not our home. I'm sore that my wife don't sleep in the same bed as her husband. I like when he call me his wife. Pas plus, he say. That mean no more. We getting married and you are coming home with me, he say. Can you ask me nice, I say? And he do.

Sweetie, I know people say me and Jacques the only ones for each other because there ain't no other ones to choose. But I also know this is the man for me because he match me. We a puzzle that fit together. I think about you and me as little children before Mama and Daddy died. We had a hard life, but it was also a life. Like floating in the Swift River—something invisible was holding us up. It was God, but it was also us. I ain't feel that since y'all left. Like I was being held by something I couldn't see. That's how this feel.

After all that running, turns out we were close to another part of town. When we finally make it to the road, we in a daze. Lots of folks pass us by, staring hard, but Mr. Holloway see us, wet and dirty, and offer to ride us home in his buggy. Y'all fall off a wagon somewhere, he ask? We getting married, Jacques tell him grinning wide, like that's the answer to his question. Mr. Holloway says, Well I'll be. Congratulations to you. I didn't know there was any colored preachers around here, and Jacques says, We gonna find one.

It's late morning when we get back to Doctor's house and I know he'll be up, sitting in his office drinking coffee and staring at a bowl of porridge he always send back to the kitchen with only a bite or two missing.

I tell him like I'm telling someone who will think it's good news, even though I know he won't.

Jacques and me gonna get married, live together at the mill house in the way that pleases God. I figure now that you have Marion for cooking and cleaning, and since I do all the house calls myself and still do the books and keep the clinic in order, and since I can still come here every morning before sun comes up and leave after you get your supper, I was hoping to have your blessing, sir.

He don't look at me. He chewing on his porridge so slow I think maybe he don't hear me, but then he say, No, That wasn't the agreement we made. You broke the agreement and now you must leave. You don't work here any longer. I will be telling Howard University I am no longer your patron.

When Jacques teach me words in French, he tell me how not everything translates easy to how we say it. Words sometimes get put together different than how we would do them, so they have more meaning than we give them in English, they go deeper. French say coup de grâce, which mean in English, hit of grace. Sound like a bunch of nonsense right? For the French it mean the final blow, the last hit that kills an animal or a person, puts an end to a bad situation. The thing that's hardest to explain is the HIT and the GRACE together. That there can be mercy in ending something, putting a stop to suffering.

Doctor don't even know it but he gave me grace.

I tell him, I'll leave your house, and don't want your money or good word. I'll make it to medical school by myself. But if you talk bad about me to folks, make it so I can't earn my way by delivering babies, Ima tell everyone about Miss Rose, how you knew about her and Gerald the whole time. I'll tell how you drink all day in this house, bleed folks that don't need bleeding, give out the wrong pills, put people in danger. I'll tell about everything I know and a few things more. You don't pay me nothing for nearly two years of work I give you and now you leave me and my husband alone.

Sweetie, the only thing I took that I didn't walk through the doors of this house with is the Gray's Anatomy Doctor gave me. That book mine. I left all of Miss Rose's clothes I been wearing. If they wasn't good enough for her to bring along on her new life with her great big love, then they weren't neither for me.

By the time we left it was just about sundown. We was scared of the terrors out there waiting for a couple of Negroes at night. But we were going home.

A beetle just drop from my hair onto this letter and I decide that must be good luck. I also decide that the luck passes to whoever touches this letter, that means you.

Come live with me now? Say yes, sissy.

20

1980

We're only ten days back from almost-down-South, from camping, from getting Pop out of jail. It's all my fault; if I had just held on to that hundred-dollar bill, Pop would be driving us right now, badly whistling a blend of songs, reaching into the back seat to tickle my legs.

Ma is a bad driver. Grandma Sylvia never lets us borrow her car. She says Ma gets too distracted, loses her road focus and swerves off to wherever her eyes wander. But Ladybug is out of gas, Pop's been gone for one night, and we have to go out and find him.

The windows are up. Ma forgets to turn on the fancy cool-fan; I don't dare tell her. We're driving fast, too fast. Her chapped lips are locked shut and dotted with crusty blood at the cracks, her nostrils flared. A drop of sweat tiptoes down the side of her face, stopping next to the scab left from where she got hurt in the Adventureland fight.

I take quiet breaths to calm down. The air in here is tight and prickly—it doesn't move. I think of how Pop makes me sniff the morning when it's about to storm. He says that right before the rain and thunder come, air pressure and wind make a vacuum, make everything still, make all the smells sweet.

This is when you call to your future self and make your wishes, he says.

I smack my leg, cracking the air around Ma's silence, calling on future Diamond to make time stop, to make Pop found.

Ma jumps and the car jerks. "What the hell, baby?"

"It's gonna be OK now, Ma," I say. I tap three times on the window and yelp, putting together unrelated motions like I see Grandma Sylvia do for good luck.

When we pull up to the Campbells' house, there is only one car home. Two if you count Tommy Jr.'s go-cart; he's racing it up and down the length of the long driveway. We pull in behind Mindy's pink car so as not to disturb Tommy Jr.'s racetrack. The first time he flies by us, there is a life-sized Luke Skywalker doll in the passenger seat. When Tommy sees us, he pushes Luke out of the go-cart; the Jedi flops in a heap onto the grass, his legs tossed behind his head.

"What on earth, is he playing with a mannequin?" Ma asks. "Isn't he too old for that?"

"It's Luke Skywalker," I say softly.

"Stay in the car," she says.

I roll down the window, careful not to look at Tommy when I hear the loud buzzing of the motor coming closer. I focus on tangled Luke. Ma is at the door talking to Mindy, who holds her hand over her ugly necklace, like Ma might want to steal it right off of her body. Mindy watches Ma like she's TV, not a real person.

"Did they get in a fight?" Ma's voice breaks through the go-cart yells. "Did something happen? Please tell me!"

Mindy shakes her head. Her mouth says, "Go home, Anna."

"Do you think maybe the cops took Pop back to jail?" I ask Ma as we speed down Orchard Avenue, heading toward I don't know where.

228

She squints at me, the face she makes when she's deciding if I'm old enough to hear things, wondering how they'll stick to me, whether they'll give me nightmares.

"No. Not possible. He has to go to court first."

Her mouth switches up, like someone just ordered her to smile.

"Sweet pea, everything will be fine—we'll find him somewhere in this town."

We enter the woods from the clearing behind CVS. This is where you can hop on a trail that stretches across town past our house, to the mills, all the way upriver.

We start off on the worn path, sprinkled with soda cans and candy bar wrappers, pausing every now and again to yell, *Rob! Pop!*

"Is he hiding from us?" I ask Ma when she stops to pee.

"No. He's just . . . lost."

But I know he's not lost. Pop knows these woods like he was born a tree, he always says.

Soon, the litter goes away; we're off the packed dirt and on to the forest floor. It's thick green and cooler, and the smell is as familiar as my own body. Ma gets more and more frantic even though we both know where we are. We run, looking down to avoid an ankle twist in holes covered by leaves; we look up so we don't plow headfirst into a birch, or get whapped in the face by a branch. Trying not to get hurt is all that fills my head; we run until I forget why we are running.

"Our daughter is here with me! Dammit, Rob, I want you to see her. Look at her!" We stop so she can shout. "I'm not OK with this!"

It's late in the day by the time we get to the house where Pop grew up with his dad and his Aunt Clara. The house has been empty since before I was born, like someone decided it wasn't for people anymore. The tree stumps out in front are surrounded by beer cans;

someone had a party. In the only oak left standing, there's a thick rope that hangs from a branch. It used to be a swing that a French man named Jacques built for Pop. Pop always makes me say *Uncle Jacques*, and reminds me that he was my uncle, too, even though I never met him.

Ma runs up to the old porch, bursting through the door.

"I changed my mind!" she yells, voice cracking. "It's not what I wanted!"

I wonder, what did she want before?

The inside of the house is dirty and crooked; the ceiling sags, the floors are at an angle. There are things still here: A kitchen table, but no chairs. A few old *Ebony* magazines. A sofa with the center cushions stained black, a hole chewed down into it, like a magical Narnia portal, but ugly. There are faded paintings on the walls of places I know are in Swift River. There are squares where paintings used to be. Either someone left here in a hurry or they decided their new life didn't have room for their old things.

"Let's go down South," Ma yells, running into the kitchen. "We're not better off without you!"

"Diamond is here with me! We can leave right now. Take my mom's car."

"But I like Ladybug," I say to her. I know Pop does, too. She might scare him off saying the wrong thing. She shushes me with her eyes and tears off to search the upstairs.

There's a white pony on Pop's bedroom wall. It's wearing a funny red cowboy hat. I wonder if that hat made Pop laugh. Ma talks to the air, but I want to talk to the house; it knew my pop when he liked horses. I look behind doors, inside thin closets, trying to imagine what it would be like to find Pop folded inside. Wondering if he could ever be Pop again.

I find Ma outside sitting on a stump, cigarette in her hand and her head between her legs.

"How could I just let him go like that?" She's saying it over and over. "Let's ask Aunt Clara for help." She grabs my hands when she sees me.

"Is she alive?" I ask.

"No, but I always feel her here. She loved your dad very much."

We close our eyes and pray to Aunt Clara.

Please, Aunt Clara, help us find him. Make him want to be found. Let him know our life won't work without him.

By the time we get back to the car, it's getting close to dinnertime. Ma turns on the radio, rolls all of the windows down. Instead of turning on to Main Street, we drive past the Tee Pee Motel and head on to the highway. It was always a thrill when Pop made this turn; it meant we were going exploring, headed toward some faraway fun.

"Where are we going, Ma?"

"Adventureland!" She laughs and also cries at the same time. "Oh, no, baby, I'm sorry. No more jokes."

"We're going to find Pop," she says when she sees me crying, too. "We're going to keep looking."

I stare inside people's cars as we pass them, wishing I could be inside: with the lady singing so hard she throws her head back, pounding on the steering wheel, or the little boy asleep in the front seat, his cheek flattened against the window. A few people look back at me and wave. I wave back, my happy smile coming at the very same time I remember I am in a sad car, a scary car.

We hit a patch of highway that is flat and straight. The sun is setting directly in front of us; it looks like it's sitting on the actual end of this road, like we could drive right off the edge of the world into

231

that hazy yellow ball. Gladys Knight and the Pips' song "Midnight Train to Georgia" comes on the radio. Pop used to tease Ma saying it was his favorite song.

"It's a sign!" Ma says hopefully, wiping her face with the bottom of her T-shirt. "Damn him with this song." She sings along.

I'd rather live in his world
Than live without him in mine
I see them first.
Sailing through the air in the dusty light.

First the buck with the antlers, his wooden thorny crown, leaping off the overpass in front of us, crashing down on the highway below, bouncing like a toy and breaking open. The rest of his tiny herd quickly follow, one deer, two deer, then a baby.

In my mind they stop, frozen in the air like a team of summer reindeer, their legs spread wide, graceful. I think my wish has come true, I have put time on pause, stopped the world from moving toward bad things, hard days.

Stay right there, deer, jumping deer, flying deer, don't come any further. Go back. Someone turn off the sun faster, make it dark and not safe for leaving, for running and leaping. Stay home.

What actually stops is us, brakes screeching, Ma's arm across my chest, the baby deer crashing into our windshield.

In the hospital they will tell us that the deer family got spooked—by a hunter, a car. As they tore across the road on the overpass, it was a trick of the eye, the way the sky was positioned above the cement barrier; they thought they were jumping to the ground close below on the other side, not off of a bridge.

Or maybe it was joy and not panic, and they simply miscalculated the distance; a family leaping into the sunset—running to, not from.

Soon they will find Pop's sneakers. Soon Ma will lie down on the grass and cry for a day and a night. She will never drive again. But the second she wakes up in that hospital bed, eyes darting wildly until they find me sitting on a chair in the corner, she calls for her husband.

Rob, Rob, Rob.

21

1987

"Are you going on a double date?"

Ma yells through the house from her post at the living room window. I hear Shelly's horn honking; she's here to pick me up for our final afternoon lesson, our return to the Black family's house.

I assume Ma is joking until I peek through the dirty sheer curtains and see that there are three people in Shelly's car—Shelly at the wheel, Mr. Jimmy in the front seat, and a guy in the back. The guy has long, jet-black hair with spiky bangs, gelled and teased out like he's in Bon Jovi. I feel sick, already thinking past Ma to the chitchat I'll have to make with a brand-new person, to how he could fuck up the groove of our driving threesome. I picture the Black family with this stranger's eyes all over them, and I feel shaky. Now that there will be a witness, what we're about to do seems silly and wrong.

"They're both too old for you, Diamond. You are not allowed in that car."

"They're work friends, Ma."

"Look at the hair on that one," she hoots. I can't remember if she gave up her pills or just hasn't taken them yet; she's biting at her lips and her pupils are big black moons. Her hands and face are smudged with newspaper ink, which means she hasn't quit the paper route yet. She's trying.

"They're taking me to work. I have a double shift," I say.

She makes a clucking sound, then settles into my lie.

"After next week, you won't need to work so much. It'll just be like a fun, after school thing."

"Ma, we won't just get a suitcase full of money after court."

"Very soon after," she says. "Something to look forward to. Don't you want things to look forward to?"

"I already have things to look forward to." I feel the fire of leaving spread through my whole body.

"I know you're keeping secrets from me, Diamond. Please stop. Please." She catches me off guard.

"I don't know. Maybe soon?" I say. She looks at me like the secrets might destroy her.

We stand in a stare-off for a minute before I get up the nerve to hand her the envelope.

"It's from Lena," I say. "To help us in court."

Her face shuffles through relief, shock, and then confusion.

"Your dad's Lena? How do you know Lena? You've been in contact with her?"

"I thought she could help, say that she hasn't seen Pop. She was nice enough to do it."

"Nice enough?" Ma says. "How kind of her to show up now." She snatches the envelope. Then softens. "Maybe you didn't realize. We're not on the best of terms."

"No, I realized."

"Then I don't know how you could do this to me."

"Because we're not the same person." I start to leave.

"You're not going anywhere." She stands in front of the door.

I move to go around her, and my size up against hers surprises us both.

"I'm your mother and you can't just go galivanting off with a bunch of grown men."

"It's work, me earning money for us," I say.

She takes a baby step aside, so I still have to brush by her on my way out.

"Jesus, my ma saw you guys," I say as I pass Shelly's open window, more pissed than I realized. It's her same old Buick, but as soon as I open the door it's like a car from a hitchhike—new smells and people all smashed together. I look back at Ma in the window, almost hoping that she'll come out and try to stop me, but she just gives a pissed-off flip of her wrist in place of a wave.

"Oh shit. See, I told you I should have picked her up first," Shelly says to Mr. Jimmy. He shrugs.

"Yeah, you should have," I say. I slide in next to the Bon Jovi guy, trying not to let my skin slurp on the vinyl seats. I'm wearing my best jean shorts. Betty gave them to me a few years ago; I couldn't button them until today. My hair is shiny, with springy curls from a VO5 treatment. I think I might look cute.

"Your ma used to be my little sister's dance teacher," Bon Jovi says. "They called you Fishbelly, right?"

"Diamond, this is Rick," Mr. Jimmy says.

"Hey, Diamond Girl," Rick says in a cheery way that makes me unsure if he is trying to make fun. He's wearing a tattered jean vest with a white tank top underneath and jean shorts cut off at the knees. He's not fat, but it looks like he's wearing clothes that used to fit different. He has nice eyes with dark, thick lashes under the bangs, puffy lips. I instantly remember him as a kid, minus the hair, always looking like he'd been slapped across the face, like the world was a constant, hurtful surprise. His sister, Donna, with her stiff pas de bourrées and shitty attitude. Their failed family farm, their dad's fuzzy John Deere tractor tattoo across a deflated bicep. And I remember older Rick as part of the popular druggie crew at school. He was best known for: bodychecking people into lockers, practical jokes, and fingering a bunch of girls in the school chorus. A month before his graduation, he tried to set off what he thought was a firecracker in Mr. Russo's chem lab, but something went wrong and he blew off one of his own fingers. This was three years ago.

"Are you two friends?" I ask him, pointing to Mr. Jimmy as Shelly bucks the car into the street. She's applying lip gloss in the rearview mirror while driving.

"Sort of," he says. "Well, yeah."

"Both hands on the wheel, Shelly," Mr. Jimmy says. She takes extra-long to finish and throws the lip gloss into her purse.

"Rick was his student," Shelly butts in. "That's how Jimmy gets all of his friends."

"Hey, Shell," he says softly. "No license for you!" He cracks up, turning around to give Rick a high five.

"Dude!!!" Rick shouts. "You're wild."

Shelly punches Mr. Jimmy's shoulder, hard. It's playful, but also how you'd smack your brother or boyfriend. He's our teacher. I still can't believe it sometimes. I try and catch her eye in the mirror. Are they trying to fix me up with this Rick guy? What goes unspoken between friends still astounds me.

"You're still in high school?" Rick asks me.

"About to be a junior," I say.

"Where you gonna work after graduation?" he asks.

"I'm going to college." It's the first time I've said it out loud to anyone other than Shelly. A rocket ship launches in my chest.

Rick's eyes go wide and his head snaps back, just a tick; he looks me up and down at least twice while he spikes out his hair with his hands. He has thick silver rings on all of his fingers, like they're trying to take your eyes away from the missing one.

"I'm going to study botany," I say, at first just to get a reaction and then *boom*, because that's what I'm gonna do. There's not a more powerful shield against the tiny flash of disgust I see as his eyes wander across my body. I want to tell him every good thing I'm about to do, all the ways I am sharp as a goddamn tack, as Grandma Sylvia would say.

"Wow," he says. "You must be wicked smart."

"She's a brainiac!" Shelly yells from the front.

He smiles at me directly, right on me.

"Wicked cool," he says. Most people stare, but don't necessarily look at me. His mouth is open and I see just a hint of that surprised, slapped-face kid coming through.

"I hear we're going spying," he says to me.

"That's not what it is," I say, but can't find other words for it.

"This is Diamond's day," Shelly says, finally looking back at me in the mirror.

"We're gonna go mini-golfing first," Mr. Jimmy says. Shelly squeals and pounds the steering wheel, as surprised as me. Mr. Jimmy can't stop grinning.

It's three o'clock on a regular workday and the place is practically empty. There is an elderly couple out there swinging clubs in slow motion; each wears a miniature top hat, their own private joke. Two employees in Putt-A-Round shirts play on their break, cigarettes stuck to their bottom lips. We ask for a discount on the eighteen holes, presenting the ticket girl with only the simple facts for justification—there are four of us. She shakes her frizzy, home-permed head, shrugs, but then takes five dollars off.

I've never mini-golfed in my life, but I'm shockingly good at it. On my first try, the ball scurries over a green hill and through a windmill, hanging a left to land a few inches from the hole. Two strokes. Same for the next one, and that ball had to go all the way around a volcano. That's what they start calling me: Two Strokes.

I throw my hands in the air, victory.

"Are you OK? About us following that guy and stuff?" Shelly asks me at the Sahara Oasis hole. "You seem weird."

I cycle through all the things: dead family, new family, hometown I never really knew. New home? New friends. *Pop.*

"Same weird as always," I say. She's happy with this.

In between the fourteenth and fifteenth holes, she pulls me into the bathroom. I'm worried she's going to tell me that they had sex.

"Don't be mad, but I told Jimmy we were going to Florida." She grabs my face and sprinkles it with tiny kisses. "Don't be mad, OK?" Nobody ever kisses me except for Ma. I stay frozen so she won't stop.

"I think he wants me to ask him to come with us, but like, no way, right? It's just me and you, right?" She holds me by the shoulders.

"Me and you," I say. My thoughts drift to the Black family. I picture them at a Florida beach, teaching the little girl how to ride the waves.

We make our way to a red plastic picnic bench next to the maze entrance, and Mr. Jimmy gets us a tray of Cokes and corn dogs, his treat. I start to tell a story I practiced, about this woman from Ma's paper route who pees in her own yard, but someone interrupts, and we never get back to it. We talk about *The Lost Boys* and who would be the secret vampires in Swift River (me), a Hulk Hogan–André the Giant rematch, then Rick says something about once getting crabs from a locker room and things get awkward. So I say something funny about my mom being crazy, and that really breaks the ice. We laugh about awful things: Mr. Jimmy's dad used to bite him as punishment. Shelly's mom left without saying goodbye. Coke comes out of my nose laughing when Rick imitates Shelly saying *Lila is such an evil bitch*. This is how private jokes get made, I guess. We splash around in the mini waterfalls and the rubber duckie pond until we get kicked out.

We head back to the Black family's house. Inside our happy car bubble, Shelly fiddles with the radio, but there are no good songs. She begs for the Rolling Stones on the tape deck and Mr. Jimmy gives in. He doesn't usually allow cassettes; says they use up more of the battery. I hold my breath and pray it's not the album with "Brown Sugar" on it, where Mick Jagger sings *Scarred old slaver, know he's doing alright. Hear him whip the women, just around midnight.* I'm afraid that Shelly might love the chorus too much to notice. *Brown Sugar, how come you taste so good? Brown Sugar, just like a Black girl should.* I want Shelly to hate this song. I want to taste so good. I want a song to be *for* me. Luckily, Mr. Jimmy pops in *Goats Head Soup*, and we sing about love and a girl named Angie.

By the time we get there, it's four thirty. We park across the street from the house, just a little way down, where we can see clearly inside but also stay hidden. Our plan was to get there right before the dad got home from work so we could watch him get out of the car, see him from the front—but the car is already in the driveway. Rick pulls a cassette of Pink Floyd from his vest pocket—*Wish You Were Here*—and tells us he knows the whole guitar solo to "Have a Cigar."

"He's in a band," Shelly says to me with an eye roll before popping in the tape. Rick air strums the chords to every song—delicate finger movements, not hair-flipping wildness. No one talks and this seems OK. It's the end of the day and the light is kind and the car is full of possibility. I almost forget why we're here. I almost forget that I don't really know why we're here.

"This guy must not have a job," Mr. Jimmy observes after about thirty minutes.

"They're probably new in town," I say. "I bet he's still looking for one."

"Or he works a night shift," Shelly says.

"What are we supposed to do?" Rick asks.

"Wait until we see them. So Diamond can get a better look at the father."

After about an hour, the little girl comes out in a light pink bathing suit, her hair braided and clipped by a dozen or so crisp white barrettes, plastic flowers sprouting from the dark soil of her scalp. Ma once tried to style me like that, but my hair is too fine; the barrettes slipped out as I shook my head. I remember savoring the *click click* of plastic on plastic for a few minutes before they were gone.

There's a blow-up pool in the front yard like the one me and Ma use, but smaller. The little girl plops down inside of it, and within a few minutes her mom comes out to fill the pool with a garden hose. The mom is tall and graceful, with teacher-good posture and the trim body of a person who does aerobics. She wears a bright orange and green head scarf; her face wide and smiley without smiling. I know she is beautiful, and I battle my brain as it compares her to the beauty that I know in Swift River, placing her in a pageant next to girls like Janey LaFarge and Gabi Garland and Pammy Kempf.

There aren't many cars that drive down this street, but the ones that do go slowly, turning their heads to get a better look at mother and daughter.

"Her skin is so glow-y," Shelly says. My whole body clenches.

"Look how white their teeth are," Rick says, running his tongue over his own yellow Chiclets.

"Why do they always wear their hair sticking up in little clumps, all over?" Mr. Jimmy asks.

"That's fucked up, the way you said that," Shelly says.

"What? I just wondered," he says. "Only the kids, though," he clarifies. I put my hands over my ears; it's too much.

"Those are braids, dipshit," Shelly says. "Look what you're doing to Diamond."

"OK, so I don't know the right word for them, but I was just asking, why do they do that?"

"It's a fair question, if we're spying and shit," Rick says.

"We're not spying!" I say.

The mom sprays the little girl lightly with the hose; the little girl squeals. I am mesmerized by their normalcy. They are a unit, uncut by the people here, not yet squeezed to bursting inside of the mountains and the smallness that surrounds us. They are as regular as we are awful for being here.

"She reminds me of that *Cosby Show* mom," Rick says. "She ain't taking no shit."

I look away in case he starts wagging his finger or doing the *Wha-choo talkin' 'bout, Willis?* imitation.

Pool full, the little girl lays back, squealing again as her head hits the coolness. As she floats in the shallow water, the memory comes: Ma and Pop holding me in the down-South ocean bay, hands cupping my back, showing me off to the sky. The last time I felt like I belonged anywhere was right there under that never-ending blue, with them.

I think about what Swift River would be like if the Black people hadn't left, if it was full of normal, like this family, if roots stretched back to olden days when my people filled the streets and went to church and worked in their gardens and ran a whole mill.

Run, I want to say to the mother, the father, the daughter. *Take your glowing skin and your happiness, leave behind the plastic pool and the pretty shutters and go to where people look like you. Where you won't be stared at, poked at, judged, ignored.*

As if she hears my thoughts, the girl sits up, spots us, and waves. The mother doesn't look to see what she's waving at, doesn't move her head at all, and it hits me that she already knows we're here.

"Duck down!" Shelly yells, and we all slump. I am ashamed, deep-down ashamed, embarrassed to be in this car with these people, to have brought them back here, to see what, exactly? I am on one side, the side of the head-turners in cars, and that family is on the other. I look at Shelly's loving face, checking on me to make sure I'm as stoked as she is, and I know that I want to be in that yard with that family more than anything in the world. I want to fast-forward to Florida, to know who I will belong to once I'm gone from here.

The father comes out of the house holding a small blue towel. He's shorter than I remembered, with an open, uncomplicated face. *He's never been punched* is what Pop would say. The mother shakes her head as soon as she sees him, says something we can't hear that makes him head right back inside. Within minutes he comes back out with a colorful beach towel.

"So, like, is that him?" Rick asks. "Is that your dad?"

I think about a world in which the answer is *Yes*, and I zoom through my life, backward and forward, a tornado gathering weight and debris as I consider what this choice would mean. Then I think about *all* of the possibilities, all of the choices.

"My dad is dead. He died in the river seven years ago," I say, and know this is true. "That's just a regular ole Black man."

Everyone looks stunned.

"Oh. Di, I'm so sorry," Shelly says, like he just died yesterday.

"I'm sorry for your loss," Rick says.

"You sure?" Mr. Jimmy says. "You *do* have the same eyes."

Suddenly my face is wet, and I only know I'm crying because of how everyone is looking at me. And then I can't stop.

"Aw, Di. It'll be OK!" Shelly says. "Remember our special thing that's about to happen?" She leans back from the driver's seat to grab my hand. She winks at me, and for some dumb reason all I can think of is that we're at the beginning of *The Wizard of Oz*, each of us still playing the part of regular people in black and white; Shelly's wink a reminder that we're about to become different people, explode into color.

"Have some of these." Mr. Jimmy hands me a family-sized bag of Doritos. I eat them one at a time and then two and then near-fistfuls, still crying. Everyone looks straight ahead, bug-eyed and silent.

"It's OK, we didn't want any," Rick tries to joke.

I can't think of anything to say out loud that isn't too much truth for this car. I just want to be alone with more food. I hold the bag over my mouth and pour in the last of the broken Dorito bits; almost instantly my stomach flops and all of it races back up through my body, into my throat. I barely get the door open before puke comes blasting out of me.

Shelly jumps out of the car to hold my hair, rub my back. Orange vomit with corndog chunks splatters her legs.

"Sorry," I say. Mortified, I bend down to wipe it off of her with my hands. "No, Di," she pulls me up, gets me an old T-shirt from the trunk, and lets me clean up first. When I get back in the car, Rick offers me gum.

"It's Hubba Bubba," he says like he's handing me a hunk of magic. I look over toward the house again, and it's just the pool out there; the family is gone.

"You feel better now?" Shelly asks.

"Yes," I say.

Everyone gets quiet.

"So, we're done here?" Shelly sounds a little disappointed.

"Yes," I say.

"Sorry to be the buzzkill, but we have to get back to town to finish the lesson," Mr. Jimmy says.

"This is a driving lesson?" Rick says. "Shit."

"Seriously, Jimmy, we're out here spying on people. We're not even in the student driver car," Shelly says.

Shelly trades seats with Mr. Jimmy, who is done pretending this is a lesson; he drives us around for another hour. He has his arm around her headrest. Shelly leans into it, just a little; they seem like a couple and I feel relieved to be back inside our weird normal.

"Let's go to my house," Rick offers as we circle Main Street for the second time. His dad is on a fishing trip, his mom at the casinos in Falls Church, and his sister in her apartment above Bubbles Laundromat; that means an empty trailer all to ourselves. We stop off at a liquor store and Rick grabs a twelve pack of Bud, a pint of peppermint schnapps, and some jerky. Every now and then Ma lets me drink sips of her beer, but I've never had schnapps. I've never been drunk. I've never been to a trailer park. There's something about saying Pop is dead that makes me feel like an orphan living wild, no one to answer to.

Torchlight Mobile Home Park sits behind a meadow on the edge of town, just past the highway entrance ramp across from the Tee Pee. You can see it from the road, but it's set way back; from a distance it looks like a mini city of white, identical boxes, organized in a grid like an alien colony from the future. It's a place people sometimes use to draw a line between broke and poor, regular townies and trashy losers. Grandma Sylvia always said that the difference between us and them was one bad month and to quit being judgy. Pop said it was about a mentality, not a bank account.

As we get closer to Rick's, the trailers stop looking identical and little homey touches pop out: potted flowers, a wooden bench, a few steps up to a front door with lanterns on a pole, ivy growing on walls. Some look like regular houses, others like a freight train car flew off a track and landed here—plain and dirty from travel. Rick's is somewhere in between: white with a blue stripe around the bottom, hard-packed dirt and gravel around the house where others have grass, an empty flagpole stuck in the ground. In front, there are a couple of lawn chairs around a fire pit, wood stacked neatly against the house.

"Wait out here," Rick says. "I gotta clean up." It makes me like him more.

We stand awkwardly next to the lawn chairs, but no one sits down. I feel that passing-by-the-Elks-Lodge fear in my jaw, my teeth. I wonder if it's the same for Shelly and Mr. Jimmy; they look uncomfortable, too.

"Get out!" someone shouts, and we all jump, then quickly realize it's a couple fighting. We laugh. Neighbors' windows are open and private sounds are so close it's like they're all living together out in the open. We hear a mom and son arguing about a broken curfew, dishes clanking in a sink, a long fart, complaints about the fart. Zeppelin is playing somewhere, and I feel a moment of relief that I know the words: *Someone told me there's a girl out there, with love in her eyes and flowers in her hair*, like this will protect me if someone asks what I'm doing here, where I come from. *I'm from this town*, I always say. *I was born here*.

Rick's trailer is bigger inside than I expected, and hot; the kind of stuffy where it seems like the smells might turn solid in your mouth. Our feet smack on the sticky linoleum floor and we all pretend that's not happening. My eyes grab at everything, and I realize I don't remember the last time I was in someone else's house. On one side of the living room, there's a sheet-covered sofa and a recliner; on the other, a small, portable TV on a wooden dresser. Family photos stare at us from every wood-paneled wall, making the place feel full of people. Rick's guitar peeks out from a corner, almost completely hidden by boxes that are stacked to the ceiling and overflowing with papers. In the kitchen area the white refrigerator juts out like a giant, so covered with gray fingerprints it looks like a design. On the back wall, a wood panel with a knob is slightly open, like a superhero passageway to a secret lair. Rick watches us taking it all in, looking nervous and out of place in his own home. We all stay standing. I'm surprised by the silent Mr. Jimmy; usually adults at least try and make it less awkward.

"Let's sit outside," Rick says. "Watch this." He opens up a window and sits the portable TV inside it. Once we're back in his yard he pulls the lawn chairs up to the side of the trailer, around the TV.

"Drive-in movie," Rick says, excited, like a kid. Only two channels come in, so we watch the end of a *Tic Tac Dough* rerun. Then *PM Magazine*, then *Scarecrow and Mrs. King*. A group of kids riding barefoot on bikes pauses to watch along with us.

"So does this count for their driving points?" Rick laughs.

"They're officially done," Mr. Jimmy says. "Nothing left but the DMV driving test."

Me and Shelly scream.

"You're good drivers," he says. I feel proud.

When it gets dark we make a fire.

It seems like we've been together for a long time. We tease each other and the jokes come easy. They call me Two Strokes. Even Mr. Jimmy looks handsome in the firelight. He and Rick drink beer and throw the empties on the ground. Me and Shelly swig from the schnapps bottle, and peppermint curls down my throat like hot lava. It makes me feel wavy and light.

Rick appears with his guitar and starts to play. It's like I'm starring in a movie about a group of friends. Rick looks sexy when you squint your eyes; he's the boy you end up with after the popular one rejects you. He's the one you were supposed to be with all along. Together, we all look like the end of the movie. I try and imagine the Black family here with us and it won't work. Pop always said I sit inside the crack that splits the world in two.

Rick plays "Shooting Star" by Bad Company. Shelly starts to sing along in her way. I surprise myself and jump in with harmony. Everybody gasps and Rick stops playing.

"Wait, Shelly, shut up for a minute."

I keep singing.

"I didn't know you could sing like that," Shelly says, looking hurt, but also like she's never seen me before.

"It's just my regular voice," I say.

"You can be my backup singer," she says.

"Her voice is way better than yours," Rick says. "You should be *her* backup."

Shelly looks at Mr. Jimmy, who shrugs like, *I can't argue with that*.

Everything shifts.

"By this time next month we'll be on the beach," Mr. Jimmy says. Shelly punches him.

"He's just kidding, Di."

"Beach where?" Rick asks.

"I haven't even told my ma yet," I say, nodding toward Rick. I'm fuming.

"We're going on a secret trip, man. Don't tell anyone. These girls will be living with me in my Florida pad."

"What are you talking about? We're living with Shelly's mom," I say.

Mr. Jimmy looks at Shelly and smiles.

"It's not funny, asshole," Shelly says. She looks down and jams a finger to her mouth for a cuticle chew. "Di, Lila says we can't stay with her. There's not enough room. I was gonna tell you."

"Oops," Mr. Jimmy says.

"Fuck you for that," Shelly says.

"I can sleep on the floor. Or I can find somewhere else to go. It's your mom. You should be there," I say.

"Lila said *no one* could stay with her. There's not enough room," she repeats.

"Ohhhh," I say.

"She's such an evil bitch. I'm sorry, Di."

My head is hot, my thoughts tumbling down a hill till they land in a ditch. I'll sleep on the beach before I'll live with Mr. Jimmy. What will happen to Shelly? Can she still sing on the cruise boat? Can I actually sleep on the beach? Where will I shower and get ready for school? I wonder whether Lila was ever an option for us.

Instead of using words, I swig the schnapps and spit into the fire. It whooshes up into everyone's face like dragon breath. I saw Pop do that once.

"Black magic woman!" Mr. Jimmy laughs and throws his head back, the holes in the back of his mouth taking over his face.

"Don't say that." Shelly slaps him on the arm.

"I got a waterbed," Rick says to me. "Wanna see?" I'm mad that he doesn't even try to sweet-talk me, but I go anyway just to get away from Shelly and Mr. Jimmy. And I've never seen a waterbed.

He leads me back to the secret lair behind the kitchen, and it opens into a room filled entirely by the waterbed. The mattress sits inside a brown, vinyl-padded frame, and a velvety bedspread is tucked in tight around the edges, except for one side; you can see there are no sheets underneath it. Wooden shelves tower over the bed, in place of a headboard; they're filled with plastic plants and angel figurines.

Rick dives into the bed and it tosses him around like he's on the belly of a big sea monster. I get on the bed more gingerly, hoping the waves won't throw him onto the floor. Rick stretches his arm out, nearly touching me, and I can see his wet armpit hair stuck together in a delicate cone-shaped swirl. We bob like we're floating in the river. He's proud of this bed.

"Sing to me, Two Strokes."

I sing "Sara Smile," by Hall and Oates.

"I can't believe how good you are," he says, shaking his head. "You should be in a band."

A fan in the windowsill turns its head, making its way around the room to blow on us every ten seconds. I close my legs and squeeze tight, terrified the breeze will catch and carry my end-of-day crotch smells.

"Where's the bathroom?" I say, and Rick points to another panel in the kitchen with a knob on it. To my horror, the trailer quivers as I walk through it, like the house could break; I could break this house. He doesn't say anything mean. Inside the closet-sized bathroom, I squat over the tiny shower stall, wet some tissue and wipe my privates, first washing off a dirty soap sliver to add some suds. Grandma Sylvia called my privates "little lady." No separation of parts—just one name for the place she told me was special. It pulses as I think about Rick back on the bed. I squeeze out a dab of toothpaste and swish it through my mouth, erasing the last trace of Dorito vomit.

"The singing flower girl," he says as soon as I get back, like he was practicing it. I look at him confused and he says, "Botany, right?" He has taken off his tank and vest. He's skinny and pale, with wild dark hair around tiny pink nipples. He has a bit of a pooch, like an old man. He remembers I love botany.

We start making out. His tongue whirls around my mouth like it's looking for something it lost. We each have ten lips and ten tongues and there is spit everywhere. I start to feel warmth and wetness in my underwear. My vagina feels like it's growing, getting fatter.

"I don't mind this," Rick says, lifting my shirt to rub at my belly. I grab his dick; it perks up to the size of a pig-in-a-blanket.

"Neither do I," I say, even though I don't know if it's small or big.

He laughs and puts a finger in my mouth. It tastes like vinegar and dirt. I think I'm supposed to suck on it, so I do. It's amazing to watch what this does to his face.

I tear my fingers through his hair, like we're in a soap opera, like I've wanted to do this for a thousand years. It is surprisingly fine and soft; the crusty gel turns to dust in my hands.

My jean shorts and underwear are off, and the fan feels good on my skin. He slides one finger up inside me and it's rough and prickly. He adds another and then a third. I pull them out.

"What," he says, smelling his fingers before he wipes them on his shorts.

"It hurts," I say. "I think you have a hangnail or something."

"Let me try again," he says.

"I don't like it."

He is on top of me when he asks, "Will you suck my dick?"

I shake my head *no*. I can barely breathe.

"Can I do you?" he asks. "No fingers."

Now I'm looking at his eyes underneath his bangs, his tongue flicking. He moves my legs farther apart. I've never felt anything so good in my life.

"Diamond," he moans my name, and I feel such a rush of care for

252

him, it's an ache somewhere deep. I want to cry. But instead something bursts in me and I'm shaking.

I can't believe my body can feel this much for someone I barely know. My body has its own mind. My head wants to rest against his chest. My hands want to touch his tiny nipples. My big legs are wrapped around him; I don't care about the sweat inside the folds. For the first time, I feel like I'm in the adult world. I want more of whatever this is. I wonder if this is the beginning of how people get stuck to other people. I think about what Ma said about her first kiss with Pop, how she knew right then she wanted to be with him forever. Pop always said he'd kill anyone who touched me, and now I feel weird for thinking about him in this moment and then bad because I will never have a dad protector to watch over me. Lena comes into my head along with a pinprick of sadness. I want to tell her about all of this. I want to tell her how much I miss my dad.

There are no streetlights here, just house lights and electric lanterns. I come outside and the half-dead fire is by itself, a few glowing chunks with no Shelly and Mr. Jimmy beside it. A couple feet away the car is rocking gently. I see Shelly's legs in the air, her bare, dirty feet, toes pointed like a dancer's against a window. Low moaning oozes out into the dark, then gummy smacking sounds. There's Mr. Jimmy's moon-white naked ass, his legs cut off at the thigh by his pants, which are only pulled halfway down. The guys in front of the trailer across the way are smoking a joint while they watch. They cheer as soon as they see me, an audience for an audience. "Fuck her good," they yell.

Shelly, oh, Shelly.

I'm a terrible friend to not have said, *No no no, don't do this.* I waited for it to happen, certain that it would and certain I couldn't stop it, so why not be entertained by it? I'm not used to people, not

253

used to having an impact on anyone but Ma. Not used to caring. I think about our cruise ship dreams, our slinky, sparkly dresses, our perfectly pitched duets, the cheering. Julie McCoy offering us champagne in between sets. Even on stage, we'd feel the gentlest rocking from the waves beneath us, like being on the waterbed, but more steady.

Well that's the end of that, I think. I wonder if this is the spirit of Pop moving through me: restless Pop, breakable Pop, Pop always with his heart someplace else.

My face hurts from Rick's stubble rub; my vagina feels large and swollen, and even though it's inside of me, it's like a new limb. I'm happy that I didn't have sex with him, like this will protect me against some dark force.

"See you soon, Two Strokes," Rick says, still shirtless as he pulls the TV out of the window.

"You won't," I say, "but thank you!"

I'm hungry and decide to wait for Shelly and Mr. Jimmy to be done so we can go to Denny's. Just like friends in the movies do after a night on the town.

22

August 24, 1987

Hello my kin,

I love that you appreciate how one dirty baseball can hold so much family history inside it. Will you keep it someplace special? Don't tell anybody, but I sleep with one of Mama's lacy hankies right under my pillow! And I see you put it together that your ma and pop got married in that same place that was so special to Aunt Clara and Uncle Jacques. It's important to have those connections that stretch from one generation to the next.

I was sorry to hear about how much your ma's back hurts. I'm sure that's hard to talk about. I've been thinking about the two of you going to court, standing tall in front of those people who've had all that power over your lives for so long. Diamond, I'm just proud as a peacock—proud of you, proud to be your family. I hope everything goes alright.

You've asked me a few times now why I didn't come to your ma and pop's wedding, and I will tell you the truth about that. But first I have to tell you the truth about me, because it's connected to that day and what happened. Tilly is not just my travel partner, she's my *partner* partner. My lady. I'm a lesbian. I want to give it to you straight, so to speak.

I kept telling myself that I wanted you to meet Tilly first, so you could see how wonderful she is for yourself, how she is beautiful inside and out. How she's always doing considerate things, like putting gas in my car, tucking treats in my pockets. How she makes these listening noises when people talk, like she's always interested even if you're boring. How she can pull apart a tangle in your mind and set it right again. How she can give you the hardest truth and it never hurts (I call her the Velvet Hammer). How her whole face is like a smile. You'd see it. *Then* I'd tell you. But I know better, Diamond. Tilly doesn't have to prove herself to anybody, especially not a sixteen-year-old girl she's never met, no offense. This is an old habit.

Also, secrets can have so much power, over time you start to protect them like they're family. When you lose them it's like somebody died. You start to love your secrets more than you love people, which for me isn't hard. People make me uncomfortable, Diamond. I don't really like them. All my life folks see me, eyes on the ground, hands in pockets, speed walking down the sidewalk, and they say, *Where you in a hurry to, Lena? Where's the race? Looks like you in first place, Lena!* But I'm not rushing off *to* something, I'm in a hurry to get *away from* someone, everyone. I cross the street to avoid small talk with a neighbor, pretend I don't see a co-worker waving in my direction.

Your dad leaving changed something in me. Nothing has ever felt as good or true or solid as the years I had with him. I see the world through a haze. Sometimes I don't feel a part of anything.

I always knew I liked girls, though. I never in my whole life dabbled with boys. I was never in denial, never took on a boyfriend

to try to get the gay out of me. I have a hard time forcing my body
to do things it doesn't want to do. My face tells on me. I'm one of
those people! If I try a bite of food someone has prepared for me
and I don't like it, my nose wrinkles up and I say, *No thank you.*
I can't smile at people when I don't feel smiley toward them—it
hurts my jaw. I lied to people about who I was for so long—lied
before I even understood I was lying—sometimes I think this is
why my body insists on telling the truth.

In Woodville there was exactly one person people said was
gay—an older man they called Big Gay Titus. He was damn near
six and a half feet tall. Nobody could say how they knew, since
he never had a boyfriend or a lover (or a wife or a girlfriend, for
that matter) that we heard about. Just a way about him, they said.
Back then nobody talked about being gay in a direct way, but if
you were listening closely, even as a child, you could hear it. *She's a
funny woman,* they said. Or, *Something ain't right.* Or, *He's that way.*
Mr. Titus took the hit for everybody. Got called a sissyman and a
punk to his face. My daddy and his brothers used to brag about
how they would pull Mr. Titus's pants down in the hallways of
their high school, tie 'em up in knots around his big feet, and then
watch him wriggle around on the floor, trying to free up those long
legs. Or how they'd pay a bum to try and kiss him. Or how they'd
leave a plop of cow dung right outside his front door so someone
would step in it as soon as they greeted the morning. They did that
far into adulthood, I'm afraid.

I never understood why Mr. Titus stayed in Woodville. He
died there, all by himself. His mama was still alive and had to bury
him, put on a service that only her church friends showed up for.
Whenever I see a tall man I think of Mr. Titus, and I make my
mind stay there long enough for the guilt to crawl in. I don't know
why it was me who deserved to get out and not him. Why my

Woodville life went untouched by people suspecting "my ways," calling me "funny," why I was left alone. Mama used to say *Don't shame the race* every time I stepped out the house. You always had to think about that. Still do. I never did bring shame to Mama's doorstep.

I got away from Woodville by taking a job as a bookkeeper at a law firm in Atlanta, and suddenly I didn't have a secret I *had* to keep anymore, at least outside of work, anyway. Up until then, I always thought secretly liking girls was what made me so different, made me feel so alone. This will sound crazy, but I also thought my secret gave me a kind of a superpower. Diamond, when I tell you I had good luck, I mean a tornado would have moved *around* me. It was like I was a witch or something. Things always went my way. My brothers used to tease me, call me Broom-Hilda. You ever see that cartoon? I never got sick, ever. Never fell and cut my leg. Can you imagine making it through childhood with no scars? It was what made me want to be a nurse. I felt guilty! Up until Atlanta, I was always in the river swimming with the current.

When I first arrived, I'd walk everywhere, inhaling all the ways it wasn't Woodville. There were people everywhere all hours of the day and night; hotels, movie theaters, a park in the middle of tall buildings, people strewn across it like it was the beach. And the shopping centers! You could fit all of Woodville's downtown inside of one. I even walked through the most dangerous neighborhoods, the mansion-filled ones with gates in front and bushes carved into exaggerated kindergarten shapes, where the white folks called the cops on you. I was just daring my luck to run out. It was a thrill, Diamond, I hate to admit it. I bought a used motorcycle when I got tired of walking, and spent whole Sundays riding through the suburbs, sometimes out to the Kennesaw Mountains.

I discovered there were clubs and restaurants where gay folks

met each other without getting hassled. There was even a church
where white gay folks were welcome. But some of those places
were as racist as anywhere else. If you wanted to be around just
Black gay folk you went to house parties and BBQs. A few weeks
after I moved there I made my first Black lesbian friends, got
regular invitations to their happenings. That's when I realized
it wasn't my secret that made me feel so alone, it was just me.
Something odd and insistent in me.

I met Laila at a house party. She worked at a record store.
Boy, could she talk your ear clean off, but she also had interesting
things to say, knew about music in a way that was almost scholarly.
She was fine as can be and could dance her butt off. I stood by the
kitchen hugging the wall and watched her go. Back then I didn't
know how to flirt so I just stared! It's a wonder she ever gave me
the time of day. Laila was my first love, my fire love. Mama always
said you get one fire love that have your heart in flames, and then
you get your water love. Your water love is the one that fills you
up, the one that stays. Tilly is my water love. A Pisces, too! You'll
understand it someday when you're older.

Laila and me fell for each other hard, and suddenly I was
unprotected. No other way to say it: I traded my superpower for
her. The day after our first date—which was also the first time that
I was out in public with a girl I was dating, not just pretending we
were friends—I got real sick, for the first time ever; a fever like a
volcano, hot lava racing up through my body. Laila said it must
have been the shrimp we ate at Paschal's, but I knew what was
really happening: my secret magic was leaving me. I know, that
sounds crazy coming from a grown woman, but I swear, from then
on, my luck changed. I had Laila, but I also had chronic migraines.
I broke an arm. I accidentally set fire to the kitchen. I caught
summer colds. I was just a normal weirdo who didn't like people

except for Laila. See what I mean about secrets? How much we give over to them? Even just writing this here, telling you about it, makes my stomach feel tight.

A week after our first date, Laila moved into my little room. A month later, I sold my motorcycle so we could afford to rent our own spot. By this time we had other lesbian couples who were friends, and they loved being around us. Everyone flocked to our house. They came for Laila and they tolerated me.

The way I loved Laila scared me. She was a gypsy type—she had grown up with a mom who moved them from place to place every few years when a relationship with a boyfriend would crash and burn. I always had the feeling like I was running behind Laila, trying to catch up, even though I know she loved me, too. It seemed like there was nothing that could devastate her, nothing that she would miss enough to "die without," which is how we think we're supposed to talk about love. I wouldn't die without her either, but I *needed* her.

I got the invitation to your ma and pop's wedding a month before it was happening. I spoke to your pop and Aunt Clara for the first time in years. Diamond, it felt so good to hear his voice, to be connected to my Robbie again after so long. They wanted to keep the ceremony small, just family (I got the feeling they didn't have a lot of friends up there). I considered whether I'd drive or take the bus. If I took the bus, I could relax, read my magazines, but also I might end up sitting next to someone eating tuna and talking my ear off. If I drove, I could stop off at diners along way. I do love a good diner, especially diner food in the South. It was an easy decision, and I got to researching the most famous diners in my Mobil Travel Guide, marking the map all up the East Coast, plotting out where I'd stop for each of the three meals I would have on the road each day.

It wasn't ever an option for me to bring Laila to your parents' wedding, Diamond. Not in my mind. My relationship with your dad was the purest love I ever had. He was my first true partner, the only person I ever felt tethered to. Every other connection I'd had to a human had been . . . tenuous. The last time I saw him was the last moment I didn't feel like I was alone in the world. Could I get that feeling back again? I couldn't risk wrecking things, couldn't tolerate even the thought of his disappointment in who I turned out to be. I pictured Laila in one of her pantsuits she'd make out of old curtains, bright and jungle patterned. Her Northern ways (no offense) and bawdy jokes, the laugh that demanded you laugh with her, the way she hugged everyone she met. She didn't always wear a bra. No. Nope. I couldn't do it.

Another worry, a deeper one, was tugging at me. If Robbie said something foul about Laila or two women being together, I'd have to defend my girl. I'd have gone to war for her. Same for Tilly—*nuclear* war for Tilly. I didn't want to have to pick sides.

Then Laila got so excited and just assumed she would be going, and I didn't know how to tell her otherwise. She wrapped up a few of her classic albums as a wedding gift—Sarah Vaughan, Nina Simone, Peggy Lee—collectibles, really. It was very thoughtful. I made your parents a patchwork quilt using some of my mama's old blankets and shirts. And then I put all my anxious energy about telling Laila she couldn't come directly into planning out this glorious, solitary road trip. I kept praying she would lose interest, like she so often did in things that weren't sparkling right in front of her. Hoped she would barely remember by the time I was ready to go, then I would tell her casually I was going on my own, maybe even while I was headed out the door, like I was going to the Quick Mart. I rehearsed it to such a degree that I tricked my own mind. I'd found myself wondering, *Did I already tell her?*

I had not. And when the moment finally came, she was more hurt than mad, which made it worse.

This is your cousin who was like a brother to you!

We visited her mother's house on the regular, so while she had compassion for my situation, she was also exasperated by it. I told her, come on now, you don't even like long car rides. And she says, test me out and see what happens. We had a standoff. She did her hair, put on her nicest dress—she looked like Dorothy Dandridge when she got done up like that—and sat on the sofa with an overnight bag. Oh, she looked beautiful, Diamond. I came and sat down next to her with my road trip snacks in an old pillowcase—I'd packed it the night before and hid it in the bottom of the refrigerator. She snatched it from me and looked inside: one egg salad sandwich and a small bag of chips. Just enough to get me to the first diner. She held that egg salad sandwich and looked back at me like I'd punched her.

By the time you get back I will be gone.

She was dramatic like that, so I pretended she didn't really mean it. Laila was a person who disappeared after a fight, went off to "cool down" in some mysterious calming place where she could be with nameless people who "got her." I didn't ask questions because I usually needed a break my damn self. She'd come back after a day or so, and we'd be new again.

It was early Friday afternoon by the time I got out of there. I'd only been on the road for a few hours before the sky got dark and the rain blurred out all but red break lights in front of me. I pulled into the first rest stop I saw. It had a Howard Johnson's restaurant. I was disappointed to miss out on the first scheduled diner by at least fifty miles, but also too hungry not to eat. In all of the hubbub between me and Laila I'd gone off without my road snacks! I remember being soaked, the bright fluorescent lights, the forced-cool restaurant air and vinyl booths making me feel even wetter, colder. I gobbled up a steak special that was greasy and overcooked. Nothing worse than being full with bad food! Made me so grumpy I didn't even want to sit and read magazines, like I planned. I had to admit that I wished Laila was there with me. She would grab my icy fingers, put them inside her warm hands, and blow heat into the center. She was always trying little ways to make my body feel better when she couldn't reach my mind.

Walking through the parking lot on the way back to my car, I could see eyes and movement through fogged up windows; I guessed we were all waiting out the storm together. I listened to an oldies station on the radio and fell asleep thinking about my daddy, who loved a good love song. He taught all of us girls how to dance proper with a man.

When I woke up, the rain had just stopped and the truckers were coming out of their rigs—men of all ages and colors. I watched as they high-stepped through the wet grass into the woods at the edge of the rest area, staying far longer than it took to urinate and be on your way. Whatever they were doing—that was their business, not for me to judge. But it was something else that made me uneasy watching those men stream in and out of the thickest part of the trees. Something that gave me the feeling of an undercurrent, a riptide, if you've ever been in the ocean. I opened the car windows and the odor of cologne and wet Georgia mud drifted inside. You know that way rain moves the smells of a place around, rearranging them so what's right there with you is coming from someplace far away?

I had a powerful sense that I needed to go home. And then I couldn't remember what that meant. The smells, the lump of bad steak in my stomach, the dead-eyed men buckling up their pants as they emerged from the thicket, this stranger-filled resting place that felt like nowhere. It had me scrambled. And then not knowing where home was made me want Laila so badly I could cry. She knew how to carry home around with her.

I went to start my car and it was dead—wouldn't even give me a wheeze, just a click and silence. See what I mean? Bad luck. I decided to call Laila from a pay phone outside the HoJo's entrance. Maybe she could call a tow truck or come get me. We'd find a cute little motel to stay the night, wake up tomorrow and be new again. We could go to the wedding, or to my next diner, or we could just disappear together.

The phone rang and rang. And I just kept calling back. I was crying by then, and I'm not a crier. I couldn't tell you how many times I tried, but it was a lot. If you've ever been desperate to reach someone and they don't answer, you know how that ringing fills up your whole head with every worst thing possible. Finally someone answered.

I'm helping her pack, Lena. It was Laila's friend Janene.

She's really leaving? In all of our fights she'd never packed her things up before.

Are you surprised? Janene said, and suddenly I knew I missed the thing that would clue me in to how this was the final straw. I missed all of the straws before the last one. Or maybe I didn't? I felt embarrassed, imagined all of our other friends coming over and looking at my raggedy pillowcase with the egg salad sandwich and chips—evidence of my selfishness, proof that I was such a coward, I'd focused on snacks and diners and not losing my love, my Atlanta life.

I got a jump to my battery from one of the dead-eyed men and then sat in that car for a good hour, praying that my magic would come back and set me on a path where I could have all the things I wanted and not hurt anyone. Was like trading the devil for a witch, as they say—there was no choice that wasn't a bad choice. Since I never made it to the wedding, you can probably guess that I ended up heading back home. By the time I got to Atlanta I'd lost both Laila and your pop. I let go of them both. Sometimes when you do someone wrong, it's too overwhelming to figure out how to fix the hurt, and you end up being the one to leave. To be honest, I felt better after that. I was alone again, and that was what I knew.

Me and your pop never spoke of it, and I'm ashamed I didn't even call to say I was sorry. Even though I knew he could be so fragile. At that point I hadn't talked to him in a few years. The last time we spoke we were both still in high school. He was having a hard time with those white kids. He'd gotten into some kind of accident, plowed his daddy's car headfirst into a wall. I don't know if he had been drinking or what, but Aunt Clara and his father considered sending him back down South to us. But then he fell in love with your mother and couldn't nobody take him nowhere. He had his Annabelle. I never hated her because she was white, I just wished your daddy had more options. But you can't deny it—she saved him.

The last time he called me—for bail money to get out of jail after he got arrested—I wired it to him. I should have gotten in my car and drove to see my poor Robbie, wrapped him up in family. I could have spoken into his grown-man ears straight through to that gentle little boy. Reminded him who he used to be, where he came from. He needed that. I have so much regret.

I've tucked two photos in here for you. They were both taken by Aunt Clara. One is from the day your daddy arrived in Swift River, and the other is from his high school graduation. In both, he's standing next to *his* daddy, Robert Sr. Truth be told I was surprised by how scared your grandaddy looks in the arrival day picture! He was always such a tough cookie. Your daddy was the

265

only one who wasn't afraid of him. I used to catch them giggling together, rolling around on the floor in tickle fights. Robbie looked like his little twin, like a time machine popped out a kid version of a grown man. Your grandaddy was a *good father*. Robbie was very loved.

I imagine your daddy had stopped speaking by the time that photo was taken. Did he ever tell you about that? He didn't speak for almost a year after he got to Swift River. We begged Robert Sr. to let us take him back. But Aunt Clara was more like his mother than a big sister, so in his mind, he was bringing his boy home. Aunt Clara was home.

The graduation photo is my favorite. Look at Robbie making one of his funny faces, Robert Sr. kissing his son's cheek; fearless daddy love, this-child-is-*mine* love. And looking sharp! A Black man in a suit—especially an elder—always makes my eyes well up.

Thank you for the school picture you sent. I think you're beautiful, and I'm not just saying that. You have that same shine you did as a little girl. I have your new picture up on my refrigerator. Tilly's refrigerator is covered with photos of her nephews and those colorful magnetic alphabet letters they play around with, spelling out silly phrases and love-filled messages. Mine was empty until you.

Being here in Woodville makes me uneasy, like I'm in between places, waiting to start my life again. *Your hometown makes you and breaks you and makes you again.* Daddy said that to me. I wonder if that's how you'll feel about Swift River if you ever leave it? I'm working on getting back to Atlanta, to my Tilly. You haven't lived until you've sat on her porch, sipping on her sweet tea! I do hope you come visit us there. They say Atlanta is the Black mecca of the South. Atlanta was Dr. King's town. That's a whole other history for me to tell you about.

In this package you'll also find another letter from Aunt Clara to Mama, sent over thirty years after the one before it. I haven't found another one after this one, so it may be the last. And I don't know what happened in between—whether the letters are lost, or Aunt Clara and Mama were lost to each other. It was *business between sisters*, Mama used to say, instead of *butt out*.

I've also included a special little book—Aunt Clara's delivery log. Forty years' worth of babies, all their parents' names. I wonder if you'll recognize them?

Here's the last thing, the best thing. You see that old paper in the envelope? Be gentle with that one. It belonged to your daddy and he didn't even know it. It's yours, now. It's all yours. Could you ever have imagined? It's your inheritance.

Love,
Auntie Lena

23

June 17, 1954

Sweetie,

I'm getting the house ready for Robert and his little boy, gathering up everything you told me the child would like. I made peach cobbler, canned some okra and tomatoes, pickled cucumbers. Got all the makings for scrapple and corn cakes. I painted a sweet little pony on his bedroom wall. Don't you laugh at me, he look just like Mr. Trotter! There's also a wooden rocking horse, made specially by my husband. Jacques can barely whittle a stick, so you know how hard he worked on that thing. I saved your marble collection and Robert's yo-yo. I never could let go of the things you children left behind. Listen to me calling you grown folk children! Never could stop doing that neither. I finished up that quilt for the boy's bed, made from pieces of your clothes, Mama and Daddy's, too. I put my radio in his room. I hung up a photograph of you.

Sweetie, I know you raised this boy like you gave birth to him yourself. I know you're sore at me, and I don't really know what to do with that. Robert Sr. asked for my help and I feel like I have to give it. But I know it broke your heart. And your little girl Lena's, too. I'm sorry.

I promise you he'll be safe here, or at least safer than he was in Woodville. Folks here let us live in peace, now. I delivered half of 'em myself. Was the first human to touch them, breathed in the same air they swallowed for their first breath. Got them ready to be held by their mamas. I was their guardian ushering them from one world to the next. Yes, they leave us be.

Since the hospital opened in Springfield, I don't catch as many babies as I used to. I'm licensed now, had to get trained to do what I've been doing all my life. I mostly do calls for the poor folks who can't afford a doctor. A few of 'em don't even have running water or electricity. But my babies are healthy. My babies come out fast. In the hospital they make the mother lay up in the bed. It's unnatural! A mama gotta move. I move with my mamas.

The wee bit of money I get from the babies, plus Jacques' work taking care of the books at the mill—it's not enough to live on. We get a little something from the lumbermen working Jacques' land. Jacques does yard work for the rich folks up on Orchard. I do some house cleaning. We sell our canned vegetables and my pies at the town square on Saturdays. It all comes together to make a life for us. Everybody likes us, treats us kindly. Most of 'em even call me ma'am. There will be more than enough of everything for Robert and the boy.

I didn't tell you this before, what with all that happened down in Woodville, but Jacques had to leave Swift River, for now. The government up in Canada trying to take his land, saying he don't have the right legal papers. They want to keep laying down their railroad tracks right through the middle of our 100 acres. They want to push his lumbermen right into the lake. He has to go fight for it. That was his daddy's land, his inheritance.

To tell the truth, Jacques doesn't want to come back to Swift River. He wants me to come up there and start a medical clinic. He says life is just easier there, easier to make a living, easier to be a Negro. He wants

to build a house on our lake, plant a garden, then sit back and wait to
retire, just like white folks do. He says we're lightning bugs got caught
in a jar. The jar is Swift River. I don't know. There's something about
a ma'am and a sir after so many years of boy and nigger gal. You get
to thinking it's some kind of prize. You take pride in being light behind
glass. Or maybe it's just the devil you know. I'm sure I sound like some
kinda fool, but I'm telling you the truth about what's on my mind. Who
would we be up in Canada? How will they know I'm a trained doctor
if I have no degree to show for it? How will they ever understand what
I gave up to stay behind? But I was ready to try, for Jacques, ready to
leave Swift River. And then I got the call from Robert. Who knows,
maybe once I get them settled, once this boy is grown enough? Maybe
they'll want to come with me.

I surely didn't think I would be in my fifties helping to raise a
young boy. Jacques and me made our peace with not being able to have
children a long time ago. I tell you, it got to where we were happy not
to have little ones running around. We like to do things just cause we
can—we stay up all night reading, go swimming at lunchtime, walk
all the way to Ashfield on a Sunday just to buy some brandy. Drink the
brandy under the stars. That's how we planned to live the rest of our
lives. I'm not bitter about putting that aside, I'm just saying that we're
all sacrificing so this boy can have a better life. This poor boy, his first
mama dying before she could even lay eyes on him, and now he's losing
you. I'm going to tell him that he was so loved by God, he got three
women to take care of him, to teach him, each passing him along like
a precious gift, one to the next, each giving him something special that
he'll surely need on his journey to greatness.

That song I used to sing to you when you were a little girl, I'm going
to sing it to little Robbie in French. Tell him it made his mama dance
and clap her little hands.

Ma petite lumière.

This little light of mine, I'm gonna let it shine. This little light of mine, I'm gonna let it shine. This little light of mine, I'm gonna let it shine. Let it shine, let it shine, let it shine.

You were the closest thing to having a child that I ever had. You and Robert Sr. You, my sweetie pie, will always be my baby, my best thing. And I promise you, I'm going to treat little Robbie Jr. like he's a prince, the future of the family, like the whole world belongs to him.

Love, your sister,
Clara Da Costa

24

Ma, we can't skip over this part. Our whole life together is burrowed inside the details of this day.

Look at us. In our going-to-court dresses. I remember you had starched and ironed them, but they weren't entirely clean. Every time you lifted your arm to fiddle with your freshly cut bangs, I could see old sweat stains under your pits. Little things like that made me love, not pity, you.

We slid into the courthouse like we'd already lost. We were too scared to think good thoughts—our whole bodies were hurting from days of clenched muscles. Earlier in the week we'd spent precious paper route money on manilla folders and a label maker from CVS; raised letters on sticky plastic spelled out *court forms* and *important proof*. Our files looked neat, even if Grandaddy's ratty leather briefcase was embarrassing in the light of other people. We'd studied those papers until we knew the police report by heart, could recite Lena's letter like a monologue. We unwrinkled them, tucking them inside encyclopedias stacked on top of each other. We thought that even with all of this, we might still get it wrong. We imagined insults and disgust, laughter in our faces.

And then it didn't hurt.

The courtroom looked tired instead of ravenous, worn-down wood and worn-down people, pictures of dead judges in a room full of empty metal folding chairs on a peeling linoleum floor. Our judge, an older man with giant white dentures, looked over our files and lisped, *Looks good.* The woman in the registrar's office next door stamped the death certificate saying, *You two enjoy this beautiful weather.*

That was the thing about a racist town. It got to decide when it would be kind.

"Well, that was easy." You sounded disappointed. We had prepared for a fight. "That woman looked lowly. How much do you think she makes an hour for stamping death papers?"

"I don't know, Ma."

"Did you see her dirty fingernails? *Always* take care of your nails, Diamond."

"I will, Ma."

"The judge looked like he borrowed someone else's teeth, don't ya think?"

I wasn't in the mood.

"Isn't it strange that no one said *Sorry for your loss?*"

Yes and no.

After, we sat on a bench in the grassy town common in front of the courthouse. It was where they celebrated holidays, held craft fairs; where that baby Jesus covered in bird poo and the paint-chipped wise men hung out for six months each year, the manger doubling as a farm stand on summer weekends. You lit a cigarette, holding your arm straight out to the side in between drags. I swatted the smoke away but didn't move. Per usual.

"I'm not sure how to feel," you said. I understood. It was unusual for you to express an emotion before it was fully baked.

I could tell you were back on your Tic Tacs by the way you sat in a comfortable slouch, no longer wooden and sharp angled from the deep ache you had carried for seven years; it was on pause. You were fuzzy, unbuttoned.

"I wasn't thinking ahead. We should have saved money for a celebration," you said.

You held up a ten-dollar bill, waving it teasingly. "We can either take a taxi, orrrrrr we could hitch and use the money for some lobster instead."

You were always so deluded when it came to a splurge. To money in general, really.

"Guess what, Ma?"

"Tell me," you said, leaning in closer.

I pulled the stiff, brand-new license out of my purse.

"I can drive." I just laid it on you.

You squinted at the card, looked at both sides.

"This is one of those fakes, so you can buy booze?"

"I learned how to drive, Ma."

You looked confused. And then the whole summer of my secret-keeping passed over your face. I wanted to die. But also I wanted to live.

"Oh" was all you said.

"You're not going to say congratulations?"

"Well, yes. I was just about to. Congratulations, Diamond."

You got up, started walking. You looked forlorn.

"Where are you going, Ma?"

"We have to get home, don't we? Unless you're driving us in our new car?"

You stopped short. Probably realizing that the insurance check would actually come in a few weeks. That you *could* buy a new car. That the faraway plans were closing in on us.

"You're too good to hitch with your ma now?"

I was. Fresh perspective had started to seep into my consciousness, the kind that comes with a foot out the door, a zoom out from your life. Hitching was not normal.

I went along anyway. I was trying to give you as many yeses as I could.

A car slowed down to pick us up; there were two guys in the front seat.

"Let's do it!" you said. "I guess Van Halen, Camel smokes, and for the twist—a car seat!"

You were trying to make fun, be light.

You were also breaking our safety rules and I told you that.

"I think I know one of them from high school," you said.

We got in and they pulled off before our doors were all the way closed. You were wrong on all counts. Andy, the driver, and Jeff, the passenger, put in a Journey tape. Nobody smoked and the music was loud enough that we had to yell introductions, making everything sound like a performance of cheer and politeness. They were obviously younger than you.

"You two are all dressed. up," Andy said. "I felt sorry for you looking like that on the side of the road."

"Don't I know you from Swifty High?" you said.

"Naw, not me. I never met you. I'd remember," he said.

There were two mini license plates stuck to the dashboard. One said *O'Shea* and the other said *Rules*.

"That your family name?" I asked. I wanted to ground us. Bring in the ancestors, mark our places.

He paused. "Yep." He said it in a prideful way. "I'm an O'Shea. Five generations here in Swift River."

"My great-aunt, Clara, was a midwife. She delivered your mother, Constance," I said. "And your aunt, Mary."

Aunt Clara had always noted when her babies had babies. I was proud, too.

The O'Shea guy whipped his head back at me. "What the fuck?"

"How the hell do you know that?" you chimed in.

"I have her delivery logbook. Auntie Lena sent it to me."

"Oh, she's 'Auntie' now?"

"My great-aunt charged fifty dollars for each delivery around that time," I told them.

"No fuckin' way. You got the wrong family," he said.

"Ain't your mom's name Connie?" Jeff said. O'Shea didn't answer. The energy in the car shifted.

"My daughter just got her license." You tried to shift it back.

He grabbed on. "Good for you, girl. Let's go do donuts in Dogfish Park. See what you can do."

"Oh, no thank you, we have to get home. My husband is waiting for us."

"Your husband is running around a few towns over with a new bitch." He laughed. "Everybody knows that."

That was the thing about a place like this. It can render a man so invisible, they see his ghost everywhere.

This is a ghost story.

"I'm a widow, goddamnit!" you screamed. You pulled out the death certificate. "Have some respect!"

You'd never said "widow" before. Not until that piece of paper. But you knew. What really happened to Pop. You'd always known. Even before he did it, you knew it would happen. I've never figured out what to do with that. The anger would migrate many times in my life, but you should know that it stayed with Pop the longest; that's where it lives now.

"This little girl lost her father!" You pointed at me. I'll admit it felt good to be included, to be in mourning, at last.

The next part isn't so clear.

O'Shea was driving fast. I remember Jeff turned on a hunting and fishing report, artfully, in the way a parent might switch things up to calm a child. You were narrating what you saw out the window like you were auditioning to be a tour guide and your life depended on it. *Over there, you can see that Walker Communications are expanding their headquarters. Remember when we had to use their operators to make every goddamn call? And you know they listened in. Hello, operator, can you connect me to the Zinns' house and can you at least stop the heavy breathing while we speak?* You were fast-talking, your voice high. All the air was coming out of you; these were the final squeaks. *There used to be a snack shop in the post office parking lot it was run by a blind man do you remember? When did they take that down? What happened to him?* You yammered on.

Were they driving toward our house? In the opposite direction? Sometimes I can only remember the end of the story clearly; my brain assembles the rest like a collage, truth and an alternate reality mixed in together. I know it felt like we were buckled in for something awful. And I was scared, but not in the familiar way that came with a ride gone bad.

It was you that scared me.

We got to the corner of Beech Street; it wasn't *not* on the way to our house, but O'Shea had already bypassed the quickest route. You leaned over and whispered, *When they slow down near the next corner, open the door and jump out. Then run like hell.* I shook my head. That was ridiculous. *One, two, three . . .*

I can't remember if you pushed me or I leapt.

In one version of the memory, O'Shea reached back and threw me out of the open door while the car was still moving fast. In another you went first and Jeff grabbed me, yelling, *Don't! Just let her go.*

But I know that I hit the ground and then the car screeched to a stop. Jeff jumped out to close both doors, careful not to look at me down on the ground. I couldn't see you; the car was blocking my view. In those few moments, oh Ma. I've never felt panic like that. The blood throbbing in my head knocked out my senses, erased the fact that I was an actual person, separate from you.

Ma! Ma!

Was I screaming it?

Mommy! Mommy.

They peeled off. "Stupid riverbeasts!" The road dust made the car a blur, a mirage.

You were sitting straight up in the weeds far off to the side of the road; in another context you might have been having a picnic. You looked over at me on the other side, baffled, like you'd lost track of yourself.

"Ma, are you OK?"

When I got up to go to you, I realized I was scraped up on one side. It hurt, but it wasn't worse than anything I'd gotten from a bike spill. It was all that weight, I understand now. It cushioned the fall.

Wild goldenrod was all around you. Pop told me that this particular kind was called "fireworks"; they looked like frozen tails of an exploding rocket. You were in the center of that gorgeous eruption, bleeding badly from your arm.

"Sweet pea, are you hurt? Oh, look what I did." You reached for me but the pain in your arm bit you like an animal.

"You need stitches, Ma." A piece of glass from a smashed bottle on the road had cut you deeply.

I ripped off the sleeve of my dress. I'd seen someone do that on an episode of *Charlie's Angels*. I tied it around your arm to slow the bleeding.

"Oh goody, another scar," you joked.

* * *

Somehow we made it to the field where they held the county fair every fall. There was a pay phone right next to the phantom entrance. We could never have walked the rest of the way to the hospital.

You tried Mrs. DeStefano. No answer. You refused to let me call an ambulance.

"Can you call your librarian friend?" you asked me. You must have felt desperate. You hated her "do-gooder crap" directed at your daughter.

"No," I told you. I didn't know it yet, but I would later come to understand that I needed to not know Betty. If we were close, she would have broken my heart.

I called Shelly.

We were sitting on the edge of the field when she pulled up. You were bleeding right through the fabric tied around your arm.

"Oh my god, Mrs. Newberry!"

"It's not so bad," you comforted her. You dusted off my dress, spit-cleaned the dirt off my face. I let you. It was the first time you and Shelly had met; you slipped into mothering like a uniform.

Shelly had crimped her hair; it looked like waffle fries. It looked like trying. I was so happy to see her.

I asked her if I could drive. I wanted to show you. And I was proud of Shelly's immaculate, fruity-smelling car, as if it belonged to both of us. We were a "we." My first one after you.

You moaned on the bumps. I remember you framed inside the rearview mirror, your head flopped to the side, like you got tired of holding it up. That plus the bloody makeshift bandage made the whole thing look like a page out of a comic book; you could have had XXs in your eyes.

The pink-and-orange early eve swirled in through the windows.

"This is nice." You lifted your head, and I saw you taking in a new kind of freedom. You looked soft; there was an opening in your face.

"If you guys ever want to borrow my car or anything, you totally can. You can go on double dates." Shelly looked back at you. "You're such a babe, Mrs. Newberry."

"Oh, I'll never be with anyone else," you said. You meant it. You were alone for the rest of your life.

"I'm really sorry you lost your husband. Today must have been hard," Shelly said.

I know this will sound bad, but I looked back at you and thought, there once was a Ma who would have been horrified at the sight of this woman. It wasn't because that's how *I* felt, but because I finally saw you as a person caught in a loop that might never break and straighten, who once wanted something you might never get. I was afraid you would stop wanting altogether.

"Tell me some town gossip, Shelly," you said. You were pulling yourself out of the pile of people who get talked about.

"Someone stole the Indian chief at the Tee Pee last night," Shelly said. "What the hell, right?"

I zoomed out some more.

"Thank god I'll be in Florida by next week." Shelly gave me a side-eye that said, *You could still come with me.*

I'll admit I doubted she'd ever leave. But she did. She went alone. First to Jacksonville, then Tallahassee, and then Houston, and then I lost track. I heard that her ex-lover Mr. Jimmy, our driver's ed teacher, is a security guard at the Swift River Valley Bank.

It turns out that leaving wasn't the hard part for Shelly—it was *landing*. She had that specific kind of rootlessness that comes when you're orphaned by two living parents. Where you flit and float, and there is an invisible pull to the earth, but you are jilted by gravity. I always imagine her driving a convertible by the sea, the wild wind in her hair and at her back, just like we'd planned. I hope she is singing somewhere, wearing something slinky that glitters. I hope she grew new dreams.

"You guys are brave. It's so dangerous to hitch," Shelly said with genuine admiration. It was the first time I'd ever heard this said out loud, a mini bomb of truth.

Ma. It *was* dangerous. And it was a choice.

"I love you," I told Shelly as we got out of the car. I meant it.

"I'll miss you when you go," I said. And I did. She was my friend.

⟿

You got ten stitches and a bottle of Percocet.

"This dress was a good choice, don't you think?" You were brushing it off like the whole court day and hell ride never happened. Time passing was the great eraser for you; a few hours could wipe clean any amount of unpleasantness. You weren't always like that. That was how Pop used to be. Tragically optimistic with a dash of amnesia.

We went out to the yard, sat in lawn chairs while we iced our sore places with bags of frozen corn. You had one fancy ice pack from the hospital, but you wanted to save it.

It was the gloaming hour; we were inside of it, drinking the colors.

"Remember when you were four and we drove across the state to the coast? We went whale watching. Remember?" you asked.

I did remember the boat, how Pop propped me up on his shoulders as we looked out at the ocean, the biggest open space I'd ever seen. Giant humpbacks circled us, and Pop leaned over the railing, yelling in astonishment. He held on to my little legs and I grabbed fistfuls of his Afro like a horse's rein. I remember the feeling that he wasn't holding on tight enough, that he might drop me in the ocean, where I would fall right into the giant blowhole. It was the first time I felt the confusing love of a slippery hold. You watched us and clapped with glee. You couldn't tell I was scared.

"Let's go back there," you said, dreaming in reverse. "There's still time before school starts."

"I'm going on a road trip with my Auntie Lena." I gave it to you straight.

"Oh, you *spoke* to Lena, too?" You looked hurt. "When were you going to tell me?"

"I didn't want to mess up court." I hadn't told you yet that Aunt Tilly was coming, too. It would have made you too jealous.

"You have to ask me for permission! I'm still your mother."

"Can I go on this road trip, Ma?"

"Where are you going?"

I pulled out the official piece of paper: the deed to my Uncle Jacques' one hundred acres of land. My hand was shaking.

"Pop's Uncle Jacques died a few years ago, and since he and Aunt Clara never had kids, he left all his Canada land to Pop. Uncle Jacques' family only knew how to reach Aunt Clara's sister, Sweetie. They sent Sweetie the notice, but she'd stopped opening mail from Aunt Clara decades ago. Lena says missing her was too painful. And she was still hurt that Aunt Clara got to raise Pop. There was a whole bag of unopened letters. This was in one of them."

You grabbed it. Started to cry.

"This was where Aunt Clara lived before she died," you told me. "After she raised your father, she finally went back to be with her husband. They had five years together before she passed. She left a few months after me and your dad got married."

"I don't know if it's real yet, but there's a lake and everything, Ma."

"Oh, Diamond, if your father knew . . ."

The space filled up with what that could have meant.

"Do you want to come with us?" I asked. I already knew you would say no.

"What about the insurance money?" you said, as if that were an alternate destination.

I didn't understand it then, but you would never let yourself take that money if I wasn't there to enjoy it with you. That wasn't the plan. You saw it as my inheritance. Later, you would give me all of it, and then later still, I would give it back to you, a little at a time. For some reason you would accept the installments, the baby steps.

"No, I'm just going to stay here. Enjoy the rest of summer. Maybe start up our old garden. You and Lena should have that time together, get in all your howdy dos."

"Are you sure?" I asked. A little part of me wished you would beg me to stay.

"I'll be OK," you said. For the first time I considered that you might not, and that I had to leave anyway.

"Ma, want to buy an above-ground pool with the insurance money?" I tried our language to cheer things up.

"That reminds me," she said. "I almost forgot my surprise."

"Surprise?"

"Go look behind Pop's car."

You had propped them up against the side of the car, hidden from street view—two beautiful bikes. One red, one blue.

"I borrowed some money from Lottie. Now I can pay her back for a change."

I didn't know what to say.

"Do you want the red one or the blue one? I thought you'd want the red because that was the color of your old bike but then I thought you might want a fresh start with the blue, but really, you can have whichever you want. We can ride them together when I get these stitches out."

Ma, I didn't thank you. I couldn't bring myself to do it, couldn't tell you how much it meant to me. It felt like a concession, like absolution. I wasn't ready.

But I told Pop as I sat in Ladybug. *I got a new red bike. It's a ten speed. It's so nice I don't even want to ride it. Something happened to Ma and me and we're pretty banged up. I'll never hitch again. I got my license.* I screamed the best part.

We have land, Pop! We have family!

Everything seemed possible.

Thank you, Ma. Thank you.

I misremembered something: Later that night, I let you sleep in my little bed again, curled into my back. Your pulse kicks had just begun to settle. I could feel the shape of your breath on my neck and tried to match its pace; it was musky from carrying the day. You were wearing a long nightgown and were slathered up in Jergens, just like Grandma Sylvia. I forget that she belonged to you, too. You whispered, *I love you. My sweet pea. Your father grew you in the garden, and you were the most gorgeous sweet pea we'd ever seen. We knew we couldn't eat you; we had to keep you.* You hadn't said that in years, probably since Pop was still alive. You were a widow now, a woman who could casually reference her dead husband in non-guilting ways. It was ordinary and also you had climbed a mountain.

By the time I woke in the morning, you had gone back to your own bed. I could hear you coughing, long and airy, like you were trying to huff a demon out of you. Years later, after Atlanta and Canada and New York, after my daughter was born, after we became pen pals and then strangers. After you were gone. I would wish, fiercely, that I had rolled over to face you that last night, curled into *you*, our noses touching; taking in all of that ferocious love even if it choked me. What would one little turn really have cost me? In the moment, something inside me took over, knew that all the little turns could crisscross the globe ten times over and add up to a whole life. Instead, I reached back to cup your head, just for a second— an abbreviation for something tender that made no promises—and went to sleep.

———◈———

Aunt Tilly says that our instincts, our deepest intuitions, are really our ancestral memory; our people speaking through us. Aunt Clara and Uncle Jacques, Aunt Sweetie and Grandma Sylvia. Pop. My sweet, breakable daddy. They said, *Go north, go find that lake. Take a swim.* And so I did.

Picture me, breaststroking through the cold water until I find a warm spot. I do a handstand, showing off my legs to the clouds, my skin a soup of you and Pop. In my head I hear you clapping and yelling, *Bravo, sweet pea! Bravo!* in that way that a mother would praise you for a sneeze well done.

I come back up for air and plant my toes into the silty mud-bottom.

25

August 20, 1967

Dear Sweetie,

Wish you could be here with us. We're having the time of our lives!

Love,
Dr. Clara Da Costa

AUTHOR'S NOTE

There is no town called Swift River in real-life New England, but the Swift River Valley in Massachusetts was the general area I had in mind when I created the fictional mill town of this novel. The Swift River Valley occupies the ancestral lands of the Nipmuc/k people, who refer to the area as *Quabbin*, or *meeting of many waters*.

The Tee Pee Motel is invented, although the atrocities that it offensively attempts to memorialize are very real. The incident Diamond describes is now referred to as the Great Falls Massacre. Both the massacre and the motel exist within the same racist ecosystem Diamond grows up seeing as normal. They are meant to represent the geography of violence she inhabits, the horrors that are all around her, in the air she breathes.

I wrote *Swift River* over a period of many years, and in that time I was profoundly moved and inspired by a number of books, most notably Claudia Rankine's *Citizen* and Isabel Wilkerson's *The Warmth of Other Suns*. The impact of their words and their scholarship was immeasurable. But *Swift River* truly came to life after I discovered the late James W. Loewen's remarkable book *Sundown Towns: A Hidden Dimension of American Racism*. The book is an essential study of white supremacy in action, documenting thousands of white communities outside of the South from which Black and other marginalized people were systematically excluded—and often driven out of the townships' limits—through discriminatory laws, harassment, violence, and terrorism. As a result, these "sundown town" communities were essentially all white. While the book focuses on the period from the late nineteenth century through the early aughts, sundown towns still exist in various forms in the United States today. I discovered, through Dr. Loewen's research, that my predominantly white hometown in western Massachusetts is right next door to what is now thought to have been a sundown town. The echoes of this were felt all through my childhood.

As I was reading the book, a detail jumped out at me: sometimes, an exception would be made for one or two Black people to live in these towns, particularly if they were seen to be providing an essential service to the white community. I knew instantly that I would make Swift River a sundown town, and that Diamond would be the descendant of the only Black person allowed to stay after the violent expulsion of the rest of the town's Black community. This history changed everything, gave Diamond's story its roots and soul.

Throughout the novel, I have taken liberties with strict historical and geographical accuracy when I felt it would better serve the narrative. The ugly history of sundown towns, and the many years of denial and obfuscation that can allow a community like Diamond's to exist, are firmly rooted in the real world. Towns like Swift River still exist all over the country. Diamond's story is just one of many.

ACKNOWLEDGMENTS

Thanks begin with my agent and champion, the incomparable Julie Barer, for believing in me and this story, for transformative editorial guidance. Julie just *makes it happen*. To Rumaan Alam, who generously helped with this match. A massive thank you to the Book Group and my UK agent, Caspian Dennis.

To my brilliant editor, Carina Guiterman: thank you for your patience and passion and vision, for loving Diamond and bringing out the absolute best in me. To my Simon & Schuster family for giving me such an incredible literary home. Special thanks to Brianna Scharfenberg, Danielle Prielipp, Sienna Farris, Imani Seymour, and Amy Medeiros. Thank you to my UK editor, the remarkable Sharmaine Lovegrove, for your ideas and advocacy, for giving this novel a voice around the world. To the entire team at Dialogue Books.

There would be no *Swift River* without my dear friend Jacqueline Woodson, who brought me back home to my writing and supported every step I've taken on this journey.

Deepest gratitude to my #1 reader, my compass and treasured friend, Mathea Morais, president of the Diamond Newberry fan club, and to Ellery Washington for superb notes and profoundly helpful conversations. Thank you to my friend-readers for their time and insight—Dawnie Walton, Robert Lopez, Sally Franson, Leslie Schwartz, and Margaret Brown. Extra special thanks to Curtis Sittenfeld, who has also been such a compassionate mentor; to Angelica Baker and Clare O'Brien, who saved me and this book over and over; to André Des Rochers, my attorney and brother for life; and to Linda Villarosa, a supporter and believer from the beginning.

Showing up with right-on-time, much-needed wisdom: Amy Bloom, Tonya Lewis Lee, Christian Campbell, Sidney Clifton, Kali Holloway, Susan Steinberg, Shaun Walker, Jean Petrucelli, Michael Bloch, and Jana Welch.

Thank you to my Columbia cohort—Crystal Hanna Kim, Andrea Morrison, Iman Saleh, Naima Coster, Cory Leadbeater, and Sam Graham-Felsen. It was a joy and honor to grow with you as a writer and human. Thanks to professors Paul Beatty, John Freeman, and Victor LaValle, each of whom had a profound impact on the writer I am today.

Thank you to my lifelines, my loves: Gabriele Glore, Hopi Noel Morton, Jane Morgan Di Spaltro, Melony van der Merwe, Shane W. Evans, Christina Pearce, and Kelley Nicole Girod, with special thanks to Diane Houslin, Robin Reid, and Evolyn Brooks for their thoughtful notes, to Michelle Reid for Clara and Jacques's dock on a lake, and to Jyllian Gunther for manuscript reads and reminders that nothing was more important than finishing. I feel blessed beyond belief for my entire CJC framily, especially April Mathis, Alex Beech, Kamari Wheeler, Alex Mulzac, and Jonathan McCrory. Thank you to Amy Friedman, my one and only mother-sister-friend, my rock, and one of Diamond's first cheerleaders.

Thanks to my Scott-Smith, Widoff-Woodson, Villarosa-Welch, Zinn, and *Descendant* families. Thank you, Byron Glore.

To name a few from my hometown crew: Jenel Roberts Lanuza, Gretchen Brown, Sara Haselton, Jamie Summ Langley, Rhys Liv-

ACKNOWLEDGMENTS

ingstone, Kerri Vassar, Michelle Blanchard, Nicki Petersen, Amy Gibson, Nicole Laporte Murdoch, Stephanie Gusan Duclos, and Pat Garland. To Mr. Richard Russo, my high school English teacher and the first person to tell me I had a voice that needed to be heard.

Thanks to MacDowell, Vermont Studio Center, and Baldwin for the Arts for their generous support, for giving me a sanctuary where I could feel like a real writer. Thank you to Brooklyn Writer's Space for giving me a writing home. Thank you, *CRAFT*, for being the very first to publish my words.

I received essential expertise and research assistance from Lynda Gravatt, Nashira Baril, Adrienne Whaley, Liz ColdWind Santana Kiser, Diane Dix, and the Nolumbeka Project. A special shout and deep bow to Benilde Little for such life-giving notes and care.

I'm grateful for my cousins, with extra thanks to my forever angel, the Honorable Howard K. Chambers, and my angel here on earth, Kodi Seaton. Love to my extraordinary niece, Ava Maya Chambers, a bright light in this world, and my magical godson, Moses Williams.

To my activist/educator parents for raising me in a never-dull home bursting with books and curiosity, kindness, and integrity. You supported each professional-path turn with such love and enthusiasm, but you knew my heart and wanted most for me to be a writer. Mom, you are my anchor and beacon, Dad, my greatest teacher.

To my wildly talented brother, whose world-changing ways are endlessly inspiring, whose overflowing ideas added so much color to this story. Thank you for being my original partner in this life.

To the ancestors, the roots of my tree: my grandparents, especially my Grandma Sally, my aunts and uncles. To all those I never met, but always feel. This book cracked wide-open when I let you speak through me.

To Christine, my sissy, everything I ever do will be for you. Un-

ACKNOWLEDGMENTS

derneath the most emotion-filled sentences I write are grief and love for you. Thank you for showing me what true artistry and devotion to craft looks like, for having faith in me, for knowing that this story was destined to get out of my head and into the world. We did it, sweetie.